MOONSHINE MURDER

Book 14 of the
'Hawkman Series'

by

Betty Sullivan
La Pierre

Others in 'The Hawkman Series'
by
BETTY SULLIVAN LA PIERRE

www.bettysullivanlapierre.com

THE ENEMY STALKS
DOUBLE TROUBLE
THE SILENT SCREAM
DIRTY DIAMONDS
BLACKOUT
DIAMONDS aren't FOREVER
CAUSE FOR MURDER
ANGELS IN DISGUISE
IN FOR THE KILL
GRAVE WEB
THE LURE OF THE WITCH
SHADOWS IN THE NIGHT
THE ARCHER

Also by Betty Sullivan La Pierre

MURDER.COM
THE DEADLY THORN

Permission to use photographs of
"Copper Moonshine Stills"
given by Colonel Vaughn Wilson
www.coppermoonshinestills.com

TO MY DEAR MOTHER

MOONSHINE MURDER

#14 'Hawkman Series'

CHAPTER ONE

Young Randy Hutchinson rode his bike at breakneck speed down the hill, then onto the road leading into the residential area. He slowed at Tom Casey's place, and eyed the woman in the yard bending over the flower beds that stretched the length of the house. Taking a deep breath, he turned into the driveway.

***

Jennifer heard the crunch of rocks and glanced up. She studied the young lad for a few moments as he straddled the two-wheeler. He needed a hair cut and wore very tattered clothes, even though he appeared clean. "Well, hello. I don't think I know you. What's your name?"

"Randy Hutchinson."

She stood up and dusted off her hands. "I don't recognize the name Hutchinson. Do you live around here?"

He pointed toward the way he'd come. "We have a cabin way up there on a hill. Don't get down here much."

"I see. Did you just move in?"

Randy shrugged his shoulders. "Sort of. I guess you'd say that, since we're still bringing up stuff for the place."

"Welcome to the neighborhood." She held out her hand and smiled. "I'm Jennifer Casey."

"Thanks," he said, grinning shyly as he jumped off the bike, dropped it to the ground, and took hold of her fingers. "Is Mr. Hawkman your husband?"

Jennifer laughed. "How'd you know him as Mr. Hawkman?"

The boy wrinkled his forehead in question. "Isn't that his name?"

"It's his nickname. His real name is Mr. Tom Casey."

"Didn't he used to be a spy? And doesn't he have a pet falcon?"

"My goodness, you certainly know a lot about him for being new to the area."

Randy shuffled his worn sneakers across the pebbles on the driveway. "Kids talk a lot, and some of the guys told me they think he's some sort of god."

Jennifer stifled a giggle. "He's a nice guy, but I don't think I'd classify him as a god."

"Is it true he's a private investigator?"

"Yes."

"I'd sure like to meet him."

"Tell you what, hang around here for a few minutes and I'll see if I can find him."

His eyes grew wide. "Really?"

Jennifer disappeared into the house, went back to Hawkman's office, and poked her head into the room. "You've got a visitor."

Hawkman glanced up from the ledger he'd been working on. "Who?"

"A ragamuffin boy about ten years of age. Says his name is Randy Hutchinson."

"Is he from around here? I haven't heard of anyone named Hutchinson in this area."

"Guess they're a new family, living way up on a hill in a cabin."

Hawkman frowned. "Usually we hear about the new ones, before they're even settled."

"I'm very curious too. The boy knows a lot about you, for a newcomer."

"Oh?"

"He called you 'Mr. Hawkman' and asked if you were once a spy, but now a private investigator. He told me he learned it from the kids. Oh, he also said you're some sort of god."

"What!"

"I'm just telling you what he told me."

"Oh, my, I better go out and set this kid straight."

He dropped his pencil into the crease of the book and stood. "Lead me to him." Before they got to the front door, Hawkman took hold of Jennifer's shoulder. "Let me peek through the kitchen window and check him out."

He scrutinized the boy through the glass. The youngster had long dishwater blond hair, which definitely needed cutting, and appeared tall and skinny for his age. His jeans and tee-shirt were very ragged. Hawkman turned to Jennifer. "Looks poor, but clean."

"My thoughts exactly."

He opened the door and stepped outside.

The boy's blue eyes lit up. "You're exactly what I imagined. My friends told me you were tall, had an eye-patch and looked like a cowboy."

Hawkman smiled. "Glad I didn't disappoint you."

"Do you really have a falcon you carry on your arm?"

"Yes, would you like to see her?"

"Oh, man, yeah."

Hawkman took him around to the back of the house and showed him Pretty Girl, who put on a big show of squawking and flapping her wings inside the large aviary. "She wants to go hunting. I try to take her out once or twice a week."

Suddenly, Randy's mouth turned down at the corners. "I've got to go. Thanks for showing her to me."

Hawkman glanced at the boy. "Did I say something wrong?"

"Oh, no, sir. I just gotta go. Can I come back sometime?"

"Sure."

They walked back around the house, and Randy jumped on his bike and took off up the road. Hawkman placed his boot on the brick wall of the flower bed next to Jennifer. "That boy had more on his mind than just meeting me."

She stopped digging in the dirt, and glanced up. "What makes you think so?"

"Something about his being so eager, then suddenly turning it off like a water spigot and saying he had to go. He seemed troubled, but didn't have the nerve to say any more."

She dusted off her hands, and sat down on the wall. "What in the world would bother him to such a point? What did you talk about?"

"I told him I took Pretty Girl out to hunt once or twice a week. Why would such a comment cause the boy to melt down?"

"You sure you didn't say something negative?"

"I'm positive." He pointed a finger. "I have a feeling we haven't seen the last of Randy. In fact, I'm going to ask around, and see if anyone knows about this family."

"I'll do the same, as I got the impression, they've been here for a few months, and I thought it strange we hadn't heard anything about them."

"Where'd he say they lived?"

She pointed west. "He said in a cabin, way up in the hills."

Hawkman frowned. "Most of that property is privately owned. Maybe they're renting a place. Off the top of my head, I don't recall any sort of a cabin, just homes."

Jennifer shrugged. "You know boys; he might have thought it sounded more manly or rustic to say cabin."

Hawkman dropped his foot from the brick and moved toward the front door. "From the looks of his clothes, I don't think there's much money in the family."

"You can't judge by what he's wearing; those might be the ones he uses for outdoors."

"True. Maybe I'm reading something into the boy which isn't there."

She smiled. "Very likely."

He glanced at his wife, then went inside.

Jennifer returned to digging the soil in the flower bed, her mind churning with thoughts of the young lad. She hated to admit to her husband, that she, too, had reservations about the youngster when he rode onto the driveway. Yet, she couldn't put her finger on it. He seemed a tad shy at first, but when she spoke to him, his demeanor and expression lightened considerably. She wondered, if she hadn't been outside, would he have come up to the house? He was definitely more interested in Hawkman than her. The fact he'd mentioned her husband being a private investigator did throw up a red flag.

She finally stood, and groaned. This bending over was killing her back. The biggest bed was now done, she'd work on the other two tomorrow. Putting her implements into a bucket, she set them in the corner, and went inside.

CHAPTER TWO

Before retiring, Hawkman locked up the aviary. He didn't always take this precaution, but tonight he decided to follow his instinct.

The night had turned warm, so when Hawkman and Jennifer went to bed, they opened the sliding glass door and the window above their heads. An owl hooted in the distance and the critters of the dark made their ways across the lawn, occasionally climbing onto the deck, only to be frightened off by a loud squawk from Pretty Girl. The water from the lake lightly rippled against the shoreline, making a soft soothing sound.

Jennifer dropped off to sleep almost immediately, and Hawkman could hear her deep steady breathing. He lay staring at the ceiling and watched the leaping shadows made from the moon's reflection, as it bounced off the water. Turning from side to side, he couldn't get comfortable and wondered if they should buy a new mattress. He kept glancing at the alarm clock and the minutes were ticking off rather rapidly. When the hands hit midnight, the squawks of Pretty Girl rent the air to the point it sounded like a war zone.

Hawkman jumped from the bed and Jennifer bolted to a sitting position. "I've never heard her make such a racket before. Something's wrong." He grabbed his gun from the holster slung over the chair and hurried out the sliding glass door. Crouching behind the aviary, his gun poised, he peeked around the corner. Not seeing a thing, he slowly moved to the side, then to the front of the cage.

"Easy, girl," he said, softly to the bird as he checked the interior of her cage. The moon gave plenty of light and he could see no snake had entered her domain. She continued to flap her wings and squawk, but less intensely. Suddenly, Hawkman heard a crunching noise like wheels on gravel. He charged around the side of the house and when he leaped around to the front, he spotted a bicycle turning the corner at the fence line and high tailing it down the road.

When he returned to the bedroom, Jennifer looked at him wide-eyed. "What caused all that ruckus?"

"I'm not sure, but I'm going back out and examine her cage better." He hurried into the living room and flipped on the outside light. Removing both the falcon's water and food, he brought them inside. He poured the dry pellets onto a paper towel, scrubbed both bowls with a detergent, rinsed each thoroughly, then filled them with fresh water and food. He returned to the aviary, swept out the floor, replaced the containers, then locked up the cage.

Wrapped in a robe, Jennifer stood at the door, watching his endeavor. "What do you think occurred? You act like Pretty Girl's food and water could have been poisoned."

Hawkman walked back into the house shaking his head. "I don't know, but didn't want to take any chances."

"Did you see anyone out there?"

He nodded. "Yeah, a person taking off on a bike."

She put a hand to her mouth. "Could you tell who it was?"

"No. The silhouette looked too big to be Randy. However, nighttime can play tricks on your eyesight."

Jennifer pointed at the cabinet. "You better put the falcon's food into some sort of tight container in case it's contaminated. I sure don't want Miss Marple getting into it."

"You're right. I'm going to take it to my office tomorrow and see if I can detect any toxins in the food." Hawkman placed the falcon's food into a zip plastic bag, slipped it into the jeans jacket he'd be wearing tomorrow, and buttoned the flap. He patted the pocket. "That should keep our nosey feline safe."

She took hold of Hawkman's arm. "If Randy came back, why would he want to scare Pretty Girl?"

"I doubt he figured she'd carry on so. He might have wanted to take her hunting, and found out I'd padlocked the cage. When he tried to force the door, then Pretty Girl let us know. Don't think she wants to be handled by anyone but us. If I'd left the door open, the boy would have discovered the wrath of a falcon."

"I'd hate to see him learn such a lesson, if he's the culprit." She pulled Hawkman toward the bedroom. "Let's see if we can salvage the rest of the night. Working in the soil yesterday has made me sore all over."

"I'll try; can't say I'm going to get much sleep now."

Monday morning, Hawkman joined Jennifer in the kitchen for a cup of coffee. "I feel like I've been run over by an eighteen-wheeler. My eyes feel full of sand and my body's sluggish."

"I know the feeling."

"Has school dismissed yet for the summer?"

"No, I think they still have one or two more weeks. Why?"

"Think I'll stop by on my way to work, and see if Randy Hutchinson's enrolled."

"Remember, he could be home schooled. Many people participate in our area. They have a large group who meet once a month."

He frowned. "Hadn't thought of that. Still think I'll drop by; since I know Mrs. Simpson, don't think she'll mind my asking."

Jennifer set a plate of scrambled eggs and toast in front of him. "Oh, she won't. You'll find her very accommodating."

He sat down at the kitchen bar and ate. "If you have a chance, ask around and see if anyone knows about this family."

"It's on my list. I'm attending the women's auxiliary this morning, and it will be a perfect place to gather any information."

"Yep, get a bunch of women together, and you're certain to find out any gossip, true or not."

Jennifer furrowed her brow and glared at her husband. "You act as if men don't gossip."

He glanced at her cautiously between bites. "Well, I didn't mean it quite that strong."

"Regardless, I'll see what I can find out."

"Thanks."

Hawkman got out of the house quickly, as he figured he'd overstepped his bounds. He journeyed up the road toward town, and pulled up the driveway leading to the small school's whitewashed building. No space appeared available, so he parked behind one of the cars he assumed wouldn't need to be moved, and hopped out of his vehicle. His timing seemed perfect, as about ten kids were outside in the small play area, running after balls or swinging on the one monkey bar set.

He found Mrs. Simpson behind the desk of the one-room school, grading papers. She'd been widowed many years ago, and had taken over the job of running the school shortly after the loss of her husband. Her appearance fit the typical schoolmarm: hair pulled back in a small bun, and a solid colored brown dress. She glanced up at Hawkman over the top of her rimmed reading glasses, and her firm mouth broke into a big grin.

"Oh, my goodness, Mr. Casey. It's been a long time since I talked with you. To what do I owe the pleasure of this visit?" She quickly rose, and grabbed an adult size chair from near the wall and scooted it toward him. "Please have a seat."

"I won't take but a minute of your time. There's a young lad who stopped by my house. Says his name is Randy Hutchinson. He acted as if his family had only been in the area for a few months. Is he by any chance registered to attend here?"

She opened a ledger on her desk and ran a finger down the margin. "I didn't think I'd heard of him, but wanted to make sure. There are many families who are home schooling now, and unfortunately, I couldn't tell you which ones. It's really cut down on our enrollment."

"So you've never heard of this family?"

"No, I'm sorry I can't help you. Is there a problem?"

"I'm not sure. However, that's not your concern. Thank you for your help."

She stood and took his hand. "So good to see you. Please drop by more often. Maybe even bring your falcon for the children to see. You still have one, don't you?"

"Yes, I just might do that. I'll let you know first."

"Is Jennifer still writing mysteries? I hardly have time to read for pleasure with all the paper grading, and my eyes are not what they used to be."

Hawkman smiled. "Jennifer is still glued to her computer, compiling her stories."

"Give her my regards."

Hawkman left the school house when a loud bell rang, and the children filed back inside from the playground. He wondered, as he drove toward Medford, if pursuing this boy and his family would be worthwhile. So far, nothing bad had really happened, except the incident last night, which could have been no more than curiosity for a young lad from anywhere. Yet, something gnawed at Hawkman's gut, and he decided, when he got home from work, to venture up in the hills to see if he could find where they lived.

   When he reached the office, the first thing he did was run some test on Pretty Girl's food. He found nothing indicating it had been tainted, and felt releaved.

CHAPTER THREE

Hawkman remained in his office all day, going over the notes he needed for a court case coming up tomorrow. He didn't like testifying, but it came with the job. It also meant he'd have to wear a suit and tie, which always reminded him of his days in the Agency.

Clyde, owner of the doughnut shop below, had the ovens at full bore, and the aroma of delicious pastries wrapped around Hawkman's nose. Finally, when he couldn't stand the temptation any longer, he went down to the bakery.

The jingle of the bell on the entry door caused Clyde to look up, and a smile wrinkled the flour spattered face. "I wondered how long it would take before you arrived."

Hawkman grinned, as he noticed the dab of flour on the proprietor's nose, and his

usual dark eyebrows were now white.
"When you're baking, you must put your
whole body and soul into the procedure."

Clyde laughed. "Yep, I love it."

"I can tell."

"What can I do for you?"

Hawkman made his choices, paid, and
went back to the office. Pouring himself a
hot cup of coffee, he munched on the
goodies as he reviewed the case. He
decided to leave a little early, as he wanted
to make a run up into the hills before dark,
and see if he could spot the cabin where
Randy said they lived.

He unplugged the coffee pot, rinsed out
his cup and placed the trash into a sack.
Picking up his briefcase, he left the office,
tossed the debris into the dumpster behind
the building, and climbed into his vehicle.
On the way home, he kept trying to picture
the area west of his house where he might
find a hidden cabin tucked into the trees.
The only place he could figure would be
near the old abandoned railroad tracks
where supplies were brought in during the
building of the Copco Dam back in the
1920s. Some of the workers might have
thrown up a structure to stay protected from

the elements and wild animals while the construction took place.

The back road, a shortcut to Highway 66, was narrow and overgrown with weeds, plus a locked gate across a private area kept people from using this route. He might have to use the four-wheeler, as he doubted he could get through the rugged terrain with his big SUV. Tonight might be a dry run, since he hadn't been up in the area since Sam, his son, went off to college.

His mind wandered back to those good times. Sam used to straddle the fender of the old truck with his gun, and as they drove along the road, he'd shoot ground or "digger" squirrels, as they called them. Hawkman chuckled out loud at the memories. Those were the fun days.

He finally drove over the bridge and wondered if Jennifer had talked with the women about this new family. Leaving the Land Cruiser in the driveway, he took his briefcase and went inside. Miss Marple sat on the ledge of the big window overlooking the lake. Her gaze seemed focused past the falcon, out to the dock where her mistress stood sweeping. This surprised Hawkman, as the breezes were still too nippy in May for Jennifer to enjoy fishing. He glanced out and watched her spread red pepper around the edges. Laughing, he poked his head out the sliding glass door.

"Are the otters messing up your fishing area again?"

"I wish they'd move these blasted little devils back to the ocean where they belong." She stomped up the gangplank, placed the broom on the deck, and the pepper on the table, then came inside. "They've made such a mess. If we had a warm day, I'd want to go down and fish, but I don't like wading through their poop."

Hawkman gave her a kiss on the cheek. "Let's hope your remedy will keep those little varmints off your favorite place."

"I'm not sure anything will work, but it's worth a try."

They walked over to the kitchen bar together. "Did you have the meeting today with the women's firehouse auxiliary?"

"Yes, I have a few tidbits to tell you."

"Should I hear you out, or make a run to the area before dark?"

"I think you need to listen to this first."

He sat down at the kitchen bar. "Before I forget, Pretty Girl's food was clean. Now, I'm all ears."

"This mysterious family took up most of the discussion. We barely had time for the business part. It appears several of the members have encountered one or more of the Hutchinsons."

Hawkman raised a brow. "How many are there?"

"One of the women met Randy and described him as very charming. However, she couldn't get a straight answer out of the boy about where he lived, except in a cabin up in the hills. The same thing he told us." Jennifer raised a hand. "Oh, and he asked her where Mr. Hawkman lived."

"Interesting."

"Then one of the other ladies saw an older boy, who appeared to be around sixteen. He took off when she came out of the house."

"What was he doing?"

"Hanging around her chicken coup."

"How does she know he belongs to the same family?"

"She doesn't, but she'd never seen him before."

"Doesn't mean a thing."

"Except, he headed west at breakneck speed."

"On foot?"

"No, on a bicycle."

"It's still hard to connect the two boys as possible brothers. With school out in certain parts of the country, he could have been a visitor."

Jennifer nodded. "True. However, several of the women have seen these two boys at one time or another riding around. A couple said they were missing a few things in their yards."

"Such as?"

"A small black pot on her front porch she used for plants. Another said she had her canvas wood carrier by the back door with a couple of logs in it to use the next day. When she went to get it the morning, she couldn't find it."

"It sounds like we might have a family of thieves among us."

Jennifer shrugged. "Hard to say. These women could be absentminded."

Hawkman grinned. "Very possibly."

"Anything else I might find of interest?"

"Yes. Ike and June were out taking a walk; they noticed a narrow plume of smoke coming through the trees to the West. They knew there were no homes in that area, but it looked like it came from a chimney. Worried about a forest fire, they kept an eye on it for several minutes, then it dissipated. They have no idea what caused it, and remain baffled."

"Wonder if they've seen it again?"

"She didn't mention they had."

Hawkman rose from the bar stool. "Looks like we have a mystery on our hands. I'd thought about taking the four-wheeler out and searching the area near the old railroad track, but I think I'll just take a dry run up the back area in the Land Cruiser and do a little scouting first."

"I'll go with you."

"Okay."

Jennifer threw on a lightweight jacket and they left in Hawkman's vehicle. As they drove westward, Hawkman told her about the memory he had of Sam on the fender of his truck shooting digger squirrels.

She laughed. "We had some fun times with Sam as he grew up."

The road became more difficult to maneuver and finally Hawkman stopped. "If we go much farther, I won't have a place to turn around. We're not far from the gate. Why don't we get out and hike to it? Maybe we'll see some signs of life."

CHAPTER FOUR

Hawkman and Jennifer trudged up the hill, each looking for signs of human activity on the ground or nearby.

Jennifer stopped to catch her breath. "It will be hard to see any bike trail, unless the boys use the same one. The weeds would pop right back up if they didn't go over the same spot each trip. I don't see a thing indicating people have walked or ridden up this way in a long time"

Hawkman stopped, and wiped his forehead with the back of his sleeve. "I think you're right. It depends on where the cabin is located. I figure it's near the old railroad tracks, and used to house the workers when they built the Copco Dam. Since the boys always head west, we're probably too far north."

"Kids will find the shortest route to wherever they're going."

"Let's head back. No sense in hiking any farther."

They trooped back down the hill to the SUV, and went home.

Jennifer bounded out of the vehicle. "I enjoyed our adventure, even though it didn't produce any answers. It's been a long time since I've been up that road. Maybe you can take the four-wheeler up the other way tomorrow."

"Can't. Have a court date; but maybe the end of the week. I expect the trial to last only one day."

She snapped her fingers. "Oh, that's right. I need to check your suit and see if it needs pressing."

Hawkman threw up his hands. "Honey, don't worry about it. The wrinkles will fall out the minute I put it on. Besides, who's going to notice?"

His tirade fell on deaf ears as she'd already headed for the bedroom, soon to come out with the garments over her arm. She set up the ironing board, had the suit, shirt and tie back on the hanger, before he could say much more.

"Man, you're fast."

She smiled, as she put everything away. "You may call me the miracle woman."

He grinned and shook his head. "I'm lost for words."

She stood on her toes and gave him a kiss on the chin. "It's because you agree."

***

Tuesday morning, Hawkman left the house dressed in a suit, but carried a duffle bag packed with more comfortable clothes. He drove straight to the courthouse, took his seat in the room, and waited for several hours before the lawyer called him to the stand.

Once he testified, and the trial ended, he drove back to the office. He thought about his testimony against Cindy Brown, the dangerous young woman in his last case. He knew she needed help, plus deserved punishment for her actions with the compound bow. It relieved him to hear the judge sentence her to mandatory psychiatric care and other restrictions. The girl definitely had a problem.

Since Hawkman spent most of his day in court, he could hardy wait to change clothes. He stuffed the suit into the small suitcase, knowing Jennifer wouldn't be too happy; but he'd forgotten to bring any hangers. Once comfortable, he made a few phone calls, then left for home.

When he walked in the door, he found Jennifer at the kitchen bar, phone glued to her ear and writing on a sheet of paper. Her intent expression gave him the gut feeling something serious had happened.

He waited patiently, curious to know the origin of the call and the purpose. When she hung up, she turned to him.

"I just got a report you'll be interested to hear."

"What about?"

"It could involve the mysterious new family. You'll have to decide."

"I'm listening."

"What's strange is we didn't hear one of these happenings since our bedroom faces the lake, and we usually have the sliding glass door open."

"I'm game, what event?"

"The taking of one of the store boats from the pier two nights ago. They found it floating in the middle of the lake."

"How does any one know it just didn't come loose from its mooring?"

"Because it was late when Ike heard a motor and looked out his window. As you know, we seldom hear boats at night. If we do, they usually have lights. All he could see was a silhouette of a person puttering down the lake."

"It's baffling; like you say, we didn't hear the motor start up. However, he could have rowed out a distance before starting it. At least the person didn't wreck the boat. Maybe he just needed a ride home."

"Are you making excuses for a person stealing a boat?"

Hawkman reared back his head. "Of course not. There must be a reason for this strange behavior. Obviously, he had no intent of taking the boat home. Instead, he just let it float away, knowing it would be found."

Jennifer nodded. "Okay. Have it your way." She glanced up at her husband. "The next incident also occurred at night, and there was probably no crime committed, but it's odd."

"I'm ready."

"Marjorie Jones, who lives in the last house west of us, couldn't sleep last night. She lay in bed reading when she heard the clop of horse's hooves and rolling wheels going down the road. She thought it odd to hear such a thing at eleven o'clock. So she turned out her light and peeked through the window. To her amazement, a man and a woman, who appeared to have a baby in her arms, with two boys in the back, were riding in this old wagon with wooden wheels drawn by a horse, going west. She'd never seen these people before."

Hawkman scratched his head. "They must have gone right by our house, too. If they went to town to shop, they'd have left in the wee hours in the morning and no one would have seen them depart. These are some strange stories you've hit me with, combined with the others from the ladies' auxiliary. I feel I'm living in another era."

"Me, too."

"It actually sounds like we've got homesteaders living in the area. What bothers me, is there's no land available. It's all privately owned. So how are they getting away with it, if that's what they're doing?"

"You think they might have permission to live on the land?"

"Hard to say. They're certainly being evasive. I'm definitely going to find the cabin and talk to them."

"Should you go alone?"

"What danger could I get into by dropping in to say hello?"

Jennifer frowned. "I don't know, but I don't have a good feeling about the venture."

CHAPTER FIVE

Hawkman and Jennifer lay in bed, wrapped in each other's arms. He kissed her on the nose. "You're one hot little mama."

She laughed and ran her hand down his chest. "You're not so bad either." Then she raised up on her elbow. "I want to go with you to find the cabin."

"Is that what you've been thinking about during our love session?"

She grinned. "Not entirely. But what about it?"

"It's not easy riding two on the Polaris."

"We've done it before on the four-wheeler."

"We were on a trail. I'm not sure there's anything but rough terrain where I'm going. What if it proves to be dangerous?"

"If both of us went, we could make it look like we're just making a house call to welcome a new neighbor. As a precaution, I'll carry my gun."

"I don't know, Hon, It rubs against my grain."

"If you go bounding in there alone, you might get shot. With a woman aboard, maybe the person would have a second thought about shooting."

"I want to make it a friendly call. My whole idea is to find the location of this place, then go to the court house and look up who owns the piece of property. I'll contact them, and see if these people are there legally."

"What if they aren't?"

"I'll talk to the sheriff, and let him handle it."

"You think they have electricity?"

"I doubt it. They're probably cooking over the fireplace, which means sparks from the chimney could ignite a forest fire. Could be a dangerous situation."

"Back to the original discussion. Can I go?"

He laughed and pulled her into his arms. "Do I have a choice?"

"Not really." She snuggled against his neck. "Are we going tomorrow?"

"What are your plans for the day?"

"Staying at home."

"Let's go in the morning. I don't have any pressing business at work. So if we find the place, I'll have time to run to the courthouse; and find out the recorded proprietor."

She yawned. "We better get to sleep. Tomorrow will be a full day, and we probably should get up early."

***

Wednesday morning, Hawkman and Jennifer donned jeans, boots and carried light jackets over their arms to the kitchen. They had breakfast, then Hawkman slipped on the wind-breaker, and strolled to the side yard, where he drove the four-wheeler out from under the lean-to. Jennifer stood at the entry, until he stopped in front of her, then she hopped onto the back.

She wrapped her arms around his waist. "I hope we find the cabin."

He gave her a thumbs up as he revved up the engine, moved down the driveway and turned west. They rode a couple of miles before Hawkman slowed a bit and studied the road. He shook his head. "I don't see a sign of a road or trail."

Jennifer pointed. "Is that a clearing up ahead?"

He glanced toward the area. "Could be; let's investigate."

Hawkman brought the four-wheeler to a stop and hopped off. Without a trained eye, the lay person would never spot the bent grass. He dropped down on his haunches and examined the indentations. "It appears thin wheels with a heavy load have been through here."

"Would the mark still show after several days?" Jennifer asked.

"Very possible."

"Could it have been the wagon our neighbor saw?"

"Yes, especially, if the boys ride their bikes through here; and knowing kids, they'd try to stay in the track, making it a game of skill."

He climbed back on the Polaris. "Let's see where it leads."

Turning into the forest, the vehicle climbed through the tall grass with little effort. Hawkman followed the path. At times, the trail grew faint, and he made the decision to keep in the area where openings between the trees were wide enough for a trailer to pass. It seemed they bounced over the terrain for a good thirty minutes before Hawkman crested a hill and brought the four-wheeler to an abrupt halt.

"Why'd you stop?" Jennifer asked.

"I just saw a reflection up ahead in those trees."

"What do you think it is?"

"Could be a gun."

"Maybe we're close to the cabin, and the sun is reflecting off of a window pane."

"I don't think so; it moved. This vehicle is not quiet and I'm sure we can be heard a mile away."

"Are we going to move on?"

"You want to take the chance?"

"If we don't, we'll never find where Randy lives."

"Okay, hold on."

Jennifer quickly grabbed hold of Hawkman as the vehicle jerked forward and bumped over some stones. He continued to slowly follow what he thought to be a faint trail through the trees, which would break out occasionally into an open area, leaving them vulnerable. Hawkman eyed the region where he'd seen the bright flash of light, but saw nothing which could have caused it. This made him more suspicious and wary of their surroundings.

"I can smell food cooking," Jennifer said.

Hawkman sniffed the air. "Me, too."

Suddenly, a shot rang through the air, and Hawkman maneuvered the four-wheeler behind a big oak tree. "Hit the ground!" he ordered.

Jennifer literally fell off the Polaris. Keeping low, she crawled behind the tree trunk. Hawkman followed suit and rolled in front of her, shielding her from harm.

"Where'd the shot come from?" she asked, nervously.

"Up front. It went over our heads like a warning." He stood and stepped out in the open.

"Hawkman, be careful," she whispered, her eyes wide with fear.

He cupped his hands around his mouth. "Who's out there?"

"What are you doing here?" a loud gruff voice boomed from the shadows.

"Taking a ride," Hawkman answered.

"You're on private land," the voice said.

"You the owner?"

"No, but I have permission to be here. You don't. So get your butts off the property."

At that moment, Jennifer whirled around when she heard a branch snap. She sucked in her breath as a long haired young man, dressed in worn jeans, tee shirt, and work boots, moved out of the foliage with a rifle aimed at her head.

Raising both hands, she pleaded. "Don't shoot. We mean no harm. We're looking for Randy Hutchinson. Do you know him?"

He lowered the gun. "What you want with Randy? Is he in some sort of trouble?"

"No, not at all. He just told us his family had recently moved into the area. My husband and I thought we'd ride up and welcome them."

Staring at Jennifer, he yelled, "Hey, Dad, they know Randy."

A burly man, with a large brimmed straw hat, carrying a long barreled rifle in one hand, stepped into the light and marched toward Hawkman. Noticing the man's determined gait, Hawkman stood perfectly still, figuring the blast from such a weapon would make a huge hole in your chest.

CHAPTER SIX

When Randy heard the blast from his father's gun, he dropped the tiny airplane he'd made out of a piece of paper, and glanced at his mother who sat at the kitchen table, peeling potatoes over a bucket. His baby sister lay in a handmade cradle by her side. The half-peeled spud in his mother's hand fell into the container as she quickly stood and looked out the window. Randy ran past her, flung open the door and dashed outside.

"Randy, wait," she called.

Not heeding her words, he took off in the direction of the discharge. He hoped to find a dead buck, which meant meat on the table. Instead, he saw his father step out of the dense brush and walk toward a tall man with a patch over his eye. Randy recognized his new friend, Mr. Casey, and cut back into the brush. He stayed hidden, and quietly moved along just behind the sight of his dad. Randy wanted to yell out and tell him he knew this man, but knew by his father's stubborn gait, he wouldn't be impressed with such news.

The boy had to cut back into the forest due to an open space in the trees, but he kept advancing. Suddenly, he heard his brother talking, and stopped in his tracks when he heard a woman's voice responding. He hunkered down behind a bush, peeked around the edge and there stood Earl, with his rifle pointed at Mrs. Casey's head.

Randy's heart pounded against his ribs so hard it made his chest hurt. "No!" he screamed, as he sprang from his hiding place and dived into his brother head first.

The weapon flew from Earl's hands, crashed to the ground and went off. Randy let out a cry as he crumbled to the ground.

Jennifer stood paralyzed in shock for a few seconds before she realized what had happened. "Oh, my God," she said, as she raced to the boy's side. "Hawkman, help," she cried.

Crashing through the brush, Hawkman dashed toward Jennifer, thinking something had happened to her. He found her kneeling over Randy, who lay in a puddle of blood.

"He's been hit in the thigh, and I need to stop the bleeding," she said.

Hawkman yanked off his belt and wrapped it around the boy's leg above the wound. "We've got to get him to the hospital or he might die. Have you got your cell phone?"

Jennifer reached into her fanny pack. "Yes."

"See if you can get a signal and call 911. Have them send in the helicopter behind the fire station." Hawkman picked up the boy in his arms, and jogged toward the four-wheeler, with Jennifer at his heels. "You'll have to drive; he's too heavy for you to carry."
He slid onto the back, holding the boy in his arms.

"I reached emergency," she said, as she jumped into the driver's seat, and pushed the starter.

The man who'd pursued Hawkman, stepped in front of the four-wheeler. "I'm his father. Where you takin' my boy?"

"Get out of my way, Mr. Hutchinson, or I'll run you over," Jennifer yelled, with narrowed eyes.

"If we don't get your son to a doctor, he'll die due to the loss of blood."

"How'd he get shot?"

"Ask the young man back in the brush," she said, pointing, as she turned the machine around and headed toward the lake as fast as the Polaris could go. The siren at the fire station had already spewed out several rounds of long wails by the time they pulled in front. A couple of the volunteer paramedics had arrived and took Randy from Hawkman's arms and began administering First Aid.

Soon, they heard the rotors of the helicopter hovering over the building, and using expert maneuvers, landed behind the station on the designated pad. Randy groaned as the men moved him onto the gurney and slid it into the chopper. Soon it lifted off, swung clear of the high lines and climbed into the sky.

Jennifer watched, then glanced at Hawkman who stood covered in Randy's blood. "Honey, you better go shower and change clothes."

He pointed west up the road. "I will, after we talk to them."

She turned her gaze toward the two people on horseback, racing toward the fire station. "I hope there's not a problem."

"It's a little late, Randy's on his way to get help. Let's pray he survives."

The two riders pulled their steeds to a quick stop, and jumped down. They tied their horses to the fence and confronted Hawkman and Jennifer.

"What have you done with Randy?"

Jennifer's mouth dropped open when she realized the dark brown eyes belonged to a woman.

"He's on his way to the Medford Hospital in the Medevac helicopter. We had to get him help fast. Are you his mother?"

Her mouth trembled. "Yes. How bad is he hurt?"

"We're not doctors, but knew he was losing a lot of blood."

She glanced at Hawkman. "I can see from your clothes, my boy might not live."

"He's young and healthy," he said. "He has a good chance of pulling through just fine."

Turning to the man beside her, she said, "Jeb, I've got to go to him."

He raised his hands in frustration. "Beth, how do you plan to get there? We have no means of transportation except the horse drawn wagon."

"I want you to take me into town and I'll catch a bus." She headed for the steed she'd ridden.

"Mrs. Hutchinson," Jennifer said, stepping forward. "I'll take you to Medford."

"That's very kind of you. I first have to fetch my baby girl I left at home with her older brother. Jeb will bring me back as soon as I can get ready. Where do you live?"

Jennifer pointed across the street. "I'll be waiting."

Beth untied the horse, threw the reins over its head, put her foot in the stirrup and flung her other leg across the saddle. She kicked the mount in the flanks and took off in a full gallop up the road.

Jeb glared at Hawkman. "I will talk to you later," he said, jumping on his horse and taking off after his wife.

"You're doing quite a favor for strangers who had guns at our heads just an hour ago," Hawkman said.

"She's a mother. I can relate to the feeling."

"Do you want me to go with you?"

"Only if Mr. Hutchinson decides to go. He tends to frighten me."

"Okay, I better get home and clean up, just in case."

Hawkman drove the Polaris back to the house and put it under the lean-to. Jennifer walked across the street, went inside and rummaged through the refrigerator pulling out condiments.

By the time Hawkman had showered and dressed, Jennifer had several sandwiches made and put two in a paper bag along with chips, sodas and candy bars. He furrowed his brow. "How long do you plan to stay in Medford?"

"These are for Mrs. Hutchinson. I doubt she's had time to prepare any food to take. As far as answering your question. I have no idea. It will depend on Randy's condition."

They'd no more chugged down their own sandwiches, when the noise of snorting and pawing of horses sounded outside. Jennifer watched out the window as Beth, with no help from her husband, and clinging to the small bundle in her arms, climbed out of the wagon. He did reach down and toss a small duffle bag to the ground. The minute she got out of the way, he turned the wagon around and headed back up the road.

Jennifer opened the front door. "Please come in out of the cold while I throw a few things together; then we'll get on the road."

Beth stepped inside and her eyes grew wide. "Oh, my, you have a nice place."

"Thank you," Jennifer said, as she reached over and pushed back the flap of the blanket covering the baby's face and smiled. "She's beautiful. What's her name?"

"Marcy. She's my pride."

Jennifer hooked her fanny pack around her waist, took a jacket from the cloak closet, and grabbed the bag of sandwiches. "I've made sandwiches for you, as I figured you didn't have time to eat."

"You're very kind."

"Are you ready to go?"

"Yes, I'm really worried about my boy. I hope he's still alive."

Hawkman followed the two women out to Jennifer's Ford Escape. "Mrs. Hutchinson, try not to worry too much about Randy. I'm sure he'll be fine," he said, helping her into the vehicle.

"Call me Beth. I don't cotton to the Mrs. Hutchinson stuff."

"Very well, Beth it is."

Jennifer backed out of the garage, waved at Hawkman, drove down the driveway, and just as she started over the bridge, a beeping sound penetrated the interior. She pulled to the side and stopped. "You forgot to put on your seat belt."

"My what?"

She reached across the woman and pulled the belt across her body, making sure she didn't have the baby caught, then clicked it into place. "There, now we're ready. Let's just pray we don't get pulled over by the police, as the baby should be in an infant car seat."

She glanced at Jennifer with fear in her eyes. "Would they take my Marcy away?"

"No, but we'd probably get a hefty ticket."

"I'd kill someone if they'd try to take my child."

Feeling uneasy about the topic, Jennifer continued across the bridge, and decided to change the subject. "When did you move to the area?"

"Two or so months ago."
"Do you like it?"
"No, I hate it."

CHAPTER SEVEN

Not sure how to take Beth's response, Jennifer squirmed in the seat. "What don't you like?"

"All of it. I don't have running water or electricity. It's hard. Especially with a baby. We have little money, and our clothes are threadbare. However, Jeb seems to find the cash to buy ammunition. Guess I shouldn't complain; at least he puts meat on the table."

"Where did you live before moving here?"

Beth stared out the side window. "I've said enough. How much farther before we reach the hospital?"

"We'll be there within thirty minutes." Jennifer stole a glance toward the woman with the large knitted shawl draped over her head which fell across her shoulders. She wondered if this was the warmest garment she owned. "Marcy is certainly a good baby. She hasn't made a sound since we left."

"She's starting to squirm. I'll feed her before we go in to see Randy." She shot a glance toward Jennifer. "You will go in with me, won't you?"

"Of course."

"Thank goodness. I wouldn't know the first thing about finding my boy."

Darkness had fallen by the time they pulled into the parking lot of the hospital. Jennifer found an empty slot near the front entrance and the women went inside. Taking matters into her own hands, Jennifer went straight to the information desk and asked about Randy Hutchinson. The woman keyed up her computer, then glanced at her.

"Are you the boy's mother?"

"No, but I have her with me."

"I will need to speak with Mrs. Hutchinson."

Jennifer motioned for Beth to come to the desk.

"May I have your full name, please."

"Beth Marie Hutchinson."

"Mrs. Hutchinson, your son is still in ICU. You may go see him, but the baby won't be allowed inside."

She nodded. "Where's the ICU?"

The receptionist gave instructions, and the two women headed down the hallway. When they reached the big double doors, they stopped outside.

"Let me have Marcy and you go ahead," Jennifer said.

"She might fuss a little because she won't be used to your arms."

Jennifer smiled. "That's okay, we'll manage."

Beth pushed the shawl off her head and ran her fingers through her hair. "I probably look a mess."

"You're a worried mother. Now, go find your son."

Jennifer noticed a window on the other side of the door and walked over, as she gently rocked the baby. From here she could view the patients in the ward and spotted Randy about the same time as Beth. When the boy realized his mother stood by his side, he raised both arms and embraced her. Jennifer could tell immediately, by the smile on his face, that the two shared quite a bond.

She walked down to the end of the hallway as Marcy made fussing noises. When she found a seat, she sat down and placed the baby on her thighs so she could see her better. The child opened big blue eyes and stared at her. "You are certainly a pretty little thing."

Not impressed, Marcy stuck out her lower lip, closed her eyes and whimpered. Jennifer rose and realized the baby needed changing. Since Beth had not left any diapers, Jennifer nabbed a nurse, who immediately brought her a couple. Going into the restroom, she found a changing table and unwound the blanket from around the baby. It amazed her to find the child dressed only in a flimsy wrap with a rag for a diaper. Her small body appeared rash free, and she looked very healthy. "No wonder your mother holds you so close. Keeps you warm, doesn't it, pretty little girl?"

Marcy flapped her arms as if giving thanks for the dry cloth. Jennifer wrapped the small body back into the blanket and tucked the extra diaper into one of the folds. "Okay, little one, glad you feel better. Now, let's go find your mama."

When she returned to the ICU, Beth had not left Randy's side. A chair had been supplied and she sat beside the bed, holding her son's hand. A doctor stood talking to them. Jennifer wondered about the diagnosis.

Soon the physician left and Beth stood. She spoke briefly to Randy and pointed toward the door. When she came out, Jennifer handed her Marcy. "She's been as good as gold. Especially after I changed her."

Beth's cheeks flushed. "How foolish of me, I didn't bring any clean diapers."

"No problem, the nurse brought me a couple. The extra one is tucked in her blanket. We'll stop by the store and get some when we leave the hospital."

"Randy wants to see you."

"Is he up to it?"

"Yes. He's very strong."

"I saw the doctor talking to you." She pointed at the window. "Did he give you any idea on the severity of the wound?"

"Randy lost a lot of blood, but after they sewed him up and gave him a transfusion, he seems to be regaining his strength. The doctor said he can probably go home in a couple of days. They're going to move him to a regular room in the morning."

"Good news." Jennifer started for the door. "I'll go say 'hello' to him."

When she approached the bed, Randy broke into a big smile. "Hi, Mrs. Casey."

"Hello, yourself," she said, grinning.

"That was such a neat helicopter ride."

"You remember it?"

"Oh, yeah. But once they rolled me into the hospital and gave me a shot, I didn't know anything more until I woke up in this room with a big bandage on my leg."

"Were you surprised to see your mom?"

"I knew she'd come, but I didn't know how far she'd have to travel, and figured it would be days before she got here. Thank you for bringing her."

"You're more than welcome."

"I sure miss my little sister."

"If you'll look through that window over there, I'll have your mom hold her up so you can see her."

Randy's eyes lit up. "Okay."

"I better go now and let you rest. Keep watching the glass."

He nodded and tried to sit up, but winced and lay back down.

When Jennifer returned to the waiting room, Beth had just finished eating her sandwich.

"You make wonderful food. I didn't realize how hungry I was."

"Glad you enjoyed it. Randy wants to see Marcy. I told him to watch the window and you'd show her to him."

She grinned and walked over to the glass. Holding up the baby, she made gestures with Marcy's arms and then giggled as Randy waved back.

Jennifer stepped out of the way, giving them privacy. Soon Beth turned toward her with a forlorn expression. "I guess it's time we should leave. It will be very late by the time we reach the lake."

"We could spend the night, and you could see Randy again in the morning. Maybe we'll know more about when he can come home."

"Can we sleep in your van?"

"No, we'll get a motel."

"I can't afford it."

"Don't worry, it's on me. We'll get one room with two beds."

She looked up at Jennifer, her eyes sparkling with tears. "I shall never forget your kindness."

Jennifer patted her shoulder. "Let me have the baby. You go tell Randy goodnight and you'll see him in the morning."

Beth soon returned and they left the hospital. Jennifer knew the area, so first drove to an all-night grocery store. Leaving Beth in the vehicle, she went inside and purchased sandwich makings, and since Beth nursed Marcy, she only bought diapers for the baby. She then traveled to the Best Western Motel and acquired a room. Once they were settled, and had eaten, Jennifer suggested Beth take advantage of the shower.

"Since you don't have running water at home, you'll find it a nice treat."

"You're right. Do you mind watching Marcy"

"Not at all. I'm going to call my husband and let him know our plans. Do you want me to have him notify Mr. Hutchinson?"

Beth scowled. "No need. Jeb won't care." She tossed her shawl onto the bed next to the baby.

Jennifer's bewildered gaze followed her,
as she headed for the bathroom.

CHAPTER EIGHT

When Jennifer heard the shower running, she picked up the phone and dialed home. Hawkman answered after the second ring. "Hi, Hon. Thought I better let you know what's going on. We saw Randy and he's doing good. He'll probably be moved into a regular room tomorrow, and could possibly go home in a couple of days. Right now, Beth and I are at a motel."

Jennifer listened for a moment. "No, she said it wouldn't be necessary, as Jeb wouldn't be worried. Beth actually said, he wouldn't care."

She remained silent for a few seconds. "I'm not sure how long we'll stay. I'll let you know."

After hanging up, she lay across the bed next to the baby. She glanced toward the bathroom as a beautiful soft melodic voice, singing what sounded like an American Indian lullaby, drifted through the door. "What other surprises am I going to learn about your mom?" she said, touching Marcy's chin.

The baby waved her arms and kicked her feet, knocking off the light cover across her legs. Jennifer laughed as she replaced it. "I think you recognize the song."

Wrapped in a towel, Beth emerged from the bathroom and glanced at Jennifer. "Sorry I took so long, but you were right, I really enjoyed the bath. Just wish I'd brought some fresh clothes. I had no idea we'd spend the night."

Jennifer smiled. "Me either, so we're in the same boat. You have a beautiful voice. Marcy kicked and waved her arms like she'd heard it before."

Beth laughed, as she rummaged through the pockets of her jeans and brought out a large comb which she ran through her wet, thick black hair that extended past her hips. "Not so sure I sound good, but I enjoy singing to her."

While Jennifer took her turn in the shower, she thought about Beth's long tresses, high cheek bones, dark brown eyes and bronze skin. She came to the conclusion the woman had Indian blood in her veins, especially after hearing the haunting melody from her lips. She'd also gathered there was little affection between her and Jeb. What about the older boy? Beth had not mentioned him.

When Jennifer returned to the room, she found Beth and the baby curled up in their bed, both with closed eyes. Flipping off the lamp, she crawled under the covers and discovered she felt very tired.

The next morning, the two women were awakened by the cries of Marcy. Jennifer rolled over and faced Beth, with only the large shawl wrapped around her body, rocking the baby in her arms, as she tried to get her to take milk.

"I'm sorry she woke you. I think she's sick. She seems very warm, like maybe running a fever."

"Oh, no," Jennifer said, crawling out of bed and slipping into her clothes. She moved over and sat next to Beth, then touched Marcy's head. "She's burning up. What do you think is the problem?"

"She keeps putting her hand up to the side of her head, like something hurts."

"Sounds like she might have an ear infection. When we get to the hospital, we'll have a doctor check her."

Beth continued to rock the baby, as Jennifer used the last of the groceries to make sandwiches, then took Marcy so Beth could dress. They were ready to leave in just minutes. When they arrived at the hospital, Jennifer scurried to find a doctor who would look at the baby. She soon found one and he verified Marcy had an ear infection, wrote out a prescription for a liquid antibiotic, also drops for the ear.

Jennifer picked up the medications at the hospital pharmacy, and they hurried up to the ICU, only to find Randy had been moved. Soon, they located him in a double bed room. When he saw them walk in, his face lit up in a big smile.

"Hi, Mom and Mrs. Casey. The doctor might let me go home today."

"Really," Jennifer said.

"Yeah, he said I was healing like a strong man. I'll have to be extra careful and use crutches for a couple of weeks. I told him I could do that. He said to have Mom talk to him."

"Thank goodness you're doing so well," Beth said, reaching over and patting his arm. "Our little Marcy has an ear infection."

Randy frowned and sat up to peer at his baby sister. "Hey, little girl, can't have you sick. I'm coming home to help Mom take care of you."

A man in a white coat walked into the room. "Is one of you Mrs. Hutchinson?"

"Yes," Beth said.

"I'm Dr. Freedman. I operated on Randy's wound. We feel he can go home today, if he promises to be careful. His wound is deep, but he's doing well. He's not to put full weight on the leg for a week. We'll lend him a pair of crutches, which you can return in a month. His stitches will dissolve, but if you notice he's torn the gash open or any signs of infection, get him back here as soon as possible." He ruffled Randy's hair. "You have one brave lad here."

She smiled. "Thank you."

"If you'll come with me, we'll get the paperwork done. I'll give you some samples of pain pills, then you can take him home."

Beth appeared bewildered and shot a look at Jennifer.

"I'll come with you."

With Jennifer at her side, they followed the doctor down to the main desk. He handed Beth a couple of sheets of paper on a clipboard, and a pen.

"Just fill these out and give them to the nurse who will be out shortly. She'll get the crutches and fit them to Randy."

Moving to a couple of chairs at the far side of the room, Beth whispered to Jennifer. "You have to help me. I don't know how to answer any of these questions."

"Can you read?"

"Yes, but I never learned how to write, except to sign my name."

Jennifer took the clipboard and the two women huddled as she read the questions aloud, then wrote Beth's answers. "What's your address?"

"I don't know."

"I'll put mine down," Jennifer said.

The rest were fairly easy, and Jennifer took the baby while Beth signed the last paper. She then turned it over to the nurse who brought out a wheelchair, and they journeyed to Randy's room.

He handed his mother a small bubble pack of pills, then made a face. "Why do I have to get in that thing, now that I have the crutches?"

"Hospital policy," the nurse said, helping him.

When they reached the front door, Jennifer dashed to get the Ford and brought it around to the entrance. Once they loaded Randy inside, along with the crutches, they headed for home.

Before they arrived at Copco Lake, Jennifer worried about driving up to the Hutchinson's. "I'm going to stop and pick up Mr. Casey. I don't want any trouble with your husband and older son when we drive to your place."

Beth shook her head in disgust. "If it weren't for Jeb's and Earl's shenanigans we wouldn't be in this mess."

Jennifer glanced toward the back and noticed Randy had fallen asleep. "Earl seems to have a completely different personality than Randy."

"Jeb taught him to be mean and cunning. I won't permit him to do it to Randy."

"How can you stop him?"

"I have my way."

They approached the bridge and Jennifer drove into her driveway. "I'll be right back."

She jumped out and ran into the house. Hawkman stood at the sliding glass door.

"I saw you coming, and wondered about your plans."

"I want you to go with me. The hospital released Randy early, but he has to be very careful for the next couple of weeks. I think it best we take him home in the SUV, instead of him riding home in a rickety wagon."

"Okay, I'm ready."

When they climbed into the vehicle, Randy had awakened and grinned when Hawkman crawled in beside him.

"How's it going, trooper?"

"Doctor said I'm healing really good."

"Great. You just gotta be careful for a few days."

"Yeah. Look at these." He held up the crutches. "The nurse showed me how to walk with them and said it was very important for me to keep the weight off my leg, or I could end up back in the hospital with bigger problems."

"You heed those words."

"I will."

Jennifer drove out of the driveway and turned west. After traveling a couple of miles, she turned her head toward Beth. "When Mr, Casey and I came up here trying to find your cabin, we took what looked like a trail up ahead. Is it the right way?"

"Yes. It's very rough. The wagon and horses do fine. I hope your vehicle can make it."

"I think it will; it has a four-wheel drive if I run into any problems." She glanced back at Randy.

"You hold on good so you don't jiggle your leg."

He grabbed both sides of the seat as Jennifer turned onto the bumpy terrain. Even though she drove slowly, she cringed at every bump. When they reached the area where Jed had shot over their head in the four-wheeler, Hawkman eyed both sides, not knowing what to expect.

Suddenly, Jeb stepped out of the shadows with his gun aimed at the front of the Ford. Beth quickly rolled down the window and stuck out her head.

"Put that gun down, you stupid man, it's your wife and son."

CHAPTER NINE

When Hawkman saw Jeb step out in front of the truck, he rested his hand on the butt of his gun in the shoulder holster. Twisting in the seat, he surveyed the area behind them, figuring Earl would bring up the rear. Surprised at Beth's comment to her husband, he glanced at Randy. The boy's mouth twitched as if holding back laughter. Hawkman wondered what kind of life these people led. The big question that lingered in his mind, was why Jeb seemed to be so obsessed with not letting anyone through the area. What was the man hiding?

Jeb lowered his gun and approached the vehicle. "Is our boy alive?"

"Of course," Beth said. "I need to get him home and into bed. He needs rest and has to stay off the leg for two or three weeks."

About the time Jeb waved the Ford through, Earl ran up to the window. "Good to have you home, Mom. Sorry the gun went off and hit you, Randy."

"Happy you missed us." She looked him up and down. "You certainly don't look any worse for wear."

"Had to eat what he put in front of me." He nodded toward his dad.

She shook her head, then turned toward Jennifer. "Keep going straight. I'll tell you where to turn."

Jeb and Earl stepped out of the way as Jennifer slowly guided the SUV past them. She hit a few bad bumps that made Randy groan.

"Sorry, I'm really trying to be careful."

"I know; it just caused a pain."

Beth turned in her seat. "We'll be home soon and get you to bed."

Just when Jennifer thought she couldn't go much farther as a thick forest lay ahead, Beth pointed to the right.

"Go this way and you'll see our cabin to your left."

Jennifer pulled up to the front door as close as she could, then Hawkman climbed out and went around to the side where he could lift Randy from the vehicle.

"I can use my crutches," the boy said.

"Tomorrow will be soon enough. Let's get you to bed. You've had a hard day." Careful not to put any pressure on the wounded leg, he gently lifted Randy from the seat.

Holding Marcy, Beth hurried ahead of Hawkman, and pushed open the door so he could get through without hesitation. She quickly laid Marcy in the homemade cradle, then guided Hawkman to a cot near the window, and pushed back the covers. "Put him here."

Heedful of the injury, he placed the lad on the bed. "There you go. Now, I advise you to get some sleep."

Randy snuggled under the covers. "Yeah, I'm tired."

Jennifer had followed the group inside. "Use your crutches like the doctor explained. I'll come and visit you soon."

"Randy glanced at her with heavy lids, and smiled. "I'd like that."

"We're going home now. Your mom will take great care of you." Jennifer placed the crutches at the end of the cot, then handed Beth a sack which contained medications and fresh bandages, along with the bundle of diapers.

"How can I ever thank you for all you've done?" Beth said, clutching the sack.

"Just take care of our boy," Jennifer said. "I'll be out to see you soon."

As Hawkman and Jennifer strolled out of the cabin, they met Jeb and Earl coming in.

"Hope this is the last time we have to meet with you folks," Jeb said.

With fire in her eyes, Jennifer whirled around on her heel and pointed a finger at him. "Mr. Hutchinson, get used to seeing me. I plan to come out here often to see Beth and Randy. If you so much as fire that gun of yours in the air, I'll have the law down on you so fast you won't know what happened."

Jeb stepped back and narrowed his eyes. "Don't get smart with me, young lady. I don't take to that kind of talk coming from a woman."

"Then mind your manners," Jennifer said, as she stalked around the Ford and climbed into the driver's seat.

Hawkman slipped into the passenger side with a smirk twitching at the corners of his mouth. Jennifer fired up the SUV, turned around, and headed toward the road.

"Simmer down, my bold wife. Take those bumps a little slower."

"How does Beth live with such a man?"

"He's all she's got."

She let out a puff of air, causing her bangs to rise. "You're probably right. I wonder if he can read and write?"

Hawkman frowned. "Why would you ask such a question?"

She shook her head. "I've learned so much about Beth. It's a good thing I was at the hospital with her or she'd have been humiliated."

"How come?"

"Well, the only thing she knows how to write is her name, which saved us a lot of explanations. I could fill out all the forms, and then she could sign them. She has a beautiful voice and crooned a very haunting lullaby while she showered. After seeing her long black hair, hanging past her hips, bronze skin, along with those dark eyes and high cheek bones, I drew the conclusion she's an American Indian or at least has Indian blood."

He nodded. "Very possible. Did you ever find out why they moved to the cabin?"

"No. I tried to be careful questioning her, as I wanted her trust. If I got too close to something she didn't want to tell, she hushed up or made the comment, 'I've said enough'."

"Interesting. You said she couldn't write, what about read?"

"Yes, she knows how to read simple stuff, like some of the questions on the forms, but big words threw her. I found it odd, she could only write her name, as you'd think she would have taught herself by just copying words. Of course, it could all be a ploy, so I wouldn't find out too much. She speaks well, but I gather she's had little education. Oh, she doesn't know her address, so I just put ours down. Maybe not such a good idea, but I didn't want getting Randy out of the hospital to become a big problem."

"If we get a bill, we'll just take it to them, if we don't get our heads shot off."

Jennifer soon turned into their driveway and pulled into the garage. "How'd Miss Marple do without me here?"

"She missed you, and hunted through each room trying to find where you'd gone. I even caught her crawling under the bed. Soon, she gave up, then wouldn't let me out of her sight."

When they walked into the house, the feline greeted Hawkman, but completely ignored Jennifer.

"Uh, oh, I'm getting punished. Wonder how long she'll tune me out?"

Hawkman laughed. "Enjoy it."

"These last few days have been quite an experience," Jennifer said, flopping down in her chair. "It's good to be home."

"How about a gin and tonic?"

"Sounds wonderful."

"I guess you're wondering how come things went so smoothly at the hospital since they'd just admitted a boy with a gun wound?"

"Yes, it did enter my mind. I assumed you had something to do with it."

"I filled out an accident report and faxed it to the doctors in charge."

"It certainly saved us from unnecessary questions."

"How bad is Randy's injury?"

"A clean wound. The doctor put in a few stitches, and didn't want him breaking it open. He warned him not to put any weight on the leg and to use the crutches for a couple of weeks."

"How'd the baby do during your stay?"

"Marcy's a doll. One of the best infants I've ever come across. However, she did come down with an ear infection, and we had a doctor check her. He prescribed ear drops and antibiotics, so she'll be fine in a few days. I worry about Beth. She'll have her hands full, and won't get any help from her sorry husband."

Hawkman brought her drink and took his chair. "There's something fishy about this whole scenario. Since I haven't had a chance to get to the courthouse, I'll go tomorrow and find out who owns the property. If I can contact him or her, it may help us get a handle on this whole situation."

CHAPTER TEN

Friday morning, Hawkman grabbed his clothes, sneaked out of the bedroom and closed the door. He doubted Jennifer had received much rest, considering what she'd been through the last couple of days. After he dressed, he filled Miss Marple's food dish and water bowl, whispering to the spoiled feline who'd wrapped around his leg. "I hope this keeps you from yowling. Let your mistress sleep. You have my permission to stay mad at her for another day."

He left the cat at her feeding station, downed a bowl of dry cereal, and departed. Fortunately, he only had to drive into Yreka to the county courthouse where he'd find the property listed. The only problem he foresaw would be if the land was subdivided between several owners. If his memory served him right, he remembered several years ago a discussion among homeowners about a man who'd bought a huge portion of land in the area near the old railroad. He'd heard nothing about it since, so he hoped it was still held by only one proprietor.

Arriving in Yreka, he drove straight to the courthouse and went inside. He knew a few of the people and spotted Sally behind the counter. "Hi, Sally."

She glanced up and smiled. "Mr. Casey, it's been quite awhile since you've graced our doors. How can I help you?"

"I want to find the owner of some property, but I'll need to look at a map, as I have no statistics to help me."

"Sure. Let's go to my station."

She moved through a swinging gate and he followed her to a desk tucked in the corner of the room. Motioning for him to take a seat, she slid into her chair behind the computer. "Okay, where do we need to go?"

"Slightly northwest of Copco Lake, near the old railroad tracks."

Her fingers flew over the keys, and she soon turned her computer toward him. She pointed. "Is this the area?"

He studied the screen for a moment. "Yes." Then ran his finger along a line. "I'd like to know who owns the parcels west of this road."

"How far do you want to extend the boundary?"

Hawkman pointed to a creek. "A bit past here."

Sally jotted down the numbers on a sheet of paper, then typed them into the computer. "There are two forty acre parcels, owned by a Jacob Hutchinson. There's a small house, a barn, and several outbuildings on one piece, nothing on the other."

Hawkman leaned forward and furrowed his brow. "Did you say Hutchinson?"

She nodded. "Yes, Jacob Hutchinson."

"How long has he owned this property?"

"Over ten years."

"Where do you send the property tax bills?"

She glanced at the monitor. "Medford, Oregon. You want his address?"

"Yes, please."

She took a pad of paper and wrote it down. "Here you go," she said, tearing off the sheet and handing it to him.

Hawkman stood. "Thanks, Sally. Appreciate your time."

"No problem. All part of my job. Wish more requests were as easy as yours."

He left the courthouse, baffled by the land being owned by a relative, possibly a father or a brother. Jeb obviously spoke the truth when he said he had permission to be on the property.

When he arrived home, he told Jennifer of his discovery.

She tapped her chin. "I find your bit of news fascinating. So how are you going to move on this information?"

"Jacob Hutchinson has lived in Medford for many years. I might be able to find him on the computer and get a bit of history."

"You think he'll talk to you?"

Hawkman shrugged. "All I can do is try."

"I have a feeling it's the father of Jeb Hutchinson."

"Hard to say. Could be a brother, grandfather or the dad. I'll know more when I see him in person."

"Good luck. Keep me informed," Jennifer
said, as she turned toward her computer,
and Hawkman continued down the hallway
to his home office.

He decided first to check the Medford
phone book out of curiosity, and see if the
man was listed. Not finding it in his side
desk drawer, where he normally kept it, he
wandered back into the living room and
searched.

Jennifer raised her head. "Whoops, bet
you're looking for the Medford directory. I
have it here. I forgot to take it back to your
office."

"No problem. Why did you need it?"

"Looking for baby stuff."

He furrowed his brow. "Why?"

She exhaled. "I wanted to see if Medford
had one of those consignment shops where
they sell used baby equipment. Beth has
nothing for the infant, except the handmade
cradle, which is lovely, but Marcy will soon
outgrow it."

Hawkman studied his wife. "You really like
her, don't you?"

"Yes. Also, I feel very sorry for the family. I
don't understand why Jeb hasn't piped
water into the cabin. There's a windmill near

the back of the house, and I bet if he tinkered with it a little, he could get it working again."

Hawkman nodded. "I think he has other things on his mind."

"For instance?"

"I don't know, but I hope to find out." He scooted the directory out from under Miss Marple. "Sorry, girl, I need this more than you." He chuckled. "Looks like she's forgiven you for leaving her."

Jennifer laughed. "Yes, she's followed me around all day, making sure I don't get out of her sight."

Hawkman carried the book back to his desk, and opened it to the 'H's'. Running his finger down the columns, he came to several Hutchinsons. Several had a 'J' as the first initial, but no addresses. It appeared he'd have to do a search on the computer.

After the machine booted up, he went to the secure website and put in his password. Once accepted, he typed in Jacob Hutchinson, Medford, Oregon. It only took a few seconds for the site to respond, and the name appeared on the screen. Disappointed with the sparse information, he printed out the couple of paragraphs which stated the man had lived at the same place for twenty years. No background data appeared as to what he'd done for a living or where he'd resided before. Hawkman thought this odd, but some things do get blocked. No reason has to be given. Just like the statistics on himself. There were none; he'd checked.

He shut down the computer and meandered into the living room. Finding his briefcase next to his chair he slid the paper inside.

"Did you find anything of interest?" Jennifer asked.

"Very little. I know it was the same man, as the address matched the one I got at the courthouse. I'll pay Jacob Hutchinson a visit tomorrow."

CHAPTER ELEVEN

As Hawkman rolled across the bridge heading for Medford, he glanced out over Copco Lake as the sun's beams bounced off the still water. It appeared like twinkling diamonds on a woman's finger. A nip in the air gave warning that old man winter wasn't through. He liked this time of year.

His mind went to thoughts of Randy. He'd been schooled at one time, but obviously no one seemed in a hurry to get him enrolled again. This worried Hawkman. The boy had a good mind and it shouldn't be wasted. Maybe Jennifer could talk with Beth about the possibilities of getting him back into school. He had no idea of Earl's age, but figured somewhere around sixteen.

He soon arrived at the outskirts of town; knowing the area of Hutchinson's address, he made the turns which led him into a neighborhood of older homes. A few had well-kept yards; others were overgrown, and needed attention. Once on the right street, he took the piece of paper Sally had given him at the courthouse, and glanced at the numbers. For some odd reason, when he came across the home, it didn't surprise him to find it run-down and in need of a good paint job. The lawn hadn't been trimmed in several weeks and the bushes had grown wild.

Hawkman studied the front for a moment before climbing out. He could see the flicker of light shining through the sheer drapes covering the front window. When he reached the entry and knocked, he heard the barking of a dog and heavy footsteps of someone approaching.

A man hovering around his mid-sixties, beer belly and greasy, dirty gray hair opened the door. "Yeah, whatcha want?" he asked.

A medium sized brown dog stood at his side, growling.

"Shut-up Mutt. Go lay down." He pointed his cane toward the back of the room. The mongrel lowered his head, and with his tail between his legs, retreated.

The old fellow looked up at Hawkman. "Well, who are ya and why ya here?"

"I'm Tom Casey, private investigator, looking for Jacob Hutchinson."

"The senior edition or the junior."

Hawkman scratched his sideburn. "I'm not sure. Which one owns the property at Copco Lake?"

"Is there a problem?"

"Not sure. That's why I'm here."

"You might as well come in. My legs won't allow me to stand too long."

He opened the screen door and Hawkman stepped inside. The stench almost made him recoil, and flee back to the fresh air. He couldn't tell if it came from filth, spoiled food, or both.

"Are you Jacob Hutchinson? The man who owns the property?"

"Yeah, I'm the guy. My dear old father is in his room. He's eighty-five and not doing very good."

"I'm sorry. So you own the property alone? No wife?"

"She died many years ago. So you wanna buy the land?"

"No, I just wanted to notify you there's someone living in the cabin on your property."

He waved a hand. "I know, it's my no-good son and his redskin woman. He got out of jail about a year and a half ago and couldn't find a job. Since they were living in a tent under a bridge, I told them they could live out there. Figured it'd be better since they have kids." The old fellow frowned. "Are they causing a ruckus?"

"No, but it's very primitive. No running water or electricity."

He pointed a finger in the air. "There's a beautiful well out there, all he's got to do is get off his lazy butt and get it working again."

"Why was he in prison?"

"Vehicular manslaughter. Driving while drunk as a skunk, ran over a man and killed him. The jury gave him five years, but he got out in three, due to good behavior."

Hawkman headed for the door. "I won't worry about your relatives on the property. I just wanted to be sure you knew about it."

"I appreciate your concern. If you talk to them, you tell them his old man said to behave or he'll have them kicked off. Also tell that lazy no-good Jeb, to get the well going."

"I'll do that, sir."

When Hawkman stepped outside, he gulped in fresh air, as he headed for his SUV. He kept the window down on his way home, as he felt his clothes reeked of the horrible odor. When he reached the house, he went in the side door and disrobed. He shoved all his clothes into the washer and placed his boots outside on the porch to air. Adding soap, he flipped on the machine, then peeked out to make sure the coast was clear. He streaked through the living room to the bedroom, and heard Jennifer howling with laughter as he stepped into the shower.

He finally emerged from the stall, dried, dressed in clean clothes and strolled into the living room. Glancing at his wife, he muttered. "I had a bad day."

"For heaven's sake, what happened? Did you get sprayed by a skunk?"

"Not quite that bad, but almost. You will not believe this story."

"Try me."

He shooed Miss Marple from the chair next to Jennifer's computer, and sat down.

"I met Mr. Jacob Hutchinson. A short, dirty man, greasy hair and a filthy cane. He invited me inside and I kid you not, I thought I'd puke at the smell. I didn't dare take a seat, as the couch was covered in stains, the chairs were loaded with dirty clothes, and the dog smelled of urine. I gathered the older Mr. Hutchinson was lying in a gross bed back in one of the bedrooms, probably dying. The stench still lingers in my nose, even though I scrubbed every inch of my body."

Enthralled by the tale, Jennifer stared at her husband. "Did you meet his wife?"

Hawkman shook his head. "Jacob said she'd died several years ago."

"Did you learn anything about Jeb and Beth?"

"Unfortunately, the old man doesn't give a hoot about either one of them. Jeb is an ex-con and he called Beth a redskin. So your observation is obviously correct; she is an American Indian. I gathered from the conversation, the only reason he let them live up there was because children were involved, and Jeb couldn't get a job."

"How did you approach the subject to get so much information?"

"I told him I just wanted to inform him someone was living on the land. He immediately acknowledged it, and gave me those details. Also he told me to tell Jeb to get his lazy butt in gear and get water piped into the house."

"Doesn't sound like he's willing to put any money into making the place more livable."

"From what I saw, he might not have any. Or he's hoarding it for a rainy day. Some of these eccentrics hide their money and die worth millions."

"And to think I almost suggested going with you. Certainly glad I didn't."

"I doubt you could have handled it. I almost keeled over. Probably would have had to carry you out."

"It sure doesn't sound like there's much love between him and his son."

"I don't think so. He didn't appear very proud of him. The first thing he wanted to know was if they were causing any trouble."

Jennifer reached over and patted Hawkman's arm. "Well, my dear, it sounds like you had quite an adventure."

He shuddered. "One I hope not to duplicate in the near future. I'll meet the old fellow somewhere before I ever enter his abode again." Pulling a tissue from the box, he blew his nose. "I hope this horrible odor leaves me soon."

"It may take a day or two."

"That long?" he asked, in horror.

She laughed, then frowned. "You didn't tell me why Jeb was in prison."

"Vehicular manslaughter. Killed a man while driving under the influence. Sentenced to five years, but got out in three due to good behavior."

"No wonder he can't get a job. No one wants to hire a felon. So how's he getting money? Beth said he always seems have cash for ammunition. Maybe he does get some from his dad."

"My question is, how would he get to Medford? Horseback?"

"Maybe his dad has a vehicle, and comes up here?"

"I had the impression Jacob hasn't seen his son or family since they moved in. I could be all wet. I also wonder if Mr. Hutchinson drives. The garage door was closed, so I have no idea if he has a car or not."

"The mystery deepens," Jennifer said. She rose from the computer and showed him an ad in the phone directory. "I'm going to Yreka tomorrow. I found a place closer that carries used baby items. I'll give them a call in the morning and see what they have."

"So you're really serious about helping Beth, regardless of the danger?"

"Yes."

CHAPTER TWELVE

After Hawkman left for work, Jennifer
prepared to go to Yreka. She felt a little
uneasy about what she planned on doing,
but decided Beth and Marcy were worth it.
Climbing into her Ford Escape, she headed
for town. The trip only took thirty minutes
and she knew the small shop's location.
She pulled into a parking place in front.

Since she hadn't shopped for baby items
for a long time, the merchandise fascinated
her. The last baby shower she'd attended
occurred two or three years ago. Finding a
clerk, she inquired where they displayed the
used equipment. The woman led her to the
back of the store and pointed out several
items, explaining they were on
consignment. Jennifer's gaze immediately
stopped on a small crib which would fit in
the cabin without taking up much room. She

examined it thoroughly and found it to be in excellent condition, and the price reasonable. Her attention then went to a couple of highchairs, and she finally decided on the sturdy oak with the lift up tray. Once she loaded them into the SUV, plus some sheets for the infant bed, she stopped at the grocery store, bought some things for Beth and herself, then headed home.

Feeling good about the purchases, she decided to take them to the cabin that afternoon. When she arrived home, she put the perishables away, then went to the bedroom. Removing the fanny pack from the dresser drawer, she fastened it around her waist, and slipped the pistol inside.

A chill ran up her spine as she went out the front door. What if Jeb or Earl shot at her? She threw back her shoulders and exclaimed aloud. "I'll yell at them first. If that doesn't work, I'll shoot off my gun." With a toss of her head, she jumped into the Explorer.

Traveling up the road, then turning at the small cut, she felt uneasiness surge through her body. Maybe she should have waited for Hawkman. She knew he wouldn't be too happy about her doing this trick alone. Butterflies in her stomach, she plowed ahead over the rough terrain. When she arrived at the spot where she should turn. Earl stepped out of the trees and pointed his rifle.

"Stop where you are."

"Get out of my way, Earl, I've come to see Beth."

He walked toward her, never lowering the gun. "What do you want with her?"

"None of your business. My visit is with your mother, not you."

He lowered the gun. "You wait here; I'll check with her."

"I'm not going to sit here, you twerp," she mumbled under her breath. When Earl disappeared into the woods, she gunned the Ford ahead, turned and ended up in front of the cabin where she parked. Jennifer hurried to the front door and started to knock when she heard Beth's angry voice.

"What do you mean stopping Mrs. Casey and making her wait for you to come back. Don't you ever do that again. Do you hear me?"

"Dad told me not to let anyone come through the property," Earl said.

"I don't care what your father said. She's my friend and I'm telling you what to do when it concerns people coming to see me. Now, get out there and have her come on in."

Earl opened the door, and appeared shocked. "She's here already." He glared at Jennifer as he brushed past her. "I told you to wait," he said.

"You don't tell me what to do," she spat.

Beth came forward. "Please forgive his rudeness. Come in, please."

Jennifer glanced at the cot where she expected to see the injured boy. "Where's Randy?"

"He's very restless and is out walking on his crutches. He'll be in shortly; he doesn't last too long. He says they make his underarms sore. I'm sure he's not using them right, as they shouldn't make him hurt."

"How's the injury coming?"

"Healing very nicely."

"Good." Jennifer pointed out the door. "I've brought some things for the baby. Want to help me bring them in."

"I'd love to."

The two women went outside, and when Jennifer opened the rear end, Beth gasped in surprise, and put her hands at her throat. "Oh my, a crib and high chair?"

"Marcy can't sleep in the cradle for much longer. She's really growing," Jennifer said, reaching in and pulling the bed toward her, then instructed Beth to grab the other end.

They carried it inside, and placed it against the wall at the end of Randy's cot. Beth had a smile on her face that lit up the room.

"It's beautiful, and fits perfectly."

"I also brought some sheets for the small mattress, but first, let's fetch the high chair."

"You are much too kind," Beth said, as they scurried out the door.

Once they'd placed the items in the room, Jennifer lugged in the sacks ladened with all sorts of goodies. As they unloaded them, Randy came swinging into the room, a big grin on his face.

"Hi, Mrs. Casey."

"Hello, Randy. I've got some things for you in this sack."

"Really?"

"You can read, can't you?"

"Yeah, pretty good. I used to go to school, and Mom has taught me too."

"Good." She handed him some books and a box of pencils. "These have puzzles in them, and I've brought a few toys you might enjoy."

She placed a paddle board with a rubber ball in his hand. "See if you can hit the ball. On second thought," she said, as the ball whizzed by her face, "maybe you should take it outside."

He laughed as he searched in the sack, where he found a race car and couple of different balls. "Wow, this is neat stuff." Swinging his body on the crutches, he went out the door with the paddle and ball in his hand.

Jennifer removed a toy with colored plastic animals hanging on a colorful string, and attached it to Marcy's cradle. The baby immediately grew excited and kicked her feet.

"She loves it," Beth said, touching the items so they wiggled.

Jennifer glanced at Beth who'd become silent, with an expression of concern on her face.

"What's the matter?"

"We can't accept these things."

"Why not?"

"I can never repay you."

"I don't expect any payment. These are gifts from one friend to another. Just seeing the pleasure on your faces makes me happy."

Beth ran her hands over the baby's crib, and tears welled in her eyes. "I love this."

"When Marcy outgrows her cradle, she'll be able to sleep in it for at least a year."

Both women turned on their heel when a voice boomed from the doorway. "What the hell's going on here?"

"Mrs. Casey has brought some lovely items for Marcy."

"You can't keep them. We don't take no charity."

Jennifer narrowed her eyes and glared at Jeb Hutchinson. "This isn't charity. These are gifts."

"We don't want to owe no one."

"No payment is due, if the item is a gift," Jennifer said.

"I want the stuff out of here," he said, advancing toward the crib.

Jennifer stepped in front of him. "Don't touch it. It stays in here for Beth and Marcy."

He pushed Jennifer aside, picked up the bed and carried it toward the door.

"Mr. Hutchinson, you're the most unreasonable man I've ever met, not to mention very selfish. These items make less work for Beth. Instead of making life miserable for your family, why don't you spend some time working on that windmill, so you'd have running water in this place?"

Dropping the bed, he whirled around and pointed a finger at Jennifer. "Don't tell me how to run my family. I want you out of here, now!"

"Only if you allow Beth and Randy to keep these items will I leave in peace. Otherwise, I'm calling the authorities to let them see how you treat your children."

The fire in his eyes and the contortion of his mouth would have caused most people to flee in terror, but Jennifer bravely stood her ground.

"So what's your answer?" she asked.

Jeb looked Jennifer in the face. "You drive a hard bargain. I'll let Beth and Randy keep the items, but I don't want you back here."

"I'm not promising such a thing. Beth is my friend, and I'm concerned about her, Marcy's, and Randy's welfare."

"I take care of my own, they're not your concern." He pushed open the door. "I'd advise you to go, before I lose my temper completely."

"I'll go, but I'll be back; you can bet on it." Jennifer said, leaving the cabin and climbing into her truck. The flush of anger burned her cheeks as she stuck the key in the ignition. She backed up and turned the Ford around. As she left the premises, she glanced in the rear view mirror. "Oh, dear God, no!"

Jeb had a shotgun pointed at her vehicle. Jennifer hit the accelerator in hopes of putting as much space as possible between him and her. The boom echoed through the air, and the sound of being peppered by pebbles made Jennifer breathe a sigh of relief when she realized she'd just been blasted with birdshot. Thank goodness she'd put distance between them. She might have a few tiny dents in the metal, but there would be less damage than if she'd been at close range.

What possessed him to shoot at her? She knew the man didn't like the idea of Beth having a friend, especially one who didn't take his guff.

"Did he think he could scare me off with a little birdshot," she mumbled.

She finally bounced onto the paved road and headed toward home.

CHAPTER THIRTEEN

Randy followed Jeb into the cabin and hurried across the room where he stood wide eyed as his mother met his father with fiery eyes, and a long dagger raised in a threatening manner.

Jeb stood the shotgun in the corner. "Now Beth, put that thing away."

"How dare you humiliate me in front of my friend. You acted like a jackass," she screamed, her voice shaking.

Marcy began to cry and Randy hovered in the corner on his crutches, clutching his gifts to his chest.

"She was so good to us when I fetched our son from the hospital. I couldn't have done it without her. Then she comes to see me, bearing gifts, and you treat her like dirt. Have you no compassion?"

Jeb held up his hands in defense. "I just don't hanker after charity, and I don't want people nosing around here."

Beth lowered the knife and narrowed her eyes. "Why? What are you doing that you don't want anyone to see?"

He shrugged. "Nothin'."

"You're lying." She waved a hand at him. "Just get out. I don't even want to look at you."

He put his fists on his hips. "You can't kick me out of my own house."

"It's not yours. It belongs to your father."

"Beth, settle down. I'll be nicer to Mrs. Casey if she comes back."

"I doubt I'll ever see her again. After being shot at, she'll be afraid to come visit me."

"Sure sorry I've upset you so. What can I do to make it up?"

She stared at him. "Are you serious?"

He nodded.

Pointing at the kitchen sink, she said, "Get the pump to working, so I don't have to haul water."

"I can probably do that, but it might take awhile."

"I don't care. Just do it."

He walked out the door, and she heard him yell at Earl to get a couple of shovels out of the shed and meet him at the side of the house. She smiled to herself, put the dagger away, and picked up the crying baby.

"Mom, do you think Dad will really fix it so we have water in the house?" Randy said, stumbling out of the corner.

"Yes, or he'll feel my wrath."

"Boy, I want to be on your good side."

She laughed. "You are, my son, you are."

***

When Jennifer arrived home, she still felt angry and stormed into the house. Hawkman glanced up from reading the paper as she slammed the front door, yanked off her fanny pack and tossed it onto the counter with a clunk.

"Hey, what's going on?"

"I'm so mad I could pick up a chair and throw it through a window."

"Whoa, lady, settle down before you explode. Let me fix you a drink and tell me about it."

Jennifer sat on the hearth, and Miss Marple rubbed up against her side. "I'm really not in the mood for you. Go see the man of the house."

"Boy, you must have had a bad day," he said, handing her a drink.

Hawkman lowered his lanky frame next to her, and she leaned against his shoulder. "I should never have gone without you."

"Where'd you go?"

"To see Beth."

He frowned, set his glass down on the brick, took her by the shoulders, and turned her toward him. "Start at the beginning."

She took a deep breath. "I found exactly what Beth needed for the baby in Yreka, bought the crib and high chair, then made a quick stop to pick up some toys for Randy, along with purchasing some staples for Beth. When I returned home, I decided to run them out to her since it was still early in the afternoon."

"Were you met by Jeb?"

"No, Earl halted me and demanded I stay there until he checked with his mom. I didn't like the cocky kid's attitude, so decided to move ahead. When I reached the cabin and approached the door, I heard Beth scolding

Earl for stopping my vehicle. She seemed genuinely happy to see me. We moved in the stuff and she was so excited, until Jeb came in and made a big to do over not accepting charity. I tried to talk to him, but he didn't listen and ordered me off the property, never to come back. As I drove away, he gave my Ford a good birdshot pelting." She dropped her head into her hands. "The man is maleficent."

Hawkman put an arm around her shoulders. "You've got to promise not to go up there again without me."

"What could he be hiding?"

"Probably something illegal. He's keeping people out on the pretense of making you think it's his private property, but we know his dad owns it. There are several outbuildings on the land. The wagon is probably stored in the barn, and the horses graze nearby. What the others contain is anybody's guess, unless I can manage to do some snooping."

She took hold of his arm. "He'd kill you in a minute and bury your body so no one could ever find you."

"I don't think so. He'd have to catch me first."

"Jeb and Earl keep a close watch on their place. You wouldn't have a chance."

"True, they keep up their guard, but you'll notice they're always checking the area where we've come in from the road. What if I follow the creek and come in from the back side. They'd never see me."

Jennifer stared at him and frowned. "Are you planning to hoof it?"

"Not all the way. I'll take the four-wheeler up so far, park it, then walk the rest."

She stood and put her hands on her hips. "Well, you're not going alone. I'll join you, as someone needs to cover your back."

He reached over and grasped her leg. "Honey, I don't want you in any danger. This will just be a surveillance run; I don't plan to meet up with Jeb or Earl."

"How do you know where those two will be? No more argument, I'm going." She pointed a finger at him. "Don't you dare try to sneak off without me."

Hawkman released his hold and ran a hand over his head as he let out a sigh. "You are one stubborn woman."

"Better yet, what if I drive up to see Beth, which would draw the attention to the front area while you're making the trek toward the back?"

Hawkman shook his head. "Definitely not. Jeb wanted to scare you when he used birdshot, but if he discovers it didn't do the trick, he'll use a more powerful gun."

Jennifer clenched her fists at her side. "I will not let that man bully me to the point of not visiting Beth. She needs another woman in her life or she'll wither away. Randy and Marcy need her to protect them from their horrible father."

"What about Earl?"

"I gather from Beth, Jeb's got him under control."

"How old is Earl?"

"I'm not sure, but I'd assume sixteen or seventeen."

"Remember, Jeb has been in prison for three years of the boy's life."

"He must have been out a couple of years or at least a year and a half before they moved here. Marcy's only a few months old, and I'm sure she's Jeb's. So if he had any influence on Earl beforehand, he took up right where he'd left off."

"So what you're saying is, you're going to go visit Beth one way or the other."

"Yes. If I get shot at again, they may get a big surprise when I shoot back."

CHAPTER FOURTEEN

Hawkman observed Jennifer as she got up, walked to the sliding glass door and stared out toward the lake. "How's Randy doing?"

She whirled around, as if suddenly brought out of a deep sleep. "Real good. I took him some books and a few inexpensive toys. He loved them. I asked if he knew how to read and he told me he did; he'd attended school at one time and his mom also taught him."

"He should get enrolled."

"I'll approach the subject later. Classes will be out in less than a month, I doubt it would do any good to register him now. Next year would be better. It won't take much for him to catch up to his grade level, as he's plenty smart."

He reached over and closed the draft to the fireplace. "I better go check on Pretty Girl. Seems like it's gotten chilly, I can feel a cold breeze coming down the chimney."

He went out on the deck and decided to cover the falcon's cage since a shivering wind had kicked up. He refreshed her food and water while she squawked and beat her wings. "Calm down girl, I know you feel the change of weather. I'm going to close you in so you'll stay cozy and warm." After securing her pen, he went back inside, rubbing his arms. "Man, feels like a frigid front is moving in."

Jennifer stood at the kitchen counter shaving off thin slices of a large prime rib roast she'd cooked the night before. "We're having sandwiches tonight, so you can fix your own."

"Sounds good to me," he said, sliding onto one of the stools at the kitchen bar.

"I wonder if there's smoke coming out of the chimney at the Hutchinson's?" she asked, slicing pickles, tomatoes and cheese, then putting them on a plate.

"It always amazed me how women could cook on one of those wood stoves. How the heck do they know the temperature is right when they put food in the oven?"

Jennifer smiled. "Mostly by feel. They learn from practice how hot it should be and when to add more wood."

He shook his head. "I've seen beautiful cakes, pies, and breads pulled from those iron monsters. I thought it amazing."

"Beth hates the cabin because it doesn't have running water or electricity. I have the impression she lived in a more modern place before now."

Hawkman cocked his head. "Did she tell you that?"

"Yes, she doesn't like the cabin, but she never said where she lived before."

"It would be interesting to know."

"Maybe one of these days she'll tell me."

"I know you don't want to let this friendship to wane away. However, you might have to. It's dangerous for you to go up there alone."

Jennifer exhaled loudly. "Don't harp at me about it. I'm not afraid and may go on a whim."

He slapped a piece of cheese on a slice of bread. "Will you let me know?"

"All depends."

"On what?"

"If I decide to go at the spur of the moment, I'll leave you a note."

He glared at his wife. "I don't like your attitude."

She shot him a look. "Then quit treating me like a child. You know I'm capable of taking care of myself. I don't need a chaperone."

They finished their meal in silence, then retired for the night. Miss Marple had the middle of the bed to herself.

The next few days a heavy cloud hung over the Casey household.

Wednesday afternoon, on his way home from work, Hawkman thought about their petty disagreement and decided it had gone on long enough. He realized he'd not made clear his concerns, causing her to feel belittled. Tonight he'd apologize and try to explain.

***

Jennifer sat at her computer, but instead of writing on her book, she stared into space brooding about the silly argument between them. She still bristled at his talking down to her, yet she knew in her heart he only cared for her well being. Her husband didn't understand the workings of a woman's mind. He never had. Smiling to herself, she remembered the many times he'd worked on cases involving young women, then come to her for advice. It still didn't excuse him for treating her like a young girl.

Maybe she should make another trip to the cabin on her own. It would prove she could do this. She'd carry her gun as usual, and be very cautious. The thought of checking on Beth and Randy intrigued her enough to get up from the computer, head for the bedroom, where she put her weapon in the fanny pack. She fastened it around her waist. If things went right, she'd be home before Hawkman.

She hurried out the door and went to the garage. The sun glinted off the paint of her Ford and she noticed several minute dents caused by the buckshot. Biting her lower lip, she climbed into her vehicle. If Jeb or Earl shot at her again, she'd definitely shoot back.

Having second thoughts as she drove up the hill to the turnoff, she took a deep breath. "I can do this," she muttered aloud.

Just before she arrived at the place to make the turn, an old pickup emerged from between the trees and bounced onto the road. As he passed, she frowned and studied the face of the man driving. Jennifer didn't recognize him or the vehicle, and wondered what business he had up here. Looking in the rearview mirror, she watched him putt down the road. She waited until he disappeared from view before entering the rough path which led to Beth's cabin.

Keeping a close lookout as she drove, it surprised her no one stepped out of the shadows before she reached the turnoff to the cabin. Yet she could feel eyes upon her. She parked in front and hastened to the entry. Beth opened the door before she had a chance to knock.

"I'm so glad to see you. Please come in."

"I won't be long. I just wanted to check on you and see Randy."

"Hi, Mrs. Casey." Randy, sitting on the cot, held up the books she'd brought him. "I really like these puzzles. Mom has only had to help me on a couple."

"Wonderful," Jennifer said. "How are you feeling?"

"Really good, I think I'm almost healed and can get rid of these crutches."

"Don't discard them too soon. We don't want any problems," Jennifer said, as she glanced in the cradle and noticed Marcy had been moved to the crib. "Oh, my goodness, you've already transferred her."

Beth smiled. "Yes, I caught her trying to roll over in the cradle, but the sides didn't give her enough freedom, so I put her in the new bed and she loves it. She likes it better than being held."

When Jennifer twirled the toys strung across the top, Marcy squealed in delight. "She's so adorable."

Beth looked at her with concern. "Did you have any trouble coming in this time?"

"No, I didn't see a soul."

"Good."

"You sure don't want to be on Mom's bad side," Randy piped in.

Beth shot him a look. "You mind your manners, young man." She turned to Jennifer. "I want to show you something."

She followed Beth to the small sink where she took hold of the pump handle and worked it up and down. Within a few short seconds, a stream of water spewed out the spout.

Jennifer patted her on the shoulder. "Fantastic. Now you can get a bathroom inside, instead of having to go to the outhouse."

Beth held up a finger and grinned. "That's my next project."

"I think I saw the workman leave just as I came up," Jennifer said.

Beth gave her a puzzled glance. "We can't afford to pay anyone to do this work. Jeb and Earl fixed the water."

"Did the person you see have an old green clunker of a pickup?" Randy asked.

"Yes."

"That was Grandpa."

CHAPTER FIFTEEN

"It must be nice having a grandpa to visit," Jennifer said.

Randy shrugged and made a face. "He never comes inside the cabin. He doesn't like us. I just saw the truck out the window."

Beth ruffled his hair. "Grandpa loves you and Marcy, it's me he despises."

Randy frowned. "Just because you're an Indian maiden. Sounds crazy to me."

Not knowing how to respond, Jennifer picked up a colorful blanket hanging on the end of the crib. "This is beautiful, and it's handmade. Did you make it, Beth?"

She nodded, then moved toward the center of the room. "Excuse me for a moment; I need to stoke the stove."

Jennifer watched as Beth first poked wadded paper and kindling into the fire chamber, then tossed a lit match inside. She opened the chimney damper to allow the smoke to escape, then went outside, and returned shortly with an armful of wood. Placing a couple of small logs inside, she put the others on the floor beside the stove, dusted off her hands, and wiped them down her apron, then smiled at Jennifer.

"There, got that out of the way. Once it heats up, I'll start supper."

Jennifer shook her head in amazement. "I wouldn't have the vaguest idea how to cook on a wood burning stove. Your talents amaze me."

Beth laughed. "One of these days I'll teach you. It's really easy, once you get the hang of it."

"What are you fixing for dinner?"

"We're eating well tonight. Earl shot many quail this morning, and from the bag of potatoes you brought me, I'll make some crispy fried silver dollars. We'll go to bed tonight with full stomachs."

"Since you have no refrigeration, how do you keep the game the men shoot?"

"We have a smokehouse behind the cabin. Keeps it all perfectly; no fly will land on smoked meat."

Jennifer patted Marcy's tummy and moved away from the crib, then turned toward Randy. "How are you doing?"

"Real good. I tried walking a few steps without the crutches, but it still hurts."

"I think the doctor wanted you to stay on them for a couple of weeks. You have another week to go."

He wrinkled his nose. "Yeah, I know. Just can't go very fast on them, and I can't ride my bike."

Jennifer grinned. "You'll have plenty of time to do all those things when you're healed." She headed for the door. "Well, Beth, I better be on my way, so you can start your meal."

"I'm very happy to see you. Come again soon."

Jennifer had just started to clutch the door knob when it flew open. She jumped back as her hands flew to her chest. "Good grief, do you always enter the house in such a hurry?"

"Oh, sorry," Earl said, as he bolted past her and ran into one of the other rooms in the cabin. He rushed back out in a matter of seconds carrying a shot gun in one hand, a box of ammunition in the other, and darted back through the open door.

Jennifer peered outside and wondered if it would be safe driving home. She turned and waved at Beth. "See you in a few days."

She jumped in her Ford, turned around and headed out toward the road. About halfway there, she spotted Earl standing in the middle of the dirt trail with his gun pointed at a SUV slowly coming toward her. She blasted the horn, and poked her head out the window. "What the heck do you think you're doing?"

"I'm going to stop the guy. Dad told me you're the only one I can allow through."

"That happens to be my husband, and if you don't lower your gun immediately, you're going to get your head shot off, either by me or him."

Earl's wide-eyed gaze darted from one vehicle to the next. Jennifer had poked her gun through the opened window, and Hawkman showed his. Earl slowly placed his shotgun on the ground, and raised his hands.

Hawkman jumped out of the SUV, shoved the shotgun out of reach with his foot. "You don't point a gun at me."

Earl pointed at Jennifer. "She's the only one I'm allowed to let through to our property."

"This isn't your land. It belongs to your grandpa," Hawkman said.

"He told us to do whatever we need to do to keep it safe from intruders."

"Do you plan to get arrested for murder?"

"No."

Suddenly, Jeb stepped out of the shadows, and stood on the sidelines with his thumbs hooked in the front pockets of his overalls. "What's going on with my boy?" he bellowed.

"If you don't want him arrested, you better take this gun away, and teach him the law. Otherwise, if he stops me again, I'm going to make a citizens' arrest and take him to jail."

"Earl ain't done nothin' wrong, just stopped you to see what you're doing on our property."

"There're other ways to stop a person without pointing a deadly weapon at him."

"I'll see what I can do to educate him. So what are you doing up here?"

"Checking on my wife. I wanted to make sure she remained safe."

"She's allowed to come see Beth. We won't stop her."

Hawkman regarded Jeb with skepticism. "Why the change of heart?"

"Beth convinced me she needed a friend."

"I see."

Jeb strolled forward, reached down and picked up the shotgun from the ground, and put a hand on his son's shoulder. "Come on, Earl, let's go home."

Jennifer sat in the Ford taking in the conversation, but had not put away her gun. She watched Jeb intently to make sure he didn't suddenly turn the weapon on her husband.

When Jeb and Earl passed Jennifer's vehicle, the corners of Jeb's mouth turned up in a cynical grin. "You can put your gun away, Mrs. Casey; no one is going to shoot your husband."

After Earl and his father disappeared into the trees, Hawkman and Jennifer drove home. Once settled in the living room,

Jennifer glanced at her husband. "You don't look very happy."

"I'm not. I thought you said you'd leave a note. I had no idea where you'd gone. Since your Ford wasn't in the garage, you had to have gone farther than walking distance."

"Sorry, I figured on being home before you got here. I'll let you know next time, regardless."

"Thank you, I'd appreciate it. Now, I want to ask. What's this bit about you having permission to go see Beth? How'd such an agreement come about?"

"I haven't the vaguest idea. When I reached the front door without sight of Jeb or Earl, it surprised me. Beth asked me if I'd been stopped and I told her I hadn't. Randy piped up and said something about not wanting to be on his mother's bad side. She quickly squelched him from saying any more. I had the feeling she has something over Jeb and knows how to get her way."

"It seems most women have this talent," he said, grinning.

She raised a hand. "Oh, I almost forgot. Driving to the cabin, I saw an old pickup came out of the area where we turn off the asphalt. I found out later from Randy, it was grandpa. Not knowing what the older man looked like, I didn't recognize the person driving."

Hawkman wrinkled his forehead. "Interesting. Wonder why he made a trip to his property. It must have worried him when I made the visit."

"That's not all. Kids have a way about blabbing stuff parents wish they didn't. Randy said his grandpa didn't like them as he never came inside and because his mother was an American Indian. Beth immediately corrected him by saying, he loved the children, but didn't like her."

Hawkman nodded. "Yeah, that's how he came across when I spoke to him. Nothing compassionate about that man, even to his own father."

Suddenly, a pounding and yelling 'please answer' at the front entry made both of them jerk to their feet. Jennifer quickly ran and opened the door.

Earl, white faced, stood on the stoop wringing his hands. "Mom sent me. We need your help. Randy fell and is bleeding really bad."

CHAPTER SIXTEEN

Jennifer turned to Hawkman. "Throw his bike in the Cruiser while I grab the first aid kit."

He dashed outside, and tossed the bike into the rear end of the SUV. "Jump in, Earl." He backed out and Jennifer hopped into the passenger side, toting a large case.

"I thought I'd better bring the big kit. We'll probably have to take him to the hospital." She glanced at Earl in the back seat. "How'd he fall?"

"I'm not sure, but I think he sneaked outside without his crutches and tried to ride his bike."

"Oh, no," Jennifer said, biting her lower lip. "I knew he was getting restless when I talked to him this afternoon."

Earl, not fastening a seat belt around his chest, bounced wildly, as Hawkman drove quickly over the rough path leading to the Hutchinson's place. He abruptly stopped at the front door sending up a dust cloud. First Aid kit in hand, Jennifer bounded out of the vehicle, and ran into the cabin without knocking. Jeb stood over Beth as she applied pressure to a bleeding wound on Randy's upper thigh. The boy lay bravely with clenched teeth and tears rolling down his cheeks.

Jennifer pushed her way in front of Jeb and knelt beside Beth. She gently lifted Beth's bloody hand. "You've done a wonderful job of slowing down the flow. Hold on until I grab the tourniquet, then we'll get him to the hospital."

She flipped open the lid of the case, found the polyester strap with the plastic buckle and immediately placed it about three inches above Randy's wound. Tightening it slightly, she motioned for Hawkman to come and carry the boy to the SUV. Beth quickly washed her hands, then lifted Marcy from the crib, wrapped her in a blanket and followed them outside.

"I want to come," she said, standing beside the 4X4.

"Of course," Jennifer said, and opened the door to the front passenger seat. "I'll need to loosen the tourniquet in about twenty minutes, so you sit up here."

Beth scooted in just as Jeb appeared and handed her the crutches. "He might need these."

"Maybe," Beth said.

"Give them to me," Jennifer said. "She has no place to put them."

Taking them from Beth, he placed the crutches in Jennifer's hands, and she laid them on the floorboard.

He closed the door and stepped back.

Hawkman turned the Land Cruiser around and headed back toward the road. He tried to avoid the bumps, but found it difficult. "Sorry, Randy, I'm trying not to hit all these snags, but there are many."

"It's okay, Mr. Casey."

Hawkman spoke over his shoulder to Jennifer, "What about the Yreka hospital? Could they handle this, or is it too serious?"

"Yes, I think it will just be a matter of closing the old wound. It looks like he just tore it open. Hard to tell how much blood he's lost, but not nearly what he did when it first happened. I doubt he'll need a transfusion."

Jennifer had placed an old towel they kept in the vehicle under Randy's leg. When she loosened the tourniquet, she looked at Randy. "You're doing great, no blood has stained the cloth."

"I really feel bad about being dumb. I felt so good, I figured I could ride my bike."

"I hope you've learned a lesson. Doctors don't give their patients instructions for fun. They're trying to protect you from hurting yourself again. I'd imagine now it will take twice the time for you to heal."

Randy's lips trembled, and he wiped his eyes with the backs of his hands. "I've caused a bunch of problems for you and my folks."

Jennifer patted his good leg. "Don't worry about it. You take it easy and we'll get you fixed up real soon."

She released the strap a couple more times before they pulled into the emergency parking lot.

Hawkman carried the lad inside and a couple of hours later, they were on their way back to Copco Lake. Jennifer took Marcy and let Beth stay beside her son, to soothe him. They pulled up to the cabin at midnight, and a ghostlike light flickered through the windows. Hawkman carried the boy inside and placed him on the cot. Several kerosene lamps dotted the room, making strange shadows on the walls.

Earl came out of one of the back rooms, his long hair scraggly, and clad only in a pair of ragged jeans. "Is Randy okay?"

"Yes, he's fine. They stitched him up, and he has to stay off the leg for a week." Beth scolded and pointed a finger at her oldest son. "So no taunting him, you hear?"

Earl bowed his head in shame. "Yessum"

Jennifer put Marcy in the crib, then moved to Randy's side. "If I'm in town the next few days would you like some more of those puzzle books?"

Randy's eyes lit up. "That would be great, but you don't have to."

"This time I'll get some really hard ones," she winked. "Maybe they'll keep you busy for a week."

He smiled. "Okay."

They said their goodbyes and left the cabin. Driving home, Jennifer turned to Hawkman. "You'd have thought Jeb would have been there to check on Randy's condition."

"Didn't you see the faint light glowing from the window in the building back of the house?"

She wrinkled her brow. "No. What would he be doing out there at this hour?"

"I wish I knew, but I have a feeling he's up to no good."

"So, you're suspicious it's something illegal?"

"Yep, just wish I knew what. I want to investigate those outbuildings. There are several on that property."

"Are you still interested in trying out the plan we discussed earlier?"

"Yes, but we'll wait a few days until Randy is better. By the way, since you went in with Beth to the emergency room, did the doctor buy the fact the boy fell off his bike?"

"Of course. Why do you ask?"

"I noticed a bruise on Randy's arm when he took off his jacket. It didn't appear like one a person would get from tumbling to the ground."

"I didn't notice. What'd it look like?"

"It circled his arm, like he'd been grabbed."

Jennifer twisted her head around and stared at her husband. "Do you think Randy's being abused?"

"If he saw something he shouldn't have, it's possible."

Jennifer hugged herself. "I don't like the thought." She reached over and placed a hand on Hawkman's arm. "Could Jeb have shoved Randy down, causing the opening of the wound?"

"It's only a theory. Both boys had the same story, which is logical and believable."

She exhaled loudly. "I don't like this idea you're planting in my head. Unfortunately, you could be right."

Hawkman turned into their driveway. "I'm just trying to figure out what's going on with this family. They're a strange bunch."

He stopped, letting Jennifer out of the SUV, before pulling into the garage. He took the large kit from her as they walked silently into the house.

"I know I should go to bed, but I'm not the least bit sleepy," Jennifer said, running her fingers through her curly short locks.

Hawkman put an arm around her shoulders and gave a squeeze. "Don't worry about Randy. I could be all wet. Jeb is just so unfriendly, it's hard not to think the worst of him."

She patted his hand. "I know, I don't like the man either. How Beth ever got involved with him is beyond me."

"He may have been a fine guy before he landed in jail. Now he can't find work to support his family and he's bitter."

"Why would he risk going back to prison?"

"He feels desperate, and many ex-cons can't handle the difficult situations they've put themselves into, so they turn back to crime."

Jennifer put her hands on her waist. "He could well be leading Earl down the same path, as the boy seems to worship his dad."

"That bothers me a lot," Hawkman said.

CHAPTER SEVENTEEN

Thursday morning, Hawkman left for work, feeling a bit groggy since he and Jennifer hadn't fallen into bed until close to three. He'd taken care of Miss Marple's food and water, in hopes the feline wouldn't bother Jennifer so she could sleep in.

Before going up the stairs to the office, he smelled the delicious aroma of Clyde's bakery whirling around his head. He detoured the minute his stomach grumbled, and went inside the shop. The proprietor smiled.

"I see you couldn't resist the charm of my pastries."

Hawkman grinned and pushed the brim of his hat up with his finger as he examined the goodies lined up in trays. "They've woven their magical spell on me again. Even though I blame my extra pounds on getting older, Jennifer doesn't buy it and tells me I have no willpower."

Clyde's musical laugh filled the room. "She's a good woman."

Just as Hawkman pushed open the door to leave, causing the small bell at the top to jingle, Clause raised his hand.

"Wait. I almost forgot. An old man came in early this morning, and asked about the location of your office. I directed him, then told him you normally didn't get here until nine or after. He had an envelope in his hand, so he might have deposited it in the mail slot on your door."

Hawkman raised his brows. "What'd he look like?"

Clyde wrinkled his nose. "Dirty. The smell of him lingered and I had to open the door for a few minutes after he left."

"Thanks. Glad I hadn't arrived yet."

Hawkman left the bakery and jogged up the stairs. When he opened the door, the normal mail hadn't been delivered, but a long white envelope lay on the floor. He picked it up, then quickly plugged in the coffee pot, before settling at his desk.

He examined the wrapper, which had no return address, but dirty fingerprints spotted

the outside. Slitting it open, he pulled out a sheet of paper, unfolded it, and glanced at the signature. It surprised him to see Jacob Hutchinson scrawled across the bottom. Smoothing out the top, he puzzled over the message written in unsteady handwriting. "Dear Mr. Casey, No need for you to worry about my property anymore. I drove up to check it out and everything is fine. Jeb is taking good care of it.
Thanks for your concern."

Baffled by the note, Hawkman leaned back in the chair, and scratched his sideburn. "Why would he think it necessary to write me?" he murmured.

He twisted around in his chair, stood, and paced the small office. Soon, he stopped and stared out the window, as a question bounced around his brain. Either the guy wants me to continue checking on the place, or he actually means things are okay. Which is it?

Sitting back down, he refolded the letter and stuck it back inside the envelope. He didn't know why it even bothered him, as he planned to keep a close check on the cabin regardless.

***

The same morning, Randy awoke on the cot in the kitchen, the covers tucked around his chin; he thought about the events of yesterday. His leg ached, and so did his arm. He eyed his mother, a shawl draped across her shoulders. She seemed tired as she stoked the big stove to warm the cabin. A couple of times she wiped the back of her hand across her cheeks. He wondered if she was cleaning off tears or sweat. She didn't seem happy; only when she played a game with him or got Marcy to smile did she laugh.

His dad and Earl stayed outside most of the time. Randy didn't know what they did, other than bring in game for food, or fish from the river. They sure didn't help his mom. She even had to clean the birds, rabbits and small stuff the guys shot. Dad did clean the deer or the occasional wild boar and hung them in the smoke house.

It appeared his dad didn't want him around the small outbuilding. It definitely got him in trouble yesterday when he spotted the padlock hanging loose, and attempted to go inside. His dad whirled around when he heard the door open, grabbed him by the arm, half carried him outside, then shoved him down on that rough log with the nub of a broken branch.

He closed his eyes and shuddered at the thought of how his scream brought Earl and Mom running. Dad shut the door quickly. Mom took one look at the blood soaking up her son's jeans and told Earl to go get Mrs. Casey, and tell her I'd fallen on my bike. I still don't know what's going on in that shed.

Randy suddenly felt a gentle hand on his shoulder. "Hey, young man, are you having a bad dream?"

Opening his eyes, he looked into the face of his smiling mom. He tried to sit up, but groaned. "Yeah, I was dreaming about yesterday."

"You mustn't think about it. You're going to heal good this time and you're not going to act foolish again. You must never tell Mrs. Casey your dad pushed you down. Promise me."

"I won't tell her, but why didn't Dad want me to see inside the shed?"

"I don't know, and we don't care. Some silly thing men do. I hope you never act that way."

Marcy began to fuss, and Beth moved to the crib and picked her up. Putting the baby to her shoulder, she patted her back and soon Marcy let out a big burp.

Randy laughed. "Good one, Marcy. You should feel better now." He glanced at his mom, when she quickly put the baby down and put a hand to her stomach. "Mom, are you okay?"

"Yes, I'm fine, just had a gas twinge. Maybe I need someone to put me over their shoulder and pat my back," she said, laughing.

He knew she'd forced the laugh; he could tell by the way she grimaced. "Maybe you should lie down for a while."

"I'm fine. Probably need to get some food down me. Bet you're hungry too."

Randy didn't like the way his mother went about the business of cooking this morning. Instead of her normal quick self, her steps were slow and she kept putting her hand to her waist. A couple of times she even jerked a little, then took a deep breath. He knew she was experiencing some pains. Maybe Mrs. Casey would come by today. He'd tell her about his Mom. He closed his eyes and wished Mrs. Casey would get his message.

His mother had told him many times if you want something really bad, close your eyes and wish as hard as you can. Let the gods take your message freely in the air, and they'll deliver it. He knew it was an Indian legend, but he wished really hard and prayed the gods would deliver.

"Randy, have you gone back to sleep?"

He opened his eyes to find his mother standing over him with a platter of food. "I was just making a wish."

"You need to eat so you'll heal strong. Can you sit up okay?"

He pushed up his upper body with his elbows and gently moved his legs so his feet were on the floor. "Hey, I did, without it hurting."

"That's good news." She set the plate on a wooden box next to him.

Soon his dad and Earl were at the table, chowing down like they hadn't eaten in a week. Randy watched then out of the corner of his eye, and wondered if they'd leave anything for Mom.

When Marcy began to whimper, Randy wanted to pick her up, but was afraid to move due to his injury. "Mom, put her on my bed, and I'll play with her so you can eat."

Beth smiled. "Good idea. You can usually make her laugh."

"You're such a sweet boy," Earl said, mockingly.

Whirling around, Beth, pointed a finger at him. "Enough out of you."

Jeb cuffed Earl on the shoulder. "Let's get outside before you get into trouble. I need you to keep guard."

When they left, Randy exhaled a long breath and concentrated on keeping Marcy happy while his mother ate. He didn't mind taking care of Marcy; he adored his little sister. She had a cute smile and had just started to laugh out loud. It was fun to watch her kick and flap her arms when he made silly faces. Not only had she learned to laugh, but also had learned to roll over and he had to make sure he'd bunched up the quilt to her side so she wouldn't fall off his cot. When he glanced over at his mom, he noticed she'd only picked at her food.

"Mom, why aren't you eating?"

"My stomach seems to be upset, and I'm not hungry. Don't worry. It will pass."

Randy observed his mother as she finished cleaning up the kitchen. Once she even stumbled, and grimaced as she brought the dirty utensils from the table to the sink. He couldn't close his eyes, but in his mind, he sent off his wishes again.

CHAPTER EIGHTEEN

Jennifer stood at the kitchen sink, and stared out the window, searching for any sign of the Killdeer bird. She so hoped it would be back this year. It built its nest on the ground among the gravel or rocky soil. You couldn't see the eggs, as they blended into the background and appeared as rocks. Such a clever little creature. It had its own defense system, pretending to be injured, it dragged its wing and fluttered away from the nest to distract the enemy. So far, she hadn't seen any evidence of the small fowl.

Even with the fledgling on her mind, Randy kept popping into her head as if he were summoning her. She brushed the thought away, since she and Hawkman had been there for the biggest part of last night.

Surely, if some sort of emergency arose, Beth would send Earl to fetch her.

Settling at her computer, Jennifer vowed to get another chapter written on her latest book. She felt so far behind, and a deadline loomed in the very near future. The manuscript popped up on the monitor, and her mind went blank. She even reread the last chapter in hopes it would help her focus on the story, but nothing seemed to work. Closing her eyes, she massaged her temples with the tips of her fingers, but Randy's face kept floating before her. Finally, she stood, went to the kitchen, filled a glass with ice, and dug out a soda from the refrigerator.

"Maybe a bit of sugar will perk me up," she said to Miss Marple, as the cat rubbed against her legs.

Heading back to the machine, she tried again to concentrate, but this time she swore she could hear Randy's voice calling. "This is getting weird," she said to her pet, who'd managed to jump onto the table beside the keyboard. "It would certainly be convenient if Beth had a phone; I could just call and see if everything was okay."

Finally, she gave up trying to write, and decided to drive to the cabin. It would take her no more than an hour to check on Randy, and return home. Then maybe she could work with a clear head. She scribbled a note to Hawkman, left it on the kitchen bar, picked up her fanny pack, and buckled it around her waist. Snatching the keys off the rack, she headed out the door.

She arrived at the cabin without incident, even though, she'd seen Earl sitting on a fallen limb in the shadows, his rifle resting across his thighs. Knocking softly on the door, she called Beth's name. To her surprise, Randy responded loudly.

"Mrs. Casey, hurry, come in."

Jennifer opened the door and stepped inside. "What is it, Randy?"

"Mom, she's really sick." He pointed at the floor.

Jennifer had to scurry around the iron stove to see where he'd aimed his finger. Beth lay curled in a fetal position, tears sliding down her cheeks.

"Beth!" Jennifer cried, dropping to her knees and putting a hand on her shoulder.

"I'm hurting so bad."

"Where's the pain?"

Beth made a circular movement with her hand over her abdomen. "It comes and goes, but the last pain really hit hard and I just had to lie down where I stood." She glanced at Jennifer. "I certainly didn't expect you today."

"I kept having these flashes of Randy running through my mind, like he was calling me."

Randy jerked his head around, his eyes wide. "Mom, it works."

Beth pushed herself up to a sitting position. "What?"

"Wishing for something really hard. You'd said it was an old Indian legend. I've been closing my eyes every chance I had and wished for Mrs. Casey to come. I started early this morning when I knew you weren't feeling good." He waved a hand in the air. "Now look, she's here."

Beth forced a smile. "Yes, it must have worked."

"I think I should take you to the doctor," Jennifer said.

"No, it will go away, Probably just something I ate that disagreed with me."

"Is any one else in the family ill?"

"No, but that doesn't mean anything. I'm the only female, besides Marcy, and she's too young. These men can eat anything. Even if it's tainted."

Beth pulled herself to a standing position and slowly walked over to a chair. "I'm going to be fine, believe me."

"I hate to leave you like this."

"Don't worry, tomorrow is a new day."

Jennifer frowned. "I wish you had a phone so I could call and find out."

Beth glanced at Randy and smiled. "I'll have him send a message through his mind, if I need you."

"It sure worked today, so it should work tomorrow. However, I might drive up just to satisfy myself."

"Whatever you wish."

Jennifer said her goodbyes and left. Driving home, she still had concerns, but Beth seemed to know for sure she'd be okay. Did the woman know what was causing the pain? Jennifer had the feeling she did.

When she arrived home, she went to the computer, and found her mind clear enough to get some work done on her book. She'd throw her idea at Hawkman tonight and see if he agreed with the conclusion she'd come to about Beth's strange condition.

***

Hawkman sat at his desk, and studied the monitor. Trying to find a missing person wasn't an easy job, especially when one hasn't had much sleep the night before. He leaned back in the chair, flipped up his eye-patch and rubbed his eyes. This new case he'd just taken on, was a woman in her fifties, looking for her biological parent. He never could understand why people wanted to find someone who'd given them up at birth. This woman had been raised by a loving family, and now she wanted to hunt down her real mother. He'd try, but his heart wasn't in it. After another hour of searching, he shut down the computer and left the office. Tonight he planned on an early bedtime. He prayed there wouldn't be another adventure at the Hutchinsons'.

It seemed the drive home took forever, but he finally pulled into the garage, took his briefcase from the passenger seat and walked inside. When he placed his attache case on the counter, he noticed a note from

Jennifer stating she'd gone to the cabin. He frowned, but her Ford was parked in the garage. Before any horrible thoughts could come to his mind, she appeared from the back of the house.

"Hi, Hon, I didn't hear you drive up." She stood on her toes and planted a kiss on his chin. "So how was your day? You look tired."

"Strange. Yes, I'm pooped." He held up the note. "Did you go to the Hutchinsons' place again?"

"Yes, I'll tell you all about it."

"It seems this family isn't going to leave us alone."

"Oh, why do you say that?"

"I received a letter from Jacob Hutchinson today. He even hand-delivered it to my office." He removed the envelope from the briefcase and handed it to her. "I'd like your translation of what it means."

"Did you talk to the man?" she asked, as she went to her chair by the window.

"No, he came by before I got to the office."

Jennifer remained silent as she read the missive. She wrinkled her forehead and glanced at Hawkman. "What was his point in writing this note?"

"Beats me," he said, opening the refrigerator and pulling out a beer. "You want a drink?"

"Sure."

He mixed her a gin and tonic, then moved to the other chair. "So, what's your take?"

"I'm not sure. Either he wants you to stay away, or keep checking. Hard to say."

"My thoughts exactly." He waved a hand. "Enough about Jacob. Tell me why you went to the cabin."

Jennifer told him about the paranormal callings she'd received this morning coming from Randy. "Very weird sensation."

Hawkman stared at his wife. "I can imagine. So that's why you took a notion you should go see if there was a problem?"

"Yes. I couldn't get anything done."

"So what'd you find out?"

She related how she'd found Beth on the floor in dire pain. "Randy told me he'd been sending me telepathic thoughts to come quickly because his mother was ill. Guess I received them."

"Continue."

"I wanted to take her to the doctor, but she wouldn't have anything to do with my

suggestion. She said the pain would go
away and she'd be fine."

"What do you think was her problem?"

"I'm only guessing, and want your opinion.
I think she had induced a miscarriage,
probably with herbs."

CHAPTER NINETEEN

Hawkman looked fixedly at his wife. "Since I know nothing about pregnant women, you still want my opinion about this? What I'd like to know is, why would she want to abort her baby?"

"It's too soon after Marcy. Beth doesn't need another infant to look after."

"Do you think she's done this before?"

Jennifer raised her hands in the air. "I haven't the vaguest idea, but it's very possible since several years have elapsed between Randy and Marcy."

Hawkman scratched his ear, and grimaced. "How would she accomplish this dangerous deed?"

"I imagine her being American Indian; she knows a lot about herb concoctions that do all sorts of things."

"I suppose you'll take a trip to the cabin tomorrow to make sure she's okay?"

"I've thought about it, but I don't think I will. If I become a nuisance, she won't want me around. If there's a problem, she'll either send Earl, or I'll get a mental message from Randy."

"Wise decision, dear wife." He slapped his hands against his thighs. "I almost went to sleep driving home; so I'm hittin' the sack early tonight."

She stood and took the empty beer bottle from the table. "You want something to eat before you retire?"

"Nope, had a late lunch. I just want some good old shuteye."

She leaned down and kissed him on the cheek. "Goodnight."

Hawkman disappeared into the bedroom and closed the door before the cat could follow.

"Miss Marple, you get back in here," Jennifer called. "He doesn't need your help."

The feline meandered back into the living room, hopped onto the hearth and lay down on her favorite throw.

Jennifer sat in the chair, threw an afghan over her legs, turned on the television and promptly fell asleep, not awakening until the wee hours in the morning. Blinking at the mute movie on the television screen, she shook her head, and for a moment didn't realize what woke her. She thought she'd heard clomping horses, and the rolling wheels of a wagon.

Flipping off the lamp beside her, she jumped up and ran to the kitchen window. Not seeing a thing, she figured it had already passed. Taking Hawkman's night binoculars from the dining room table, she put them to her eyes and watched the bridge. Nothing passed over it, nor did she see anything on the road across the lake. Could they have possibly been headed in the other direction? If so, why didn't she spot the wagon earlier? She finally decided she'd been dreaming, turned off the television and trudged off to bed.

***

Friday morning, Hawkman awoke refreshed, climbed out from under the covers, stretched and glanced at his sleeping spouse. He remembered peeking at the clock when he felt the mattress bounce at three in the morning. She'd either gone to sleep watching the tube, or her muse had visited her with some brilliant ideas for her book.

He jumped into the shower and by the time he dressed, the aroma of bacon had made its way to the bedroom and wrapped around his nose. "Aah, that smells so good," he said, padding into the kitchen carrying his boots.

"Figured you'd be hungry," Jennifer said, smiling.

"You certainly didn't get much sleep last night. How come you're so bright and bushy tailed?"

"I really got plenty, went to sleep in front of the television watching a boring show. Didn't awaken until I dreamed about a horse and wagon going down the road."

Hawkman glanced up at her, while pulling on his boots. "You sure it was a dream?"

"I sure couldn't find any evidence of it. I looked out the kitchen window, checked the bridge, then across the lake, and saw absolutely nothing. If it was going in the other direction, surely I would have spotted it leaving earlier."

"Yeah, sounds like you had a nightmare."

She laughed. "Why do you say that?"

"As far as we know, the only people using a wagon drawn by horses are the Hutchinsons."

She put a plate of food in front of him. "The explanation answers why I woke with such a start."

"So what are you going to do today?" Hawkman asked.

"I might go to Yreka and do a little shopping, just to keep from thinking about Beth."

"You don't expect any telepathic messages?"

"No. I have a feeling she'll be just fine"

After they ate their breakfast, Hawkman left for work. On his way to Medford, he couldn't stop thinking of Jennifer's so called dream. He had a feeling the whole thing happened. Possibly Jeb took the horse-drawn wagon out on the narrow, dirt back road. It could be done, even though it would be a rough haul, but worth it to Jeb, if his load was illegal. Jennifer hadn't seen anything, because she'd looked in the wrong direction, thinking he was leaving the area; but Jeb could have been returning home with an empty wagon and took the easiest route.

Hawkman had some ideas forming in his mind about what Jeb might be doing, but wasn't ready to discuss them with his wife, or the law authorities, until he had more proof. He also worried about Jennifer's blooming friendship with Beth. The woman could well be in the thick of things with her husband, yet hiding unlawful activities from her children, and using Jennifer as a patsy.

Another thing bothered him: what did Jacob Hutchinson have to do with this operation? Hawkman felt in his gut, the man had an investment in Jeb's project. Someone had to put up the money, and what better person than your own father. The sooner he could find out what sort of shenanigans were going on, the better he'd feel.

He decided when he got home tonight, he'd talk to Jennifer about trying out the plan they'd discussed earlier. If they calculated right, and arrived at the property near the same time, maybe Jennifer could entice the whole family into the cabin, and he'd be able to sneak a look inside those outbuildings.

***

Jennifer headed for Yreka with her list. She hated leaving the house, in case Earl came needing her, but she planned to visit Beth this weekend and hoped to find her feeling well. Sweeping the negative thoughts from her mind, she concentrated on her driving. She first stopped at Walmart where she found several harder puzzle books for Randy. He seemed to find them fun, yet they were educational, so he learned while recuperating. Passing the baby items, she couldn't resist some cute toys for Marcy, and a darling pair of booties.

Leaving the department store, she headed for the Thrift Shop. She roamed the aisles and picked out a couple of comical tee shirts for Randy, a work jacket she thought would fit Jeb, and a couple of long sleeved casual shirts for Earl. Searching through the women's items, Jennifer realized she had no idea what size jeans would fit Beth, so decided to forget those and focused in on blouses she could wear everyday. She piled her items on the counter, then went back to the housewares and browsed through racks of stuff. Finally, deciding on a couple of long-handled utensils and a canvas wood carrier, she went back to the cashier. When she deposited her purchases into the Ford, it amazed her to think all the things she'd bought totaled under ten dollars. She figured she'd be stopping here more often for her own personal shopping.

After a trip to the grocery store, she headed home, and thought about the reaction she'd probably get from Jeb. If he gave her any static, she'd tell him the jacket belonged to her husband. He never wore it and she'd planned to throw it out, but hoped he could use it. It made her cringe to lie, but if it satisfied the horrible man, it would be worth it.

Jennifer pulled into the garage, carried the groceries in first and put them away. She had to make a couple of trips to the Ford, but finally transferred all the items inside. Glancing at the wall clock she couldn't believe she'd been in town so long. Too late to start a big dinner; sandwiches were on the menu tonight.

She stepped back, put a hand to her mouth and stared at the pile of stuff for the Hutchinsons. Had she been pretentious? Would they take this all wrong? Jeb seemed to have a certain amount of pride, but Beth seemed willing to take anything she offered.

"Dang it!" she said aloud. "I'm not sure I'm doing the right thing."

At that moment, Hawkman walked in the door, and glanced at the mound of clothes. "Uh, oh, what have you done?"

"I went to the thrift shop and got carried away. I bought something for every one of the Hutchinsons, even Jeb. Now I'm having second thoughts. Jeb is not too keen on charity, and I'm afraid he's going to have a fit when I bring this load up to them."

"Well, let's talk about it," he said, placing his briefcase on the counter. "You might have just done the right thing. Show me what you've bought."

CHAPTER TWENTY

Jennifer stared at her husband with a dubious expression. "I don't understand what you mean, but here's what I bought." She moved to the chair where she'd stacked the items, went through each article of clothing, and utensils, explaining why she'd bought them. Holding up the bag from Walmart, she showed him the gifts for Randy and Marcy. Biting her lower lip, she hugged herself. "Now, I'm having second thoughts. Jeb is going to have a fit about accepting charity. I want this to be a happy experience, not a big argument among the family."

"You've played right into our plan."

She furrowed her brow. "What are you talking about?"

"Don't you remember our discussion about me checking what's going on in those outbuildings?"

"Yes, but it certainly wasn't on my mind when I went to town."

"I'm sure you never gave it a thought, but it just might work. If you can get the whole family into the cabin at one time, then my chances of snooping around will be much safer."

"When did you want to do this?"

"This weekend, but first, we'll need to work on the timing."

"How do you propose to do that?"

"Before it gets dark, I'm going to take the four-wheeler, and see how long it takes to follow the creek that runs near the cabin. I'll go to the point where I think they might be able to hear the Polaris. I'll mark the spot, then hike the rest of the way until I can see the outline of the buildings. I figure it will take about ten minutes longer than you driving up in the Ford."

Jennifer sat on the arm of the big leather chair. "What if someone spots you?"

"I won't be getting close enough on this dry run."

"Where does the property end? I have the feeling Earl walks the boundary, and he'd just as soon shoot you."

"Let's hope he's having dinner."

"You better get on the stick. It'll be dark in about an hour."

"I'm going to change into some old clothes. Don't want to get these torn on thorns."

He went back to the bedroom and within minutes returned in faded jeans, a long sleeved shirt, work boots, an old favorite hat he wouldn't throw away and a worn jacket. Sticking his stop watch in a pocket, he went out the door.

Jennifer soon heard the machine start up, and Hawkman rolled down the driveway. She glanced up at the wall clock, and wrote the time on a paper pad.

***

Hawkman drove up the road he normally took to get to the cabin, but veered off and headed toward the back path, then cut off before coming to the guard rail which supported a large chain and padlock across the front. Jeb wouldn't have to contend with this barrier as he'd get on this route farther west. Finding the stream, Hawkman stayed on the North side until he came to a shallow spot with level ground on each side. He crossed over, and continued west. When he figured the noise of the four-wheeler might be heard by the Hutchinsons, he parked in a cluster of bushes and continued on foot. He didn't come across any fence to indicate the starting of the property, but he could see the outline of one of the outbuildings. It certainly seemed taller than he remembered. Slowing his pace, he took caution as he approached and ducked behind some brush when he heard a neighing. Peeking over the bushes he could see the corral with four horses on the south side of a large dilapidated barn. The big doors stood open on the building and the wagon sat inside.

He hunched down when a figure strolled around the corner with a bucket in his hand. The animals shifted toward the person, whom Hawkman recognized as Earl. At least, he didn't have a gun in his hand.

Hawkman didn't want Earl to catch sight of him so he moved to the north and took a chance of getting closer. He had no idea

how many shacks occupied the piece of
property, but he needed to figure out which
ones he wanted to check out, and how
close they were to the cottage. Crouching,
and staying in the thick brush, he advanced
westward toward the cabin. The barn sat
quite a ways from the main house, but in
between he counted three small buildings.
One looked as if it could fall down any
minute, but the other two appeared stable,
well built, and bigger than he thought.
Those two piqued his attention. He turned
and started back the way he'd come, but
got side tracked by a commotion in the barn
area.

Scrunching down, he peered through an
opening in the bush and spotted Earl trying
to saddle one of the horses. The mount
wanted nothing to do with the procedure
and the more Earl yelled, the more the pony
shied away. Hawkman figured this was a
good time to get out of there, as the boy
wouldn't notice him. He hurried back to the
four-wheeler and took account of the terrain
around him, so he'd know where to park the
vehicle when he did this trick in earnest.
Hopping onto the seat, he started the
engine, and headed for home. By the time

he rolled onto the driveway and parked, dusk had fallen. When he walked into the house, Jennifer hurried to the counter, checked the time and wrote it on the paper.

"It took you close to forty-five minutes, longer than I expected."

"You can knock ten minutes or more off, because I had to do some scouting, which I won't have to do on the real run."

"Did you find out anything new?"

"Yep."

"Well? Are you going to make me draw it out of you?"

Hawkman laughed. "Sorry, Baby, guess I'm mean at teasing you like that."

She put a hand on her hip, and tapped her foot. "Yes, you are."

"Let me grab a beer and I'll fix you a gin and tonic; then we'll talk."

"Fair enough," she said, and went to her favorite chair in the living room.

He soon joined her, placing her drink on the table. "The four-wheeler is perfect for this job."

"Do you think you were spotted?"

"No, too much going on for Earl to notice me. He was trying to saddle one of the horses, and the animal wanted no part of it."

"Guess he's learning."

"I'd say he's trying to break a fairly gentle steed to the saddle." Using his hands, he explained what he'd found. "You know the big building you see when you drive up to the cabin, but you can't really tell what it is. It's a huge barn, not in the best of shape, but will probably stand for another fifty years. The corral surrounding it looks like it's been constructed recently, with fairly new wood. The big wagon is sheltered inside that building."

"I wondered where they kept them. I could never see much of the barn due to the other buildings when I went there."

"Those are the three small outbuildings I'm most interested in. One's about ready to fall down with the next big wind, but the other two caught my attention. They're well built, tall, wide, and I could make out a window in each one, which probably means there's a pane on the other side too."

"Do you have any ideas about what's going on inside those structures?"

"Maybe nothing, but I need to check them to satisfy my curiosity."

"So how are we to work the timing of this adventure?"

"I've got to have a head start. It takes about twenty minutes for you to get to the cabin. It also may take you a few minutes to get the family collected inside, if you can. Regardless, give me a good ten or fifteen minute start. Then you head out. Don't worry, just do your thing, and I'll work with it."

"What if I can't get Jeb or Earl inside?"

"Do what you can. I'll play with whatever happens."

Jennifer stood, and paced the floor rubbing her arms. "I don't like it."

"Honey, it isn't like I haven't done this type of thing before."

"I know, but it still bothers me. I don't trust Jeb or Earl not taking a potshot at you if they discover you sneaking around."

"I don't trust any of them."

Jennifer swung her gaze around. "You don't trust Beth?"

"Sorry, no. She could be right in the middle of everything, using you as a patsy."

"Am I that vulnerable?"

Hawkman stood and put his arm around her. "Yes, you wear your heart on your sleeve. An evil person can see right through you."

CHAPTER TWENTY-ONE

Friday night, Jennifer lay in bed staring at the ceiling and envied her husband for his ability to fall asleep the minute his head hit the pillow. It didn't matter to him what doubts had arisen about their plan for Saturday; he could turn it off and fall into a deep slumber. He'd always told her he'd take care of the problems when they presented themselves; and he could think much clearer if he'd gotten a good night's rest. She agreed with this philosophy, but tonight, the fact he didn't trust Beth, and felt she might be treating her as a patsy, disturbed Jennifer. Hawkman might not understand women's thinking, but he could evaluate their characters with expertise.

She figured his training in the Agency had given him this ability, and he'd honed it to perfection. It upset her to think she'd let her personal compassion for the Hutchinson family get in the way before she stood back and scrutinized Beth. Yet, even now, she couldn't see anything negative about the woman. She appeared to love her children, even her rogue spouse, and worked hard to make them happy. The only bad thing Jennifer could think of, was the thought of Beth aborting her child, but she couldn't believe such a thing had really occurred; only her feminine intuition had played a role in assuming the incident. Her thoughts went to Randy and Marcy, two innocent children in the middle of possible illegal activities.

Sleep must have overtaken her, as those were the last thoughts she remembered when she awoke Saturday morning. She rolled out of bed, yawned and stretched. Hawkman had already risen and she could hear him banging around in the garage. After showering, she dressed in jeans and a sweatshirt, then rummaged through the closet looking for a large sack she swore she'd stored there. She finally found it on the shelf under a stack of hats. The items she'd bought for the Hutchinsons would fit in it nicely. Taking it to the living room, she put the folded clothing on the bottom, then placed the housewares stuff on top. An uneasy feeling crept through her as she stacked the items into the bag. Hawkman had planted a seed of mistrust in her mind, and Beth would have to prove him wrong.

Jennifer fixed breakfast and called Hawkman in from the garage. He scrubbed his grease covered hands at the kitchen sink.

"Good grief," she said. "Did you have to wash in here? You've made a horrible mess."

He shrugged. "Sorry, but it would muck up the bathroom, too."

"Why couldn't you have used the hose outside?"

"Didn't have any soap."

Jennifer raised her hands in frustration. "I give up."

He sat at the kitchen bar. "The four-wheeler is gassed up and hums like a baby."

"I really have reservations about this caper."

"It'll be over and done with before you know it."

"What if Jeb won't come to the cabin?"

"Do the best you can. Maybe he'll be hunting. If he's tinkering around the buildings, and I can't check them out, I'll go back at night."

She frowned. "If he caught you, he'd have grounds to shoot you as a trespasser."

"I don't plan on his seeing me night or day."

"I wish I felt as sure as you do."

"What's troubling you?"

She put down her fork and pushed the plate away. "Your comment about not trusting Beth."

Hawkman leaned back in his chair. "Stop and think about it. Here's a woman living with a man, has three children by him, and knows he's been in jail. You don't think she doesn't know where he gets his extra money or what he's doing?"

"I'm not sure. Either she's naive, clever in hiding her feelings, or very tough skinned."

"Probably all three. I'd like nothing better than to believe, for your sake, that she's innocent about the whole scenario. Also, my gut tells me Randy suspects something."

Jennifer looked at him wide-eyed. "Randy?"

"Yes. Remember the first time we met him, and I told you the boy wasn't telling me what was really on his mind?"

She nodded.

"He's too young to know exactly what's happening, but he's intuitive, and doesn't like the feeling."

Jennifer let out a sigh. "Let's get this over with. Are you ready?"

He spread his arms and looked down at his jeans. "I'm dressed in old clothes and just waiting for you." He got up from the bar. "Give me a fifteen minute head start."

"Okay."

Jennifer checked the clock and her wrist watch to be sure they were the same. She clasped her fanny pack around her waist, picked up the bag of items, and went to the Ford. Biting her lip, she waited in the vehicle until the time had passed, then backed out of the garage, and drove up the road. Her stomach churned as she approached the turnoff. She drove slower than normal, not in any hurry to take on this challenge. When she rounded the curve, she caught her breath. A strange car was parked in front of the cabin.

She had to make a move, but not sure what. Hawkman had probably made it to the edge of the property and advanced to the barn. About that time, the cabin door opened, and Earl walked out.

She quickly opened the driver's side door. "Earl, does your mom have company?"

"It's no problem. Go on in."

"Wait a moment. I have something for you." Jennifer grabbed the bag off the seat and made her way inside as Earl held the door open. She noticed him twisting his head toward the barn when he heard the horses whinny.

"Hey, Mom, more company," he said, obviously not too concerned and followed her into the kitchen.

Beth turned and smiled. "Jennifer, good to see you. Meet Tami, an old friend of mine."

Jennifer placed the sack on the floor and held out her hand. "Pleasure to meet you. Are you from around here?"

"No."

The woman had an attractive face, but had overdone the make-up. She had piercing green eyes that made Jennifer shudder as it seemed she looked straight through her. Her long, bleached blond hair hung over her shoulders in loose ringlets. The low-necked long-sleeved dress, revealed a deep crevice of oversized breasts, which reminded Jennifer of someone trying to be super sexy. Tami's gaze shifted from Beth to Jeb, then back to her. She appeared about the same age as Beth. Jennifer thought it odd the woman didn't say where she came from, but she didn't pursue the subject. Jeb sat on the couch with a scowl on his face. He didn't greet her, but Randy raised a hand and waved from the cot by the window.

"How are you doing, Randy?"

"Fine."

An uncomfortable feeling existed in the room, so Jennifer immediately took the bag and placed it on the table. "I went shopping yesterday, and Jeb, I went to the thrift shop, so I don't want to hear anything about charity."

She pulled the work jacket out first and walked over to him. "I'd like you to try this on and see if it fits."

He glanced at Beth and she nodded her head. He harrumphed and stood. Jennifer glided the sleeves over his large arms, shifted the back up so it fit his shoulders, then pulled it closed in the front. "Perfect."

Grumbling, Jeb pulled the garment off and threw it to the side. Jennifer paid no attention, and pulled out the shirts she'd gotten for Earl.

"These are neat. Thanks, Mrs. Casey."

"You're more than welcome." She then took the long-handled utensils, canvas bag, and blouses for Beth from the sack.

Beth took hold of the cookware. "Oh, I like these, and this wood carrier will certainly come in handy." She caressed the material of the blouses. "These are lovely. Thank you."

"I'd like to have bought you some jeans, but didn't know your size."

"That's okay, you've given me plenty,"Beth said, showing the items to Tami.

Jennifer then walked over to the cot with a tee shirt and several books for Randy. "These puzzles are harder. I hope they last until you can get up and walk on your crutches."

Randy grinned. "Thank you, Mrs. Casey. I really like your gifts."

Jennifer patted him on the arm, then gave Marcy her toys, and handed the cute pair of booties to Beth. "They should fit her soon. I'd rather get an outfit for a baby too big than too little."

"Good idea," Beth said. "They outgrow them before they wear them out."

Jennifer chuckled. "You got that right. They grow much too fast." She folded the sack and left it on the table. "I'm going to leave, so you can enjoy your company. Nice meeting you, Tami."

The woman didn't smile, just nodded her head.

Jennifer left the cabin and prayed Hawkman had time to check the outbuildings. She couldn't have remained in the cold atmosphere of that household any longer. On her drive back to the comforts of her own home, she thought about Beth's strange friend.

CHAPTER TWENTY-TWO

Hawkman arrived at the area he'd marked to park the four-wheeler, then took off on foot. When he approached the corral, the horse whinnied, causing him to duck around to the side of the barn. "A regular watch dog," he grumbled.

Managing to get around to the outbuildings without the horse making another sound, Hawkman bypassed the dilapidated structure. He could now see the cabin, and frowned at the sight of Jennifer's Ford parked behind a strange car. This could cause a problem, so he'd better hurry and see what he could find inside these sheds, before someone came outside.

Cautiously, Hawkman checked the window on the side, only to find it covered with dark drapes.   He moved to the front of the middle building, where a large chain and padlock secured the door.

Leaving that one, but still keeping watch on the front of the cabin, he checked the aperture on the side of the front shed, and found it also covered. He advanced to the front, where he found an unlocked padlock dangling from the chain. Quickly slipping inside, he closed the door, but found the interior became pitch black, so he pushed it open a crack. When he turned around and saw what occupied the building, it took him by surprise. "Holy crap," he whispered. He swiftly removed his camera from a pocket and flashed some pictures, now thankful for the darkness.

Suddenly, the sound of people talking filtered through the gap in the door, and Hawkman peeked out. He recognized Jennifer's voice and figured she thought it time to leave. Stepping out of the structure, he shoved the camera back into his pocket and pulled the door closed, then dashed around the corner toward the corral. The blasted horse made a ruckus again as he passed the enclosure. Holding on to his hat, he dove for the bushes. He glanced over his shoulder, figuring the minute Jennifer drove away, the troops would leave the cabin and make their rounds. Sure enough, he spotted Earl at the corral. Hawkman kept his head down as he passed through the bushes, hoping he didn't make the leaves or limbs sway enough to make the boy suspicious. When he finally made it out of sight of the property, he breathed deeply in relief, hopped on the four-wheeler and headed home. Jennifer wouldn't believe what he'd discovered. He'd also be interested in who owned the odd car.

By the time he reached the driveway, Jennifer had already parked in the garage and gone into the house. He pulled under the lean-to, and strolled into the kitchen.

"Were you able to explore those outbuildings?" Jennifer asked, filling a glass with water. "I feared you might not have time."

"Yes, but they have a guard horse."

"A what?"

"Stupid horse that neighs every time a person walks by the corral. I imagine the family is aware of this and pays attention, so I had to scamper."

"When I arrived, Earl was outside and I noticed his ears piqued when he heard the horse whinny. He just glanced toward the barn, but didn't seem to pay much attention, then followed me inside."

"The animal probably makes the same sound when other wildlife ventures too near the pen."

"What did you find out?" Jennifer asked, sliding onto a bar stool.

"I took some pictures, so let's upload them to the computer; but before we do, tell me about the unfamiliar car. Did Jeb buy a vehicle?"

She waved a hand in the air. "Oh, my, you're not going to believe this."

"Try me."

"I didn't know how to respond when Beth introduced me to her sexy friend."

"Male or female?" Hawkman asked, with a grin.

"Female, of course. She hardly said a word. I have no idea where she's from, even though I asked. The woman never replied. The atmosphere in the house could have made your breath freeze. I wanted to get out of there as soon as I could."

"Are you sure she was Beth's friend?"

"That's how she introduced me to Tami. I doubt very seriously she'd be a friend of Jeb's."

"You never know. What do you mean by the word, 'sexy'?"

"More like a tart. Long bleached blond hair, too much make-up, plunging neckline which showed off big boobs, and painted fingernails. She's probably very near Beth's age, maybe a year or so younger; but I would never have suspected Beth running with the likes of such a woman, even though, I thought her sort of pretty in an odd way."

"Maybe she once had her eye on Jeb. He isn't such a bad looking guy. A little rough around the edges, but some women like the type. She could have made the trip when she found out where he lived."

"Who would have told her? They're certainly not listed anywhere," Jennifer said, waving a finger in the air.

Hawkman shrugged. "How about Jacob? He's in the phone book."

"Interesting thought, but since you've planted the seed of Tami being Jeb's mistress, I did notice how she'd stare at Jeb, glance at Beth, then me. Very weird mannerisms. I couldn't read her actions at all."

"Did Beth show any signs of awareness?"

"I couldn't take my gaze off of Tami, so I have no idea of her reactions."

"Another mystery in the Hutchinsons' lives." Hawkman pointed to the computer. "Why don't you boot up and I'll show you what Jeb's into."

Jennifer moved to the machine, and flipped it on. Hawkman took the cord and attached the camera. They both stared at the screen until the folder popped up, and she clicked the mouse over the top and opened the pictures.

Putting a hand over her mouth, she gasped, "Oh, my gosh. He's into moonshine."

"Yep. Those copper stills cost a bundle. There's no way Jeb could afford them, so someone else is in this operation too. I have a gut feeling they were there when the family moved in."

"The thing is huge," she said, flipping through the photos.

"Now I know why those buildings are so tall. I have no idea what's in the middle one. Could very well be another still, just not hooked up. I'm surprised to have found the door unlocked on this one."

Jennifer glanced up at her husband. "Did you have a suspicion about this?"

"I had two ideas rattling around in my brain: one was a meth lab or he was making white lightning. I'm actually relieved to find the still. Making dope is very dangerous and he could blow up the whole place. There's not as much danger in making whiskey."

Jennifer pointed to the grate under the huge copper still. "They still have to use heat."

"That's why they do the work at night. A stream of smoke comes from the vent at the top, and can be seen during the day."

"He has to have a lot of water too."

"Yep. He's hooked up to the creek that runs near the house. I saw the pipe leading to the still."

"To think Beth had to practically browbeat him to get water into the house!"

Hawkman patted her on the shoulder. "My dear, this still has been hooked up for some time. Jeb only started it up. It shouldn't have been any problem for him to get running water into the cabin."

"You think he's selling this moonshine?" Jennifer asked.

"If he is and gets caught, he could go back to jail. I figure he's selling it, even though it's illegal because that still can produce at least one hundred and forty gallons of liquor at a whack."

"My word. Who would he sell to?"

"There are bars who'll buy the stuff, if it's good enough. Also, individuals, who just like the rotgut."

"Can he make enough to support a family?"

Hawkman nodded. "The bucks could roll in, if he doesn't get caught."

Jennifer stared at her husband. "You're going to see to it that the operation is squashed, aren't you?"

"So far, I don't know if he's conducting an illegal business; but if he is, I'll bring him down."

CHAPTER TWENTY-THREE

Jennifer became quiet, and Hawkman studied his wife's solemn face. "What's the problem, Hon?"

"Because of me, we got involved with this family. Now we're going to destroy it."

"No, they're destroying themselves. You only tried to befriend them."

"What will happen to Earl, Randy and Marcy?"

"If Beth isn't involved, they'll stay together; otherwise, the state will have to find homes for the children."

"The thought makes me shudder. Randy adores his little sister, and you know they'd be separated."

"You're putting the cart before the horse. Let's take one phase of this adventure at a time."

"Okay, tell me how you're going to find out if he's selling to outside sources?"

"I'm going to have to do some surveillance."

She frowned. "Pray tell me how you're going to accomplish this feat without getting caught, and how do you plan to follow him if he goes out the back road?"

"Like I said, let's take one event at a time. I haven't planned it all yet."

***

Randy lay on the cot, looking at the puzzle books Mrs. Casey had brought him. Out of the corner of his eye, he could see Tami. He didn't like her, never did, and wished she'd leave. Earl couldn't stand her either; he'd told him so. Even his mom seemed to just put up with the lousy looking woman, but dad appeared to welcome her. Randy got the impression they had some sort of business deal, as they talked numbers a lot.

He wished he could go back to his own room that he shared with Earl, but mom didn't want him back there until his leg had completely healed. Earl liked to tease and carry on; sometimes he would cuff Randy, causing a fight. With him in the kitchen, mom could supervise Earl's actions. His mother's tone of voice brought him out of trying to concentrate on a word for the puzzle.

"I know what's going on, but I don't want to hear any more about it," Beth said.

Randy glanced at the adults facing each other. His mom had her hands on her hips and stood glaring at Dad.

"It's like talking to a wall," Jeb said, throwing up his hands and storming out the front door.

"Why do you treat him like that?" Tami said, glancing toward the entry. "I'd give my right hand to have a man like Jeb."

Beth put her face close to Tami's, almost touching noses. "You've tried before. Do it again and I'll kill you," she hissed.

Tami stepped back, picked up her big purse from the floor, and threw the strap over her shoulder. "You don't know how to treat a man; that's why you almost lost him," She swaggered toward the entry.

"I still have him. You don't," Beth growled as Tami slammed the door.

Being awakened by the loud noise, Marcy let out a howl. Beth wiped her hands across her face, bent over the crib and picked up the baby.

"There, there, my sweet girl. Everything's okay."

"Mom, how did Tami find out where we lived?"

"Grandpa probably told her. She's working out a business deal with him and your dad."

"I don't like her, and you don't either. I hope she doesn't come back."

"You hold your tongue, young man. How do you know my feelings?"

"Your voice was mean when you talked to her, like when you scold Earl and me for getting in a fight."

She smiled. "But I still like you."

"Yeah, cause we're your kids. She's not."

"Don't worry about it. You hear me now?"

"Yes, ma'am."

Randy sighed and turned his attention to the puzzle books. His joints ached from having to be in bed all the time, and he found it hard to get comfortable. He decided tomorrow he'd get up and walk around in the kitchen before he forgot how to move his legs.

Nightfall came and Randy watched his mother light the lamps, then feed Marcy as

she sang the haunting lullaby. Soon, Marcy
fell asleep and was tucked into her crib. Still
humming, Beth moved around the kitchen
straightening up.

"Randy, turn your head, I'm going to take a
bath."

The boy rolled to his side.

Beth stripped naked and washed herself
from the cistern water she'd heated on the
stove. Before slipping on her flannel gown,
she tried on the blouses Mrs. Casey had
brought and studied herself in the cracked
mirror hanging on the wall. She smiled,
then took them off, and folded them neatly.
After pulling on her night wear, she called to
Randy. "Okay, I'm through."

Randy loved for his mother to brush her
long hair. It glistened like black diamonds in
the ghostly light thrown from the lanterns
around the room. She'd bend over and
brush it toward the front, then tilt her head
back as she made long strokes on each
side, then pull the strands over her
shoulder, smoothing it as she finished up.
Taking a piece of long soft cloth, she'd tie
the tresses together at the nape of her
neck, making a lengthy ponytail.

She picked up one of the lamps, came to the cot and kissed him goodnight, then went to her bedroom. Dad and Earl never came in until the wee hours of the morning. When he questioned his mother about what they were doing, she told him not to be bothered by their activities, but he could smell a rat and vowed to find out one of these days.

Randy stared out the window at the pitch black night. It appeared a storm might be moving in with all the clouds. Not a star nor moon in sight. He could hear the whistling of the wind, and cracking tree branches which were slung against the sides of the cabin. A ghostly night like he'd expect around Halloween with witches and goblins.

He pulled the covers around his neck and crunched down into the bed, then stifled a scream when the front door flew open and banged against the wall. His heart raced until he saw his dad and Earl hurry in and push it shut. Randy quickly rolled over to face the wall, not wanting them to see he was still awake.

"Looks like a storm moving in," his Dad said to Earl, in a hushed voice.

"Yeah, and it's cold."

Earl went to his room, while his dad stopped at the sink, pumped water into the bucket and washed his hands. Splashing a bit onto his face, he sucked in his breath, "Man, that's freezing," he hissed.

Taking the towel hanging on the nail next to the pump, he dried, then journeyed into the bedroom, closing the door behind him.

Randy turned on his back and heard the bed squeak in the other room as his dad sat on the edge, then the clunk of each boot as it hit the wooden floor. His interest perked when his mother's voice came through the thin wall.

"What kind of deal do you have going with Tami?"

"She's got some contacts."

"I know what's going on, and I don't like her around. She's a slut, and would like to lure you to bed."

His dad laughed. "No way will I get into that situation again. I almost lost you over the mess."

"If there's a second time, the kids and I will disappear. I'm not happy with what you're doing."

"It will give us some money for a change. We can fix up the cabin and make it more livable."

"I'd rather we go about it legally. If you go back to jail, what will I do?"

"Beth, I don't want to talk no more. I've got to get some rest. Have to get up early."

Randy could hear the bed creaking, and figured his dad had turned his back to his mom. He let out a sigh, realizing their talk still didn't reveal to him the illegal game his dad was playing. This worried Randy, because he could hear the concern in his mother's voice. He did know one thing: his mom didn't like Tami, and the discovery made him smile to himself. It bothered him Tami had caused problems in the family before. He wondered what kind.

CHAPTER TWENTY-FOUR

Sunday morning Hawkman mowed the lawn, then decide to take Pretty Girl out to hunt. When he entered the kitchen, Jennifer glanced up from her computer.

"So have you devised a plan on how you're going to catch Jeb?"

"Ideas are forming in my mind, but I have a few days as the still was cold when I found it, so I have time before they'll be taking any into town." He patted her on the shoulder. "I'm going to take the falcon out; she hasn't hunted in a while. It will also give me time to think."

Jennifer nodded, and focused on the monitor.

Hawkman carried the perch he'd made to fit the Cruiser, adjusted it on the inside, then went around to the aviary. When he slipped on the leather glove, and opened the cage, the falcon squawked and flapped her wings, almost knocking off his hat. "Simmer down, girl, I know you're excited."

Her claws grasped onto the glove without any coaching and he carried her to his vehicle. The man and his bird drove down the driveway. Hawkman at first thought he'd take her toward the Hutchinsons' place, but decided against it, as he didn't trust Earl and his gun. He turned right, went over the bridge, then veered to the left and headed up Ager Beswick Rd., toward the house where the deaf boy, Richard, used to live. He soon parked on the side of the road, took his pet into the field, which was wet from last night's rain, and let her fly. It always amazed him to watch her soar upward, then take a sharp turn toward a cluster of trees where she'd disappear for a spell. The wind had died down, but the breeze that swept across his cheeks had a stinging chill to it.

He strolled back to the SUV and leaned against the fender while waiting for her return. Having to catch Jeb in the act of selling booze, could be very dangerous. He didn't think he should tell Jennifer about his idea until afterward, as she wouldn't go for it at all. The details were filtering through his brain when he heard the squawk of his pet. Strolling out to the center of the meadow, he whistled his call to her, and held up his arm. She circled several times before making a smooth landing on his forearm. Her beak showed evidence she'd found her kill.

Hawkman returned home and put the falcon into her cage. She appeared much more content. He swept out the aviary, filled the water tin, and put some dried grain into the food container. He dropped the clear protector down around the sides as the wind had kicked up and had turned quite nippy. He then went inside through the sliding door leading to the deck.

"Bet she enjoyed her trip," Jennifer said, looking up from her computer and smiling.

"She's always much calmer when we get home from a hunt."

Jennifer twisted in her chair. "I've got a question."

"Okay, shoot," he said, pushing Miss Marple off the seat next to Jennifer and lowered his lanky body.

"If Jeb takes his hooch into one of the nearby towns, do you think he'll use the buckboard or borrow Tami's car?"

"Interesting question. Why do you think Tami would lend him her car?"

Jennifer tapped her chin with a pencil. "I'm not sure. There's something about her sudden appearance that makes me wonder about her relationship with the family. Maybe she's a moonshine runner. Or what about Jacob making a trip out to the cabin and transporting the liquor?"

"You're full of good ones today. You've given me a few more things to worry about. Let's talk about all the options you've brought up."

"Okay, where do you want to start?"

"Did you ever get Tami's last name?"

"No."

"Hmm, makes it a little hard to research, especially since her first name could be a shortened handle. Not knowing where she lives makes it twice as hard."

"Sorry, at the moment, knowing you were charging up the back way, and then my finding a stranger at the cabin, made it difficult for me to concentrate on my objective."

He patted her on the arm. "I'm not scolding you. Everything went just fine. You did good."

She bowed her head. "Thank you, kind sir."

"You told me a little about the reactions of everyone; have you thought of anything to add?"

"No, other than she appeared very distant or cocky. I wouldn't classify her as shy, more like secretive."

"Let's skip her right now and go to why you think Jacob might come and haul out the booze."

"You said the still was obviously put in before the Hutchinsons moved in, and copper stills are very expensive. Knowing Jeb has no money, you assumed since the dad owned the property, he probably installed them." She cocked her head toward Hawkman. "What if Jeb hadn't moved up here; did Jacob have plans to make the moonshine himself?"

"Hard to say. Since he's playing caregiver to his father, he probably wouldn't leave him at night, especially since the man's apparently bedridden. It's possible he had the still or stills brought to the property. Not sure what's in the other outbuilding, but it's tall enough for another one. Anyway, he could have planned to do it himself earlier, and later decided to hire men to make the rotgut."

"I'm curious about how this moonshine is made."

"It's really an easy process, but first you need a copper still. There are all different sizes, but the one in Jeb's outbuilding is huge. You can go on the computer and find pictures of them. To make the mash, the recipe can vary, but commonly they mix corn meal and hot water in 'mash barrels'. Next they add scoops of sugar as well as yeast and malt. This mixture begins to bubble furiously and will continue to do so for several days as fermentation takes place."

Jennifer sat with her chin resting on her hands, giving Hawkman her full attention. "What next?"

"When the mash quits working it has the kick of a mule and is ready to be transferred to the still. A fire is stoked underneath, and the alcohol vapor rises to the top and condenses into liquid as it passes through the coiled worm submerged in the cooling barrel. A potent rivulet, a little larger than a pencil trickles from the end of the worm into half-gallon fruit jars. The first part is high-proof while the adulterated end of the batch is known as "singlings" or "low wine", which is set aside, poured back into the still, and cooked again. So the first drops were followed by a flow of decreasing strength, or proof. If you poured some of the lower stuff on the fire and it flashed up, it would be kept running; but if it put out the fire like water, it's time to quit. Any hot liquid remaining in the still is recovered and poured over new grain in the mash barrels to repeat the process."

"I don't get this 'worm' thing."

Gesturing with his hands, Hawkman drew a picture in the air. "From the top of the still an elbow-shaped pipe juts out and tapers from around four inches to about one-inch in diameter. Attached to the end of this outlet is a twenty-foot coiled copper pipe known as the "worm". It's looped inside an adjacent barrel kept full of cold water during distillation of the sour mash."

"Why does everything have to be copper?"

"Other metals can be toxic to the human body."

"How does a buyer know he's getting good stuff?"

"A moonshiner might advertise the quality of his brew by pouring some into a metal spoon and set it afire. Safe moonshine burns with a blue flame. If its dirty the flame will be yellow. A reddish flare indicates lead in the mixture."

"I've read where some of these moonshiners have blown themselves to kingdom come."

"There has to be good ventilation, because alcohol vapor is more explosive than TNT."

"I hope Jeb is a careful moonshiner. Those building are not too far from the cabin."

"If you noticed in the pictures I took of the still, there are vents all around the top, plus a pipe that goes out the roof. That's why they do most of their distilling at night, so the smoke can't be seen by authorities, or others who might turn them in."

Jennifer leaned back in her chair and stretched her arms above her head. "You're a good teacher, I could picture the whole thing in my mind."

"Thank you," Hawkman said. "Getting back to Jacob. I don't think he is, or will be,

Jeb's runner. So it leaves our mysterious
Tami's car, or the buckboard."
  "It also appears that Jeb entered the
picture right on time for Jacob," she said.

CHAPTER TWENTY-FIVE

Randy awoke early Sunday morning. The dawn still provided enough light for him to see the outlines of the furniture in the room. He decided to try walking around. It delighted him when he carefully stood and felt no tenderness. Taking a few steps, he smiled to himself; still no pain. He moved slowly at first, then picked up the gait and before he knew it, he galloped in a circle. Not hearing his mother open the bedroom door, he came to an abrupt halt as she stood staring at him with her hands on her hips.

"What do you think you're doing?" she asked.

"Mom, it doesn't hurt. I had to get out of bed before I forgot how to move my legs."

She smiled. "I'm glad you decided to try it. It looks like you're on your way to getting well, but I don't want you to overdo."

"I promise. If I use my crutches, can I go outside for a little while?"

She sighed. "You can't be happy with walking around inside?"

He shook his head. "Not the same."

"Let's see how you feel after breakfast."

He grinned. His mom wouldn't make such a statement, if it didn't mean she'd probably consent. Otherwise, she'd have said 'no' right off the bat.

Beth stoked the fire in the stove and had it burning before Marcy let out a cry. Picking up the baby, she sat down and began feeding her.

Earl came out of the bedroom, rubbing his eyes. "What's to eat, Mom?"

She pointed toward the cabinet. "Cold biscuits wrapped in a cloth; and there should be some leftover pieces of pheasant, if your dad didn't eat it before he took off this morning. Take one of those metal plates and warm the food on the stove. Leave some for your brother."

"Yeah, and for Mom too," Randy cut in.

"Don't worry, there's plenty here," Earl said, taking his share. "Where'd Dad go?"

"I don't know. He got up before daylight," Beth said.

"How come he never tells us where he's going?" Earl asked, between bites.

"He's the head of the household, and we don't question his actions," Beth said, looking at Earl and frowning. "I need to cut your hair. It's hanging in your eyes and touching your shoulders."

Earl made a face. "Aah, Mom, today?"

"Why not? Have you got something special planned?"

"Thought I'd go fishing, if Dad doesn't need me, and see if I couldn't get a batch for dinner."

"That's a good one; you can go after I trim your long locks."

Earl scowled and finished his food. "I'll go check the horses and be back shortly."

Beth nodded, and put Marcy back in her crib. She placed the toys around her, then watched the baby babble and grin. "You are so cute," she said.

Meanwhile Randy went to the cabinet and brought out the remainder of food for him and his mom. "You want yours warmed, Mom?"

"Yes, that would be good."

Randy didn't want to act too eager to get outside, as his mom might get suspicious of his motive, so he took his time eating, and played with Marcy a while. When his mother went into the bedroom to dress, he thought enough time had elapsed, so he slipped on a pair of jeans and the tee shirt Mrs. Casey had given him. He took a jacket off the peg near the door, and grabbed the crutches. "Mom, I'm going outside for a while," he called.

About that time, Earl came in the door.

"Did you find Dad?" Randy asked.

"No, he took one of the horses, so he's probably out in the field. Where's Mom?"

"She'll be out in a minute to cut your hair," Randy said, with a grin.

Earl doubled up his fist and waved it in front of Randy's nose. "Don't get smart. She'll cut yours next."

"Enough, boys," Beth said walking into the kitchen. She pulled out the shears and motioned for Earl to sit on the stool.

Randy went out and closed the door behind him. A cool breeze swirled around

his head and he pulled up the collar to cover his neck. He took a deep breath. "So good to be outside," he said, aloud. He glanced in all directions, but didn't see his dad, so decided he'd take a chance and venture toward the building where his dad had knocked him down. Maybe he could see inside. Randy knew the contents of those sheds had something to do with whatever made his mother unhappy.
He clomped along on the crutches and it seemed to take forever, even though the structures weren't far from the cabin.

   Randy discovered the door was padlocked with a chain and he couldn't get it open. The windows were covered with dark curtains on the inside, forbidding him even a peek. He maneuvered to the next one and found the same predicament, but from this one he could hear a strange sound, like bubbling or something boiling. "What the heck," he muttered. He moved around the structure but found no peephole.

   Figuring he'd been snooping long enough, and Earl would be coming out before long, he moved on to the corral and stood watching the horses. Soon, his older brother joined him.

"What are you doing out here, runt?"

Randy hated being called that, but decided not to cause a problem. "Just watchin' the horses. I needed some fresh air and Mom said I could go for a walk. So guess I've been out long enough."

"Yeah, she told me to tell you to get back inside, wimp"

Heading back to the cabin, Randy yelled over his shoulder. "Cute haircut,"

"Shut up, brat."

Randy snickered as he chugged along. When he got even with the second outbuilding, he glanced back to make sure Earl wasn't watching, then put his ear against the wooden side. He could still hear the bubbling noise and swore the siding felt warm to his skin. A knot hole caught his eye and he tried to see through it, but to no avail. However, a strange smell seeped through the tiny opening. Suddenly, out of the corner of his eye a movement caught his attention. He jerked his head around and spotted his dad riding a horse, galloping toward the cabin. Quickly stepping away from the structures, Randy went swinging toward the cabin entry on the crutches.

Jeb came to a stop and dismounted. "Hello, Son, good to see ya out."

"Hi, Dad. Mom let me go for a walk. Sure feels good to get outside. I went as far as the corral, so thought I better get back before she got worried."

His father opened the saddle packs and took out several small dead birds. "Take these in to your ma, she might want to fix them tonight for supper."

Randy managed to slip the small doves into his large jacket pockets.

Jeb mounted the horse and headed for the corral. "I'm going to rub down the horse, then I'll be up."

Randy noticed the lather on the beast's body, and figured he'd been run hard. His dad's shotgun hung in the scabbard on the side of the saddle. Going toward the front door, he tread a bit slower, so the birds wouldn't fall out. He glanced back toward the outbuildings and still wondered about the strange sound and odor. When he reached the cabin, he shoved open the door with his shoulder. "Hey, Mom, Dad just got home and told me to give you these." He unloaded the fowl into the sink. "He said he'd be up shortly after he rubbed down the horse. "Boy, that horse was lathered from head to tail. Wonder why Dad ran him so hard?"

"Could be several reasons," Beth said, examining the kill.

When she didn't explain her comment, Randy removed his jacket and hung it on one of the pegs by the door, stood the crutches in the corner, then went to the crib where Marcy lay on her tummy, babbling at the colorful rag doll propped in the corner. "You know, Mom, she's really adorable."

"Yes, she is. She's acting more like a person now, and fun to play with." Beth said, as she stoked the fire in the stove, then set a bucket of water on the top to heat up so she could pluck the feathers from the fowl.

Jeb walked in the door just as Beth plunged one of the doves into the steamy pail. "You gonna fix those for supper?"

"Yes, I like fresh birds."

"Save one for me, I won't be here to eat."

Beth raised a brow. "Oh, where will you be?"

"Gotta go into town. Have a meeting."

"Are you riding one of the horses? Or taking the wagon?"

"Neither."

She glanced at him. "Then pray tell me how you're going to get there, walk?"

"Tami's picking me up in about an hour."

Beth jerked her head around and glared at her husband. "Tami? When did you make this arrangement?"

"The other day when she visited us. You got so mad I didn't tell you."

"You think this is making me happy?"

Randy stared at his mother and he knew that angry look. Her eyes narrowed and flickered with specks of red fire. The corners of her mouth had turned down, and she dunked those birds one at a time in the hot water, then ripped off the feathers with one swoop of her hand.

CHAPTER TWENTY-SIX

Randy edged over to his cot and pretended to be reading the puzzle books, but shifted his body so he could watch his parents out of the corner of his eye. His mother's fury only blossomed as she worked. She banged a big skillet onto the top of the stove, slammed the cabinet door when she removed the can of lard from the shelf. Her mannerisms were swift and jerky as she took her anger out on cooking.

His dad leaned back in a straight chair, the two front legs lifted from the floor, smoking a corn cob pipe as he watched her. "Beth, I'll probably be back before you go to bed. This meeting can't take long."

"Why can't your dad take you?"

"Tami made the connection."

"I see," she said, never looking at him.

He leaned forward and rested his arms on his thighs. "If I can get some money coming in, I can buy an older pickup and we'd have our own wheels, so we don't have to depend on others."

She pointed a flour laden finger at him. "We do just fine with the horses and the buckboard. Emergencies, like Randy getting shot in the leg, were the only times we needed help."

He nodded. "I know, but I need a truck for the business."

Beth remained quiet as she coated the birds in flour. The carcass of each one sizzled as she carefully slid it into the big skillet full of hot grease.

When the sound of a horn honking came from outside, Jeb stood, put on his hat, and slipped on a jacket. "I'll see you in a few hours."

Randy observed his mother, and could see the set line of her jaw. She wasn't at all happy about this situation. He decided to say nothing, as he knew he'd be told not to question grown-ups' business.

***

The Caseys had eaten an early dinner and Jennifer happened to be at the kitchen sink cleaning up when she spotted Tami's car drive by.

"Looks like that woman I told you about is heading for the Hutchinson's place," she said, over her shoulder,

Hawkman walked to the window with the newspaper in his hand. "You mean the sexy Tami?" he said, glancing out the window.

"Yes."

"Let's keep a watch for when she drives back by."

"It could be hours."

"Maybe, maybe not. I'll watch the bridge. It was an older tan Corolla, right?"

"Right."

Hawkman meandered back to his chair and pivoted it so he faced the lake. Miss Marple sat at his feet begging for attention. "Okay, girl, get up here," he said, patting his thigh. The cat hopped up, nestled in his lap, and immediately began purring.

Jennifer finished up in the kitchen and spread the dish towels out on the counter to dry. When she looked out the window, her mouth dropped open. "Get your binoculars and check the passenger in Tami's car. It sure looks like Jeb."

He dropped the paper and put the glasses to his face. "Yep. It's him."

She walked to the kitchen bar, and drummed her fingers on the counter. "What in the heck are those two doing together? I thought Tami was Beth's friend."

"You said she had eyes for Jeb."

"I wonder if Beth knows he's with her?"

Hawkman watched the car until it drove out of sight going toward town, then placed the binoculars back on the table. "How could she not know?"

"He could have met Tami in the field. There's quite a stretch between the road and the cabin."

"True. Don't you think he's taking a chance? Earl would have probably spotted him getting in the car."

"Maybe we're making something out of nothing. This could all be very innocent."

"I doubt it," Hawkman said. "There's nothing blameless here, but how is it all tied together?"

"You think Tami has something to do with the moonshining mess?"

"Give me a good reason why you think she doesn't."

"How would a woman fit into the picture?"

Hawkman held up a finger. "Number one, she has a vehicle."

"So does Jeb's father."

"True, but Jacob doesn't like Beth. Supposedly, Tami is her friend."

"Why would Jeb care? I get the feeling the man does as he pleases, regardless of what Beth thinks."

Hawkman made a face. "You got me on that one. Maybe I should have followed them." Then he snapped his fingers. "I bet she's a contact for potential customers."

"Oh, Hawkman, you've lost it. A woman running an in-between for buyers?"

"Sure, a perfect setup. No one would suspect her."

Jennifer twisted the ring on her finger. "I don't know; it really seems far-fetched. I'd think hooch buyers would be tough old men, who'd want to deal with males only."

"Face it, none of them want to get caught, so they're protecting their butts by doing business with a woman." He put the feline on the floor and joined Jennifer at the kitchen bar. "I think I've hit on something."

"Do you think she'll haul the white lightning in her Toyota?"

"No. When Jeb is financially able, he'll buy a truck. Right now he's broke, so he'll use the buckboard and go out the back way. I have a feeling he's only been selling a little bit at a time, to ranchers and farmers, just enough for his supplies. I think Tami is the key to bigger hauls. I wish I knew the woman's last name, and where she lives, so I could find out more about her."

Jennifer picked up a pencil and wrote Tami's name on a sheet of paper. "I'll go up to see Beth next week, and I'll ask her about Tami."

"She might get suspicious."

"I'll be careful how I approach the topic." Jennifer tapped her pencil on the palm of her other hand. "I had a question right on the tip of my tongue. Oh, yes, now I remember. Beth told me they had a smoke house. Did you see it?"

He nodded. "It sits directly behind the cabin, surrounded by trees. I could smell smoked meat when I approached the corral. Didn't have time to enjoy the aroma since other things occupied my mind."

"The family seems to have plenty of meat to supply their needs, but what about vegetables?"

"There's plenty of land for them to plant a garden. It wouldn't have to be a big plot for a family of five. Their biggest problem would be getting water to the plants."

Jennifer shook her head. "Another thing bothers me about Jeb. I'm sure he shoots game out of season. Couldn't he get in trouble?"

"If he got caught. However, if he slaughters and butchers it immediately, then hangs it in the smoke house, it would be hard to prove he took a deer out of season."

"Changing the subject," Jennifer said. "Are you going to try to follow Jeb when he makes his next run?"

"I'd like to, but not sure how I'll handle it. I can almost bet he's using the cover of night to hide what he's doing. It'd be easier if he'd just take the buckboard into town during daylight hours, but I doubt he'd take the risk. So to follow at night using the four-wheeler means I'll have to get there early and hide on the back road. Unfortunately, if I tag along behind, the noise of the machine will give me away. I could hoof it, but have no idea how far I'd have to go, and that could be mighty tiring."

"Could you stake out where the back road dumps onto the highway?"

"If his client meets him before then, I'd lose out. My other alternative is to wait until Jeb gets a better means of transportation. However, who knows how long it could take."

"Sounds like a predicament to me."

"First, I have to go back to the cabin and snoop around those outbuildings. If he's started making a batch of moonshine, I'll have to calculate when he'll be taking out a load."

"How will you know?"

"As I explained to you earlier about the fermenting of the mash."

"Yes."

"It takes several days; when it quits working, it'll be transferred to the still. Then I'll figure a couple of days for him to get it bottled and loaded into the buckboard, which he'll probably do at night."

"So you plan to spy on him? What if he catches you?"

"Fortunately, there are no dogs, just the stupid horse who makes noise. I spotted a couple of good hiding places where I can see the building containing the still. If he loads the rotgut earlier than I calculate, don't expect me home until the next morning."

"When are you going to start this surveillance?"

"Tonight. When it gets dark."

CHAPTER TWENTY-SEVEN

"Once you park the four-wheeler, you'll be hoofing it into unknown territory. How do you plan to maneuver in the dark?" Jennifer asked.

"In case it's pitch black, I'm taking my Surefire LED flashlight. If I keep it pointed toward the ground, the beam should be hidden by the heavy foliage. Once I'm close to the corral, I'll turn it off."

"Why are you even going tonight? We just saw Jeb leaving the area with Tami."

"It'll be a perfect time for me to see if he's started a new batch."

"How, if the door's padlocked?"

"I'm taking my lock-picking kit."

"Sounds like you've thought of everything, except an escape route."

Hawkman grinned. "I'll find one when I need it."

"Earl would shoot you first and ask questions later," Jennifer said.

"I know. I'll watch for him. If we had better cell phone connections, I'd have you call me if you spotted Jeb and Tami coming back."

"Afraid you'll just have to watch for the headlight beams. It should give you time to get out of sight."

"Better get my stuff together and get going."

Jennifer glanced out the window. "It's not completely dark yet."

"It won't matter until I get there, which will take about thirty minutes. Should be perfect."

He slipped on a heavy jacket, then shoved the small lock pick set into one of the zippered pockets, the flashlight into another, and his small camera into the inside pocket. Pulling on a pair of gloves, he went out the front door.

Tooling up the road, Hawkman felt the same surge of excitement go through him when he started on a dangerous mission in the Agency. He loved the thrill of uncertainty, not knowing if he'd be able to accomplish the job, or get shot at. If things moved along right, he'd eventually talk to Detective Williams, even though he didn't have jurisdiction in this area, he could maybe recommend someone.

Hawkman soon came to the spot he'd marked earlier to park the four-wheeler. Darkness had fallen, but with no clouds in sight, a big moon lit up the countryside. It helped him find his way, but he'd have to be careful so his shadow didn't give him away.

The corral came into sight, and he detoured in a wide circle so as not to disturb the horses. He hoped Earl was inside, but with Jeb gone, he could well be policing the area. Cautiously making his way toward the back of the cabin, he cut across the ground. A big bird squawked and flew from a tree branch over his head. He ducked and remained still for several minutes, then continued. Inside the cozy home, the soft glow of the lanterns filtered through the glass, weaving a weird, flickering shadow on the ground outside. The windows at the back of the house were dark. Hawkman had not seen this side of the cabin and took a mental picture of it.

He eased out of the protection of the forest surrounding the cabin and hurried

into the shadows of the outbuildings. Since
he knew what the first building contained,
he scurried to the side of the second
structure. As he leaned against the boards,
he could hear a gurgling noise coming from
inside. He moved around to the front,
keeping a lookout toward the cabin and the
path leading toward it from the road.
Working quickly with the lock pick, he
opened the padlock and leaving it hooked
onto the chain, guided it with his hand so it
rested on the door without banging against
the wood. The hinges creaked loudly, so he
only opened it enough to slip through.
Warmth engulfed him, and the putrid smell
of fermentation hit his nostrils.

   Pulling the door closed, he removed the
camera from his pocket and shot some
pictures of the barrels. He then pulled out
the flashlight, shined the beam into the
bubbling yeast and wished he knew more
about the stages of making the moonshine.
From what he'd read, it took a few days for
the fermenting, and it had to stop fizzing
before being poured into the still; then one
more day before it would be ready to
bootleg.

He turned off the flashlight when he heard the distinct sound of a car engine. Reaching up to his shoulder holster, he loosened the flap covering his gun. Peeking through the slit in the door, he could see the glow of headlights coming up the road. He should have time to get out before the vehicle made the turn and cast the headlight beams onto the structures.

Just as he stepped out of the building, Earl came out the front of the cabin, carrying a shotgun. Hawkman stood frozen to the spot, in hopes the boy wouldn't look his way. Fortunately, the young man's attention went to the oncoming car, and he pulled the rifle up to his jaw and took aim. Hawkman took the moment to slip around the side of the shack before the shafts of light hit the wood siding. He heard Jeb's booming voice. "Earl, lower the damn gun, it's your dad."

Hawkman ran past the corral, only to have the horse whinny several times as the animal trotted along the enclosed fence. He hoped with the confusion in front of the cabin, no one would take notice of the horses.

He didn't worry about making a disturbance as he dashed through the bushes toward the four-wheeler. Getting his boots wrapped in a vine sent him sprawling to the ground. Yanking at the creepers, he finally unwrapped his feet and checked his pockets for the items he'd brought. He listened for a few moments to make sure no one was trailing him, then raised his body off the ground. He used the flashlight to help guide him through the remaining tangle of brush, and soon arrived at the four-wheeler. Climbing aboard, he turned the ignition, put it in gear, flipped on the lights, and headed home.

Jennifer jumped up from her chair when he walked in the door and gasped. "What happened to your face?"

"Nothing," he said, removing his gloves, then touching his cheek to find it crusted in blood. "I must have scratched it when I fell."

She handed him a hand mirror. "You better let me clean you up, and you can tell me what happened"

Leaving the room, she returned with cotton and hydrogen peroxide.

"Looks rather ghastly, but it doesn't hurt."

As she started wiping away the dried blood, Hawkman cringed. "Well, it didn't until you got ahold of me."

"Keep still. It isn't as bad as I thought."

Hawkman told her of the incident of falling. "I took some pictures of the fermentation taking place in big barrels in that other building. I figure by the end of the week, Jeb will do a run on his goods." He also told her about Earl coming out about the same time his dad arrived home. "When he pointed the shotgun at the car, Jeb hung his head out the window and shouted obscenities at the lad. If I hadn't been in a predicament, I'd have enjoyed it a lot more."

Jennifer threw the soiled cotton swabs away, rubbed a salve over his face, and handed him the mirror again. "You have one good scratch down your cheek; thank goodness you didn't hit your eye."

He glanced into the glass. "Those little scrapes are nothing. They'll heal in a few days."

She sat down beside her husband. "What do you think Jeb or Earl would do if they caught you snooping around their place?"

"If Jeb plans to run moonshine as his job, then he'd probably kill me and bury my body in the woods where it'd never be found."

Jennifer bit her lower lip. "Wouldn't they realize I'd lead the cops right to them?"

"Mark my word, they'd have an airtight story. Beth would stick to it too, and I'd lay odds she'd no longer be your friend. Remember this is her family."

Jennifer stared at Hawkman. "Do you honestly think he'd go that far?"

"Yes, I have no doubt. He's an ex-con, has no job, and feels desperate. No one is going to get in his way. Right now, he has no idea I've been poking around, and I don't intend for him to find out."

Jennifer placed her hand on his arm. "Have you mentioned this situation to Detective Williams?"

Hawkman shook his head. "He doesn't have any jurisdiction in California, but I do intend to talk to him once I have more solid information. Maybe he can give me some advice."

"The still is there."

"Doesn't mean a thing. Jeb can make whisky for his personal use, as long as he doesn't sell it. I have to catch him in the act."

"How do you plan to follow him?"

"I've got an idea or two roaming around in my head. Not sure which I'll use."

She slid off the bar stool and hugged herself. "This whole mess makes me very nervous."

CHAPTER TWENTY-EIGHT

Jeb jumped out of Tami's car, stormed up to Earl, and snatched the rifle out of his hands. "I'm putting this gun away for a few days. When you can show me you know how to handle a firearm without putting innocent people at risk, I'll let you have it back."

Earl bowed his head. "I didn't plan to pull the trigger."

"I sure as hell didn't know it. All I could see was a big barrel pointing at me. I've told you many times before, you shout a warning before bringing the gun up to position. Didn't you recognize Tami's car?"

"Not in the dark. I couldn't even tell the color. It surprised me to see headlights coming up here at night. We usually don't have visitors this late."

Jeb walked back to the driver's side. "Thanks for the ride."

"I'll pick you up tomorrow around the same time and we'll set up some dates," Tami said, with a big smile.

Jeb nodded and stepped away from the car as she backed up and left. He watched her drive away, then turned and strolled toward the second outbuilding. Pulling a key ring from his pocket, he reached for the padlock and realized the door wasn't locked. He turned to Earl. "You been messin' around in here?"

"No sir."

"How about Randy?"

"I don't think so."

Jeb didn't say any more, checked the rifle to make sure no bullet was in the chamber, leaned it against the side of the building, opened the door and reached for the flashlight he had stored in the corner. He checked the mash, nodded, then stepped out of the building, and made sure he laced the lock through both ends of the chain. He didn't want the kids fiddling around with the fermentation.

Earl had already gone inside. Jeb picked up the rifle and followed. One lantern on the table flickered with enough light so he could see. He picked up the lamp with his free hand and walked by Randy's cot and Marcy's crib. They both appeared to be sleeping. When he got to the bedroom, Beth turned over and stared at him.

"Did Tami throw herself all over you?"

"No," he said gruffly. "This was a business meeting."

"Right," she said, rolling over in a huff. Then she sat up, her brow furrowed. "What are you doing with the Earl's shotgun?"

"I took it away from him. He pointed it at the car as we drove up."

"He's only doing what you tell him. I've heard you preach more than once, not to let anyone come on the property he doesn't recognize. So how's he supposed to stop them, other than point his gun?"

"First, shout a warning for them to halt. When they do, you find out who they are and what they want, then tell the folks they're trespassing. If they don't heed your warning, then point the gun. Simple as that."

Beth threw up her hands. "Have you lost your mind. Who's going to listen to a kid?"

Jeb put out the lantern, slid into bed and turned his back to her. "I'm tired. Tami and I have another meeting tomorrow night, plus I've got work to do beforehand. I'm not arguing with you anymore."

Seething with anger, she pulled the covers up to her shoulders. "How many of these so called meetings will there be?"

"I have no idea. Goodnight, Beth."

Monday morning, Beth slipped out of bed before the sun rose. She shrugged into an old, worn, chenille robe she'd had for years and tiptoed into the kitchen. Randy and Marcy were still sleeping, so she moved on to the entry, where she quietly opened the door and stepped outside. The rose-pink light of dawn filled the surroundings and a cool breeze snapped at her neck and bare feet as she made her way to the outbuildings. She knew what the structures contained, and passed up the one with the still. When she reached the second one, she yanked at the chain, and cursed under her breath to find it padlocked. Placing her ear to the wood, she could hear the bubbling of the mash. From the rapid sound of the gurgling, she calculated a few more days for the yeast to stop working. It would probably be the weekend before Jeb took a batch of this putrid stuff to sell.

She turned to go back into the house, and one of the horses in the corral let out a loud whinny. "Oh, shut up you stupid horse,"she mumbled.

She picked up the wood carrier Jennifer had given her, filled it with some kindling and logs stacked outside the door, then carried it back into the cabin. Stoking the big stove, she lit the small branches, and once they caught fire, she closed and latched the lid.

Removing the soft cotton band around her hair, she brushed the locks, then twisted it into a small bun at the nap of her neck, and secured it with a pencil. Her day really began when Marcy stirred.

***

Monday morning, on his way to the office in Medford, Hawkman thought about whether he should make a trip to the cabin again tonight to check on the mash. Even though he knew little about fermentation, according to what he'd read, the fierce bubbling indicated it would be a few more days before the mixture would be ready for the still.

He also considered talking to Detective Williams on the situation. He knew he wouldn't have any authority over the brewing in California, but he could possibly give him some pointers. Making up his mind, as he hit the outskirts of Medford, he turned on the street which took him to the police station. He parked in one of the visitor slots and went inside. The main area seemed unusually quiet as he strolled down the hallway toward Williams' office. The door stood open and Hawkman knocked lightly on the door jamb, then peeked around the edge.

"Hey, you son-of-a-gun, where have you been?" Williams said, standing and holding out his hand.

"Working. How are things going with you?" Hawkman said, shaking his friend's hand. "Seems mighty quiet around here."

"We're trying to get ready for when school's out. Then all hell breaks loose."

Hawkman chuckled. "Celebrations of another year gone by?"

"You got it." The detective looked at him. "You usually don't just pop in here to say 'hello'. What's up your sleeve?"

"You've got me pegged." Hawkman said, scooting a seat up to the desk. "What do you know about making moonshine?"

Williams had just lowered himself into his chair, but jerked up his head. "What the hell have you gotten into now!"

CHAPTER TWENTY-NINE

Hawkman waved his hands. "It's not what you think. I've stumbled onto a situation. I'm not sure how to go about solving this mess without hurting a mother and three kids."

"Is this in Oregon or California?" Williams asked.

"California. I know its not in your jurisdiction, but thought maybe you could give me some people to contact."

"How far along are you into this investigation?"

Hawkman spent the next hour telling the story of the Hutchinsons. He emphasized how Jennifer had grown quite fond of Beth, the new baby, and Randy. She didn't like Jeb, nor did she trust the older son, Earl. He told about finding the copper still and the fermenting mash. Then he related the incident Jennifer had meeting Tami, and how they'd seen Jeb and her leaving in a car headed for town. "Briefly, that's the story. I know the law says a man can make whisky for personal use, but the minute he sells it, he gone over the line."

The detective leaned forward. "That's correct in almost every state, but first, you've got to tell Jennifer to back off. This could turn into a very nasty affair. Especially, with an ex-con, and his dad, Jacob, who doesn't like Beth. If you're right, and the old man is financing this operation, no one stands in the way. Not even the spouse, kids or friends."

Hawkman nodded. "I've already tried to talk to Jennifer, but she doesn't want to hear it."

Williams hit his fist against the desk top. "You tell her I said it. If she doesn't believe you, have her call me."

"I'll do that."

"At this time, you don't think he's running it?"

"If he is, it's only to local ranchers. I think this Tami is going to be the connection to get his hooch into the establishments."

The detective scooted a paper pad to the center of his desk, and picked up a pen.

"Since I can't help you, I'm going to give you the name of the detective in your area who can handle this." He ripped off the sheet and handed it to him.

Hawkman took the paper and glanced at it. "Detective Bud Chandler. I've read about him in the newspaper."

"He's a good man. I've worked with his group several times. I'll give him a heads up that you might be calling."

"Thanks, I'd appreciate it."

Williams leaned back in his chair. "How do you plan to follow this guy, if he delivers a batch in the buckboard?"

"I'm not sure yet. It won't be an easy task."

"Be careful and don't get yourself killed."

"I don't intend to." He stood. "I've taken enough of your time. Appreciate your help."

"Keep me informed. Very interesting project you've taken on."

"Will do," Hawkman said, as he left the office, tucking the name of the detective into his pocket.

***

Jennifer wanted to find out Tami's last name and where she hailed from, but felt she needed an excuse to go to the Hutchinson's place again so soon. She wracked her brain for a good reason and hit on the idea of baking a couple of cherry pies. Doubting Beth had the ingredients to make such a treat, she'd keep one and take the extra to the family. Jennifer busied herself in the kitchen and when the pastries were done, she smiled to herself at how beautiful they'd turned out as she put them on the counter to cool.

When they were warm to the touch, she covered them both with foil, then carefully placed one into a box. She clipped her fanny pack around her waist, carried the pastry to her Ford and placed it on the passenger side floorboard, figuring it would be the safest place as she drove over the rough path to the cabin. As she headed up the road, she wondered how she'd approach the subject of Tami without drawing suspicion.

Approaching the cabin, she thought it strange not seeing Earl with his rifle. When she pulled up to the door, she spotted Jeb coming out of the second outbuilding, and locking the door. She quickly busied herself getting the box out of the Ford so Jeb wouldn't think she'd seen him. Hawkman had told her he'd found the mash fermenting in that structure. She'd love to see it herself, but knew it was out of the question.

Randy answered her knock. "Hi, Mrs.Casey," he said, eyeing the box.

"Looks like you're doing very well. Not even using your crutches," Jennifer said.

"I use them when I go outside. Mom doesn't want me to hurt myself."

"It's a good idea. Better to be safe than sorry."

Beth put Marcy into her crib and turned to Jennifer with a smile. "Oh, my, woman, what do you have in your hands?"

"I had the urge to bake, and thought your family might enjoy a treat, too."

Jennifer lifted the pie from the container and placed it on the small table next to the stove. "I hope your brood likes cherry pie."

Randy clapped his hands. "It's my favorite. Can I have a piece now?"

Beth shook her head. "Not until after supper."

"Darn," he said. "That's a long way off."

Jennifer laughed. "There's plenty, so don't you worry, it will save until you've eaten. By the way, how are you doing on the puzzle books?"

"They're hard, and Mom is making me think about them. She said I wouldn't learn anything if she kept telling me the answers."

"Good for her," Jennifer said, grinning.

"If I can't have any pie, can I go outside?"

"Yes, with your crutches," Beth said.

Randy took off out the door, just as Jeb entered. The man didn't acknowledge Jennifer, but spoke directly to Beth. "I've got a meeting. Save me some food."

She nodded, and Jennifer saw the fire in her eyes. "There may not be any pie left when you return," she said in a sharp tone.

He glanced at the pastry. "Don't let those boys have more than one piece."

"I'll think about it," Beth said.

A horn honked, and Jennifer jumped up from her seat. "Are you expecting company?"

"No, it's Jeb's ride. You stay put."

Jennifer had a feeling Tami had pulled up outside, but she wanted Beth to tell her, and maybe she would, once Jeb had gone.

He grabbed a jacket from the rack on the wall next to the door and left without saying a word.

"Damn that woman!" Beth said, stomping her foot.

Jennifer studied Beth and could see the anger she harbored inside. "What woman?"

"Tamara Spencer."

"Who?" Jennifer asked.

Marcy let out a whimper, and Beth whirled around. "You met her the last time you were here," she said over her shoulder.

"You mean Tami?" Jennifer asked.

"Yes."

"I didn't know her full name, so you threw me. Is she local?"

"She's been in Yreka for the past two or three years. I haven't had much to do with her, because many years ago, she tried to take Jeb away from me."

Jennifer's eyebrows raised. "What brought her out of the woodwork now?"

"She says she's going to try to help Jeb get a job, and has set up appointments for him to talk to different people. I don't trust her."

"You think she's after Jeb again?"

"Definitely," Beth said, holding Marcy close to her breast so she could suckle. "I don't want her around at all."

"Have you told Jeb the way you feel?"

"Yes, I've also told Tami to stay away from him, but neither pay any attention."

"It sounds like quite a dilemma," Jennifer said, trying to be careful of the words coming out of her mouth.

"It won't be, if I have my way," Beth said, removing Marcy from her breast."

Jennifer felt she'd stayed long enough, and rose from the chair. "I better get on my way. If I go into town the next few days is there anything you need?"

"No, thank you. I'm well stocked."

"Tell Randy I said to keep working on those puzzles."

Beth smiled. "He loves those books. They've really helped him get through this ordeal."

"I'll talk to you in a few days," she said, before closing the door. Once in the Ford, she quickly wrote down Tami's full name and where Beth said she lived. Maybe Hawkman could find out more about this woman.

CHAPTER THIRTY

Randy was glad to get outside since his mom wouldn't let him have any dessert, and he sure didn't want to hear women's talk. He swung on his crutches alongside the cabin and finally arrived near the second outbuilding. Scouring the area, he looked for Earl, but didn't see him, so he remained hesitant about nosing around the structure. About the time he headed for the corral, Mrs. Casey came out the door.

"Thanks for the pie," he yelled.

She turned toward him, and waved. "You're more than welcome."

He watched her drive away, then continued his journey. When he arrived at the horse's pen, he saw Earl standing on the other side. "Whatcha doing?" Randy asked.

"Feeding the horses, dummy, can't you see?"

"Nope, looks like you're swinging on the fence. Where's your gun?"

"None of your business."

"Bet Dad took it away from you, didn't he?"

"Shut up, nosey."

"Mrs. Casey brought us a cherry pie."

Earl jerked up his head. "Really?"

"Yep, but Mom won't let us have any until after supper."

"When you gonna get off those stupid crutches so I can chase you?"

Randy threw back his head and laughed. "Soon, I hope. I miss our wrestling matches."

Earl walked around the corral. "Come on, little bud, let's go see how long it'll be until supper."

***

When Jennifer drove into the driveway, she noted Hawkman had beaten her home. "Darn, I forgot to leave him a note," she mumbled under her breath, as she hurried into the house.

She found him standing at the counter. "Sorry Hon, I thought I'd be back before you got here."

"Did you go to the Hutchinsons?" he asked.

"Yes, and I got some information for you." She handed him the slip of paper.

"Tamara Spencer from Yreka. So this is Tami's full name? You have any trouble getting it out of Beth?"

"No, it came quite easily, thanks to Jeb." She then told him the tale about Tami coming to pick him up while she was there. "If I was that woman, I wouldn't want to be on Beth's bad side."

Hawkman glanced at Jennifer. "Why? Do you think she really cares what Beth thinks? Remember, we're dealing with money."

Jennifer made a face. "Beth has a mean streak; I can see it in her expressions. Also, we're talking about a marriage at stake."

"I'm not following you."

She related what Beth had told her about how Tami had at one time tried to take Jeb away from her, but failed. "I thought something awfully fishy the day I met her, and noticed how she had eyes for Jeb."

"Doesn't sound good. You're right. A woman's wrath can be vicious."

"Right now, Beth's anger is vented toward Jeb, but it could change, if Tami gets aggressive."

"This is all very disturbing."

Jennifer walked over to the cabinet and lifted the lid on the crock pot. "Dinner is done. You want to eat now?"

"No, not just yet." Then he spotted the cherry pie on the counter. "On second thought, I'm ready."

She laughed. "I wondered when you'd spot the dessert."

"You've been busy today."

"It was my excuse to go see Beth. I made two and took one to them."

"You're quite a blackmailer."

As they ate, Hawkman told Jennifer about his visit with Detective Williams and told her about Bud Chandler, the detective he'd recommended to handle the case when he got some concrete evidence on Jeb Hutchinson. "I've read about him in the paper. It appears he does a good job at law enforcement."

Jennifer nodded. "Yes, I've heard of him too."

"I'm going to make another run up to Hutchinson's tonight."

"Watch for the car lights again. Jeb is out with Tami, and you sure don't want to get caught snooping around."

Hawkman changed clothes and left on the four-wheeler. He soon arrived at the parking spot, then walked in the rest of the way. When he approached the corral, darkness had fallen, and he again detoured; but it didn't keep the horse from neighing. "Damn horse sure has sensitive hearing," he hissed, as he ducked behind a tree trunk. He waited several minutes to make sure the coast was clear before advancing toward the outbuilding.

The aroma of food cooking floated through the air. No sounds met his ears, and no headlights appeared coming up the path to the house. Hawkman hurried to the second structure and listened. The bubbling noise had decreased quite a bit since last night. He quickly used his pick to unlock the padlock and only opened the door enough to get inside. Again he took a couple of snapshots and checked the barrel with his flashlight. Satisfied with the findings, he slipped out the door, making sure he'd fastened the padlock. When he turned to leave, his heart stopped.

"Hi, Mr. Casey. Whatcha doing?"

"Hello, Randy. Just checking to make sure everything is okay. Why are you outside without your crutches?"

"I wanted to see if walking without them made me hurt."

"How does it feel?"

"Good. No pain. How'd you get here? I don't see your car."

"I came up the back way."

"You want to come inside?"

"Uh, no. Are you good at keeping a secret?"

"Yeah."

"Don't tell anyone, especially, your mom, dad or Earl, that you saw me, not even Mrs. Casey."

"Why?"

"Cause I could get into a heap of trouble."

"How come?"

About that time, Hawkman saw a ray of light penetrate the darkness, as the door to the cabin opened. Randy turned and Hawkman, taking advantage of the moment, dashed around the corner of the building when he heard Earl's voice yell into the night.

"Hey, punk, get back inside before some wild animal eats you."

Randy twisted his head around, looked behind him, then shrugged his shoulders. "Coming."

Hawkman bolted through the brush, and sprinted all the way to the four-wheeler. He jumped onto the seat, started it up, and put it in high gear all the way to his driveway.

When he stumbled into the kitchen, Jennifer looked up from her computer. "What the heck happened?"

"I got caught."

She jumped up, ran to the window, and glanced outside. "Are you being followed?"

"No."

"Who spotted you?"

"Randy."

"Randy!" she said, in disbelief.

"Yeah, I'd just locked the padlock on the fermentation building and about to leave, when I heard this innocent voice at my back. "Hi, Mr. Casey." Believe me, my heart literally stopped beating."

"What was he doing out at night?"

"He said he wanted to try walking without his crutches."

Jennifer wiped her hands across her face. "He'll tell Beth and probably Earl, then it will get back to Jeb. This could made for a big mess."

"Maybe." Hawkman told her the rest of the conversation between him and the boy. "I don't know if he'll keep it a secret or not."

She shook her head. "Hard to say."

CHAPTER THIRTY-ONE

His nose wrinkled and scratching his head, Randy walked through the doorway of the cabin. "Is there such a thing as a ghost?"

Earl threw back his head and laughed. "Now he's seeing things. What an idiot."

Beth glanced at him. "Enough out of you. Get to your room." Then she turned to Randy. "Why do you ask?"

"I just talked to a man, turned around when Earl called, then I looked back, and he'd disappeared. I couldn't find him anywhere."

"What did he say to you?" Beth asked, concern in her voice.

"He just asked why I was outside without my crutches."

"Did you recognize him?'

Randy thought a moment before answering, and remembered he'd told Mr. Casey, he could keep a secret. "No, but he seemed okay."

Beth patted him on the head. "I don't think I'd worry about it. You probably need to get outside more. Tomorrow, you can go play without your crutches."

"Thanks, Mom. I'm going to bed right now, so I can get up early."

Beth chuckled softly and tucked him in. "Don't have a nightmare about the ghost you saw."

"He didn't scare me, he was nice. Maybe I'll see him again."

She checked on Marcy, then put one lamp near the front door, carried one with her, and extinguished the others in the room. "Goodnight, boys."

"Night, Mom," they said in unison, even though Earl was in the other bedroom.

Randy couldn't go to sleep. Every time he shut his eyes, they popped open again. He couldn't quit thinking about Mr. Casey being outside, and why he wanted him to keep the visit a secret. Why would he come in the dark and tinker with the padlock on the building with the strange noise inside?

About the time Randy's eyelids grew heavy, a squeak he recognized as his folks' bedroom door forced him to glance toward the noise. His mother, fully dressed, carrying a rifle, walked swiftly across the room, quietly opened the front door, and disappeared outside. Now where is she going with a gun at this hour? Dad hadn't returned home either. This night seemed to be turning into many unexplained events.

Sleep finally overtook the lad and he didn't catch his parents coming in the door.

***

"What were you going to do, shoot us both?" Jeb said.

"Keep your voice down. You want to wake the kids?" Beth said. "Yes, if she'd put a hand on you, I would have shot you and Tami."

"I told you my dealings with her were strictly business."

Beth whirled around and stared into her husband's eyes. "I can guarantee you, they aren't strictly business with Tami." She stomped into the bedroom.

Jeb followed, shaking his head.

***

Hawkman took the camera from his pocket. "Did you by any chance keep those last pictures of the still and fermenting barrels on your computer?"

"Yes," Jennifer said, as she moved to the machine.

"Good, I want to compare tonight's photos with those of last night. I don't know much about this moonshining business, but I'd suspect one can tell the rate of the fermentation process by the bubbling."

"Sounds logical," Jennifer said, handing him the cord to connect the camera.

He held up his hand. "Hold on a second. A car is coming across the bridge, let me check if it's Tami." Moving to the kitchen window, he viewed the tan car as it rolled past. "Yep, it's her, and a man."

"They do hold late business meetings," Jennifer said, sarcastically.

Hawkman moved back to the computer center and connected the camera. She opened the pictures, then pulled up the older batch. He pointed to the recent barrel. "Looks like it's slowed down considerably, wouldn't you say?"

"Yes, I'd agree."

"More than likely, it will be ready to put in the still by Thursday or Friday. Jeb will probably make a run soon. I can check on Friday, but I'd bet on Saturday."

"Do you think he'll make the run at night?"

"Yes, especially if he uses the buckboard, which I think he will until he can get himself a truck."

"Have you figured how you're going to follow him?"

"No, but it will come to me."

Jennifer cocked her head and stared at him. "It isn't like you not to have a plan."

"Well, I sort of do, but I'm not telling you."

"Why, because it's dangerous?"

"Let's just say, it isn't real safe, but secure enough."

Jennifer slapped her hands on the desktop. "You certainly know how to make me worry."

He walked behind her and put his arms around her. "Please, don't worry. I'm going to come home safe."

She shoved him away. "Don't try to con me. I'm not falling for it."

He backed off and put his hands in the air. "I tried."

The next couple of days were uneventful as Jennifer stayed busy with the Ladies' Auxiliary, and Hawkman spent his time catching up at work. Friday evening rolled around and Hawkman prepared to ride the four-wheeler up the back route and check on the progression of the home brew.

Jennifer ignored him and worked at her computer. Finally, she glanced at him as he filled his pockets with several surveillance items. When he took out his pistol and checked it for rounds, she broke the silence. "You obviously feel this trip might warrant the use of your gun? That tells me it's not as safe as you portrayed to me."

"I never venture into new territory without being prepared. If history is right, I could come across some very brutal men surrounding this type of operation."

"Shouldn't you have talked with the detective in Yreka before taking this on by yourself?"

"I need more concrete information before I approach him. All I have right now is circumstantial. I have no proof Jeb is selling his booze."

"Why don't I go with you? I can cover your back."

Hawkman jerked up his head. "Absolutely not. It's out of the question. Don't even pursue the subject."

She shrugged her shoulders. "Just trying to be helpful; you don't have to bite my head off."

"Sorry, didn't mean to. This is a one-man job. In fact, it might not even go down tonight."

He slipped on his jacket, buttoned it up, and went outside. Checking the Polaris for fuel, he topped it off, then headed out. Reaching the parking place, he figured he wouldn't have to go in as far, as long as he could get a view of the corral.

He'd thought earlier to slip a pair of night binoculars into the side pockets of the four-wheeler, and removed them once he'd parked. Threading through the brush, he soon arrived close enough to the pen, and put the glasses to his face. The horses were meandering around, and he could see the buckboard inside the barn. Obviously, no run would take place tonight or the animals would be hitched to the wagon.

Hawkman returned home. "No action tonight," he said, entering the kitchen.

"Have you by any chance seen Tami's car go by?"

"No, and I would've seen the headlights. No one has come over the bridge since you left."

"Good. I'm sure the buckboard is the means of transportation for the hooch. Tomorrow night will tell the tale."

"I'll be glad when this part of the investigation is over," Jennifer said.

CHAPTER THIRTY-TWO

Saturday, Hawkman tried to stay out of Jennifer's way as she spoke in curt sentences, but mostly ignored him. She definitely didn't seem happy, but he felt she'd get over it as long as he didn't tantalize her. He stayed in the garage, and tinkered with the vehicles.

Dusk soon arrived; he grabbed a sandwich, then prepared to leave. "Honey, I'm taking off; don't worry about me. It'll be late when I get home."

She approached him, put her arms around his neck. "I'm sorry, I've been such a pill. Please be careful, and promise you'll wake me when you get in. Remember, I love you very much."

He held her close for several minutes. "I love you, too. I'd never do anything to hurt you, so yes, I'll wake you when I get home."

He kissed her passionately, then pushed her back and gazed into her face. "You're so beautiful. Don't think for one minute, I'd let anything happen. I'm not about to take the chance of some other man having you."

She grinned. "I'll be waiting."

Feeling much better, Hawkman took off on the four-wheeler. He'd make a quick stop at the Hutchinson's corral to make sure the buckboard would be used, then he'd backtrack to the road leading out. Arriving at the parking spot for the Polaris, he took the binoculars from the side pack, then scurried through the brush. He approached the area where he could see the outline of the corral and put the glasses to his face. The wagon had been moved through the big door to the front side of the barn. He could see the outline with two horses hitched to the front.

"Yep, the run is tonight," he mumbled under his breath. He headed back to his machine, hopped onto the seat, turned the ignition, flipped on the lights and headed toward the back path. Hawkman soon jockeyed upon the road and drove until he came to the padlocked gate. He debated whether to hide his four-wheeler in the brush nearby, and hoof it, or go farther. Pushing his luck at being spotted, he decided to steer around the gate and conceal the machine closer to where he figured Jeb would bring the buckboard onto the trail.

Turning off the lights, he geared the machine down so it wouldn't be so noisy. His sight adjusted to the night and he could see his way without any danger. Approaching the area he suspected Jeb would use, he searched for a spot to hide the four-wheeler and soon found a small cluster of trees surrounded by high brush. When he pulled into the thicket, he could hear the scurrying of animals and the flight of birds overhead. He'd definitely interrupted a nighttime den. Shutting down the engine, he dismounted and crept toward the path which led to the Hutchinsons' place. He reasoned the sound of the horses and wagon would carry a distance in the quiet night. Searching for a good place to conceal himself, he soon discovered a gully surrounded by shrubs. He slid into it and hunkered down. It wasn't long before he realized the ground underneath his boots was soggy. Obviously, an underground stream flowed directly under his feet.

The same moment he climbed out of the mire, he heard a whinny. He quickly looked around and dove behind a fallen log. Jerking off his hat, he put it underneath him and kept his head down. It seemed forever before he heard the grunts of the horses and the thud of the wagon as the heavy cart bumped over the side ridge of the road. He finally peeked over the large oak branch and could see the silhouette of Jeb poised on the bench, reins in hand.

Thankful he didn't see Earl, he jammed his hat onto his head, then jogged after the wagon. When he got close enough to grab the tailgate, he swung himself into the back. Happy to see the tarp tossed over the moonshine containers, he quickly slid under it. Knowing when to get out could be a big problem. He had no idea if Jeb planned on going right to the place of business, or if the customer would meet him on the road. The time he needed to jump out of the wagon depended on the situation.

Hawkman felt his bones being jarred to the core on the hard floor of the buckboard. He peered out from underneath the cover and tried to see in front of the wagon between Jeb's legs and the butt of the rifle perched at his side. So far, the man had shown no indication of slowing down. Suddenly, up ahead, Hawkman noticed car lights blinking off and on. He edged to the back of the buckboard, slithered over the back side, dropped to the ground and rolled to the side of the road. Hunkering down, he ran alongside the edge, staying a few feet behind the wagon.

When Jeb slowed, and stopped the team of horses, Hawkman slipped behind some bushes and watched a man with a flashlight approach the buckboard. Jeb stepped down from the bench seat onto the tongue, then hopped to the ground. The two men talked for a few minutes, then walked to the side of the cart where Jeb yanked back the tarp. The other man shined the beam from the lantern onto the stash of rotgut.

"I'd like a taste," he said.

Jeb reached down and untied a metal cup from the neck of one of the large containers. He then unscrewed the lid and tilted the jar. When he handed him the cup, the man said, "You first."

"Sure." Jeb downed several gulps, then handed it to the prospective customer, and watched his face as he took a sip.

"Whoohoo, this is good stuff."

"Glad you like my brew," Jeb said.

"I'll take the whole batch."

The man handed Jeb a roll of cash, and the two men loaded the white lightning into the trunk of the car.

"If this goes over as well as I think it will, we'll be doing business on a regular basis," the man said, as they shook hands and he got into his car. Turning around, he sped down the dirt road, heading for Hornbrook.

Hawkman didn't recognize the man, and wondered where his business was located. He'd do a search on the bars in the immediate area on the computer and see if he could find photos of the owners. He'd know the man if he ever saw him again. It wouldn't be hard to spot someone who weighed over two hundred pounds, and stood only about five foot, six inches tall, with a bald head that glistened by the light of his own flashlight,

Jeb hopped back on the seat of the buckboard, picked up the reins, and gave a sharp yelp as the horses moved down the road to a wide spot where he turned the wagon around and headed toward home.

Hawkman followed the carriage until Jeb reached a heavily darkened area with trees over-shadowing the road, then he grabbed the tailgate and swung his legs up, slipping into the interior with little noise. He pulled the tarp over himself, figuring if Jeb happened to glance back, he'd be hidden.

When he felt the wagon turn, bumping over the dirt brim of the road, he bailed out the rear, landed on his feet, then clambered behind the trunk of a large oak tree. He watched the wagon move ahead before he hightailed it through the forest to the hidden four-wheeler.

Driving back to the lake, he came to the conclusion that following the wagon appeared less dangerous than pursuing someone in a car. He doubted Jeb had any inkling he'd had a passenger in the bed of his buggy. Hawkman rounded the corner of his driveway and parked in the lean-to. Jennifer met him at the door.

"I'm so relieved to see you home safe," she said, giving him a hug. "Tell me what happened."

He stepped inside, removed his gloves and paraphernalia he had in his pockets, placed them on the kitchen counter, then selected a beer from the refrigerator. "Want a beer?"

"No, I already have a gin and tonic made."

They moved to their matching chairs, and Miss Marple jumped into her mistress' lap.

Jennifer swiveled her chair so it faced Hawkman. "Start at the beginning."

He gazed at the ceiling. "I stepped out the door, got on my four-wheeler..."

She reached over and smacked his knee. "Not back that far."

Chuckling, he related the saga from the point where he'd checked the Hutchinson's place, then how he'd gone to the road and waited, until the moment he ended up home.

Her gaze locked onto his face, she barely blinked, listening to the tale. "You really took a chance hiding in the wagon."

"I thought it might be dangerous, but it worked out to be safer than if I'd followed him in a vehicle. He had no lights, didn't even carry a flashlight. The other guy had the lantern."

"Just one man showed up? Did you recognize him?"

"Yes, and no. Jeb didn't have a huge batch. At least, not as much as he could make in that huge still. He might have another lot ready to go for tomorrow or he's feeling his way into the market. This man definitely liked the moonshine, and bought the load. I'm going to do some research and see if I can find this guy."

"How could you see him in the dark?"

"The beam of the flashlight hit him in the face several times. His bald head glistened, and he wobbled when he walked. I'd say for a short man, he must have weighed two hundred pounds."

"Under what brand name would they use to serve the whiskey?"

"More than likely they'd classify it as the house brand. A few would know it to be special and pass the word to try it. The news would get out that it had a kick and people would flock to the bar to try it. The owner could make a killing."

Jennifer sighed. "Along with Jeb, as he builds a reputation for the best hooch around."

"Yep. Time to talk to the detective."

CHAPTER THIRTY-THREE

Jennifer bit her lower lip, and unconsciously stroked Miss Marple's furry back. "Can't you wait awhile? You're not even sure he peddled it to a place of business."

"It doesn't matter; I saw money exchange hands. He's sold the white lightning to someone and it's illegal." He leaned forward. "You act like you want me to skirt the law."

She sighed and leaned back in the chair. "I don't know what I want. I'm just worried about Beth and the children. What will they do if Jeb is returned to jail?"

"The same as they did the last time he was incarcerated." He shook his head. "You're talking with emotion and not using your head. Think about what you're saying."

"You're right. I keep seeing Randy's and Marcy's faces in front of me. I guess it's the mother instinct."

"For some reason you've been infatuated with them since the first day you met the family."

Jennifer put Miss Marple on the floor and turned toward Hawkman. "It might be because I've never been around destitute people. When I see the barren way they have to live, it tugs at my heart strings."

"Honey, I admire your thinking. However, there's nothing you can personally do about it. They've chosen their way of life."

"I know everything you say is true. It just bothers me to see innocent children brought up in that type of environment."

"You have a big heart, but I'd like you to try to push the Hutchinsons out of it. There's nothing good going on in their household, and you're only putting yourself in a position to get hurt."

Jennifer nodded, and glanced up at him with tears rimming her eyes. "I'll try, but I can't guarantee I'll be successful."

He reached over and took her hand. "That's all I ask."

"I sort of want to change the subject," she said.

"Shoot."

"You said you were going to research Tami Spencer. Did you find anything of interest?"

"Strangely, no. All I found was she moved from Portland, Oregon, to Yreka and has lived there two years. Nothing on her employment or history, just sort of a ho-hum person with no significance."

"So she's been in this area about as long as Beth and Jeb. Makes me wonder if she's been keeping track of their whereabouts."

"Very possibly, if she still holds a flame for Jeb."

"Beth told me, Tami attempted to take him from her some years ago. I have a feeling it happened before he went to prison."

Hawkman scratched his sideburn. "It would be interesting to find out where Beth and the boys lived before Jeb was released. I hunted for her too, but couldn't find a thing, like she'd disappeared off the face of the earth. However, she could have been going by an alias for the boys' sake."

Jennifer got up from her chair and paced. "I might go up there next week and see if I can find out any more. I'm afraid though, she's not going to like my line of questions."

"All she can do is tell you nothing, or to get out."

***

Sunday morning, Hawkman arose early and took Pretty Girl for a hunt. While she soared above him, he leaned against the fender of the Cruiser and thought about the Hutchinson situation. The whole mess had really affected Jennifer and it bothered him. He decided to let things simmer for a week or more. What did it matter if Jeb got caught this week or three weeks from now? It would give her a break from having to worry about whether the Hutchinsons' children would have a home or not. Normally, Jennifer was down-to-earth and realistic, but this family had gotten under her skin. She needed time to sort it out, which he knew she would, in due course.

He'd calculated that last night, Jeb had only carted out about half the moonshine he'd brewed from the huge still, and therefore, would probably make another run tonight to a different customer. Before going to the detective, he should have a couple of buyers to report. When he finished with Pretty Girl, he'd go online and see if he could find the man who bought the first load. Tonight, maybe he'd recognize the purchaser.

His beloved falcon had not returned from her hunt, and his gaze studied the tree line. Moving out into the field, he whistled several times to no avail. Advancing toward the area where she'd disappeared, he saw her suddenly emerge from the top of a large oak tree and circle high above his head. She finally descended and perched on his outstretched leather clad arm.

"What took you so long, girl?"

When he checked her beak, he could see remnants of brown fur. "Looks like you found yourself a good size prey this time. Bet your tummy is full now."

The man and his pet returned home. Hawkman cleaned out the aviary, and placed Pretty Girl on the perch with fresh water and dry food, which he doubted she'd find of interest until tomorrow. Entering the house from the deck, he noticed Miss Marple had hopped onto the large ledge of the window, licking her chops as she viewed the falcon. "You silly feline, that bird would tear you apart in a few seconds. I'd advise you to quit dreaming."

Jennifer chuckled from her seat behind the computer. "You'll never convince her."

"I'm heading back to my office. Need anything before I leave the room?"

"No, thanks."

Hawkman booted up his machine, removed his hat and stuck it on the fancy hook Jennifer had supplied. She obviously hadn't appreciated the big bare nail he'd hammered into the wall. He clicked on the icon to the special search area he had privy to, then put in his user name and password into the search area. When the web page appeared, he typed in taverns and owners, in Sisikiyou County. Hoping pictures were supplied, he watched the monitor as it went through looking for the information. Soon, the names of many nightclubs popped up on the screen. Some listed owners. Hawkman started with the ones in nearby towns. Clicking on the names of the bars, he found pictures of the buildings, and a few had photos of the owners. Just about the time he was ready to give up, a fuzzy black and white picture emerged of the proprietor of a saloon in Yreka.

Hawkman enlarged the shot and studied it. Even though he found it hard to define the features, he'd swear they belonged to the man who'd picked up Jeb's load last night. He wrote down the owner's name and the place of business, then printed out the unfocused picture. Narrowing the search down to the local bars, he printed out the list, just in case this one fell through. His gut told him Tami would do business with the locals first, because Jeb had no vehicle to transport his goods, other than the buckboard. Even if Tami had offered her car, Jeb would refuse because it would set off Beth's ire.

He did a few more searches and still found nothing on Tami Spencer, nor on Beth Hutchinson. It made him wonder how Beth made a living while Jeb did time in prison. Maybe Jennifer could find out, but he doubted it. It would probably remain a mystery forever. Shutting down the computer, he stacked the printed copies at the side and left the room.

Going to the refrigerator, he rummaged around until Jennifer finally said. "What are you looking for?"

"Sandwich makings"

"Hold on a second and I'll come in."

"Didn't want to bother you."

"It's okay, I'm ready for a bite to eat too."

After saving her work, she put the computer into sleep mode and came into the kitchen. Without hesitation, she took out leftover roast, cheese, tomatoes, pickles and other needed condiments.

"You're something else," Hawkman said. "You pulled everything out like magic."

She smiled. "That's a woman for you."

"Glad I have you," he said, giving her a quick kiss on the cheek.

She put a hand on her hip and looked him in the face. "Why do I have this dark feeling you're going out tonight?"

"Why do you say 'dark'?"

"Because it's been like a black cloud hanging over my head all day. I kept waiting for you to say something, but you never did."

"Guess I just assumed you'd know. I'd bet my last dollar Jeb didn't take all the hooch last night.   That still will brew double what he had in the wagon. He'll make a run tonight to sell to another buyer."

"Did you find out anything about the one last night?"

"I think I've found my man, but the picture is hazy, so I'm going into town next week and see if I can spot him in his tavern."

"Is he local?"

Hawkman nodded. "Yreka"

They ate their sandwiches, and made small talk as twilight fell. Hawkman prepared for his trip into the woods, then left on the four-wheeler. He made a quick run by the back of the Hutchinsons' place to make sure the buckboard was hitched to the horses. Finding it as he expected, he journeyed on to the spot he'd gone the night before, parked the machine and waited in the moonless night for Jeb to come rolling by.

CHAPTER THIRTY-FOUR

Hawkman didn't have to wait long before he heard the snorting of horses, and the rolling of wooden wheels over rough ground. He hunkered down in the shadows until Jeb passed, then ran behind the wagon, grabbed the tailgate, swung himself into the wagon and slipped under the tarp. Everything went as routine until suddenly bright lights lit up the whole dirt road.

"What the hell," Hawkman muttered. He stole a peek from under the tarp and two cars appeared, one on each side of the road, equipped with spot lights pointed at the wagon. The horses became frightened. One reared, as they yanked against the reins, causing the buckboard to jerk back and forth.

"Turn those damn things off," Jeb roared. "You're scaring the horses." He fought to get the animals under control, when finally the beams went off.

Hawkman quickly scooted over the rear and dropped to the ground. He stayed crouched for a second behind the carriage, then hightailed toward the wooded area. Car doors slammed, and suddenly, Hawkman spotted a shaft of light sweeping across the area. Dropping to the ground behind some brush, he lay very still and watched the flash pass over him. Fortunately, it kept going, and didn't move back toward his hiding place.

"Thought I heard a rustling sound," the man said, fanning his flashlight beam behind the buckboard.

The horses had settled, and Jeb jumped down from the seat. "There're all sorts of animals out here. You probably frightened one with those bright lights."

"You sure no one followed you?" he said.

The other man tapped his shoulder. "Quit worrying, Claude. Who the hell would trail a horse-driven cart?"

"Can't be too careful, Luke," the man said, walking to the side of the wagon, and peering under the cover.

Hawkman could hear the men's conversation clearly, and figuring they were preoccupied with the hidden contents, he took the risk of raising his head. The lantern glow reflected off the tarp, and made the men's faces look distorted, but he recognized both men.

Feeling a cramp forming in his neck, Hawkman quietly crawled back to the tree line where he rose to his feet behind a cedar. He could watch the men's actions between the thick limbs. They went through the ritual of tasting the brew, nodding their heads, handed Jeb a roll of bills, then carried their merchandise to the trunks of their cars.

"We'll let Tami know if we want more," Luke said, as he slammed the lid, and climbed into his vehicle.

Jeb gave a wave, and climbed back onto the bench seat of the wagon. The whole meeting took all of twenty minutes, and Jeb was on his way back to the cabin.

Hawkman jogged along the bank behind the cart, but stayed in the shadows, as Jeb kept turning around and looking into the bed of the wagon. Something bothered him. Hawkman wondered if he'd noticed the mussed up tarp. When he'd jumped out in haste, the rope tied to the cover had tangled on his boot, and he didn't have time to toss the end back into the bed. He hated to think he'd have to hoof it all the way to the Polaris, but it might come to that.

Suddenly, Jeb stopped the horses, reached around and tried to pull the canvas toward him, but it hung up on the tailgate. He finally climbed from the seat, carrying his rifle, and walked around to the back of the trailer, untangled the rope, then rolled it several times until it rested against the front board. Hopping back into the seat, he placed his gun next to his leg, picked up the reins and continued his journey.

Hawkman didn't dare hitch a ride now, as Jeb would shoot him before he could get one leg hitched over the tailgate. He had a long walk ahead. Keeping the buckboard in sight, he took long strides, but kept just enough behind it so Jeb wouldn't catch a glimpse of movement from the corner of his eye. It didn't take long before they came to the dogleg in the road where Jeb cut off to go to his place and Hawkman veered in the opposite direction to find the four-wheeler.

Relieved to turn into his home driveway, he parked under the lean-to, and went inside. Jennifer left the computer and gave him a hug, then stepped away and turned him around.

"Oh, dear, don't sit on anything, your whole backside is covered in dirt and grass. What happened?"

As he undressed in the laundry room, he related the story of the men with the spotlights on their cars. Checking the pockets of his clothes, while Jennifer swept the floor where he'd traipsed, he continued his tale.

"Do those men carry weapons?" she asked.

"I'm sure they do. I recognized the two men tonight. They own the sleazy joint on the outskirts of Yreka called 'The Hut'. They're a couple of rough slime balls, and have been in trouble with the law several times, but it doesn't seem to sway these two men to keep their noses clean. Regulations mean nothing to them. You'd never know it by Claude's and Luke's looks, they appear as innocent as newborn babes."

"I'm certainly happy you came out unscathed. We can handle dirty jeans much easier."

Hawkman took her hand. "I know you're worried about Beth and the kids. So I've decided not to go to the detective just yet."

"Thank you. I know you have to do what has to be done, but I'm glad you're going to give it a little more time. Maybe, just maybe, this is to get the family on their feet. Then it will stop."

"Honey, how am I going to convince you that it won't. This is easy money for Jeb."

She grimaced. "It's so hard for me to think that way. I know you're right; I just don't want to believe a man could put making white lightning more important than his family."

"You're going to have to come to grips with it eventually, and I'm hoping a little more time will help."

She left Hawkman to start the washing machine, and went to the bedroom. He soon followed, crawled into bed and folded his arms around her.

Monday morning, he quietly slipped out from under the covers, and decided to go to the guest bathroom to take his shower, so as not to disturb Jennifer. Today he had several things on his mind, and wanted to check out the first guy Jeb made connections with on Saturday night, as he wasn't sure it was the same person he'd found on the computer search. The name, Moss Atkins, didn't ring a bell, nor did the tavern, "The Big Mug", but he'd recognize the man if he saw him again.

When he headed for the kitchen, it surprised him to smell coffee perking. "Good morning, my sexy lady. Did I wake you?" he said, coming up behind her and kissing her neck.

She turned and grinned. "No, I have a full day; thought I'd better get up and moving."

"What are your plans?"he asked.

"I'm going to visit Beth and possibly find out how she survived while Jeb did time."

"You think she'll confide in you?"

"I have no idea. She may kick me out, and tell me to mind my own business."

"What will you do?"

"I'll leave, and mind my own business."

He chuckled. "Good thinking." Pouring some of the hot brew into a thermal cup, he pulled her close to him with his free hand.

"I'll see you tonight." Then he gave her a passionate kiss.

"Have a good day, and please, stay out of trouble," she said, giving him a swat on the butt as he headed for the door. "I know you're going to buy a bear claw at Clyde's donut shop, but I'll forgive you this time."

Laughing, he jumped into the Cruiser and headed for Medford. He knew the taverns would prepare for their nightly crowds a few hours before opening. Not sure what time that might be, he'd just drive by the pubs. Maybe he'd get a glimpse of the owners.

Knowing the location of 'The Hut', since it'd been there for years, he decided to go by there first. It stood in the middle of a huge lot on the outskirts of Yreka. Its parking lot of two rows extended all the way around the building. He pulled in and circled the structure. As he drove toward the back, he saw one of the cars he recognized from Jeb's hooch run, parked at the back entrance with the trunk open. They were wasting no time to get the brew to the customers.

He drove out of the area and then to the side of the road and programmed "The Big Mug's" address into his GPS. This bar

happened to be on the other end of town.
When he finally reached   it, he found it to
be more of an upper class establishment.
Fancy door at the entry, professional signs
in the windows, also parking in front, on
each side and surrounded by a tall redwood
fence. He circled the place and found it
locked up tight. Searching for a sign giving
the hours of business, he spotted it on the
front porch stating, "Open-5PM until 2AM".
He'd stop later, and see if this Moss Atkins
was the man he'd seen at Jeb's Saturday
night.

CHAPTER THIRTY-FIVE

Jennifer paced the floor. She needed an excuse to go see Beth, but felt offering gifts each time appeared more like charity, than friendship. She didn't want Beth to think she felt sorry for the family, which, in fact, she did, but didn't think it good to expose her feelings.

She finally came upon an idea, shrugged into a hoody, and left the house. When she pulled up to the cabin, Randy ran to her vehicle, and jumped on the running board by her window.

"Hi, Mrs. Casey."

"Hello, Randy, it looks like you're almost healed."

"I think I am. A couple of stitches fell out, so that tells me the scar is almost well."

"Yes, that's a good indicator."

"You come to see Mom?"

"I came to visit all of you. How is everyone?"

Randy ducked his head. "Okay. Mom and Dad argue a lot."

"That happens, I don't think it's anything to worry about."

"Do you and Mr. Casey fuss at each other?"

She smiled. "Sometimes."

He jumped down to the ground. "I'll tell Mom you're here."

"Okay," Jennifer said, as she climbed out of the Ford.

Beth met her at the door. "Come in. Good to see you. What brings you to our humble abode today?"

"I'm going to town either this afternoon, or tomorrow morning, and thought I'd check to see if you needed anything." Jennifer immediately headed for the crib. When she approached, Marcy gurgled with glee. "You are so cute and growing like a weed."

Beth walked to one of her cabinets and removed a small jar. She pulled out a couple of dollars, and handed it to Jennifer. "If you'd pick up a box of baby cereal, I'd appreciate it. I want to start Marcy on a little bit at night, so maybe she'd sleep longer in the morning."

"No problem. What kind?" Jennifer asked, stowing the bills in her fanny pack.

"Rice would be fine. I'm in no hurry, so you needn't rush to get it to me."

Jennifer saw an opening and decided to ask Beth a pointed question. "How in the world did you survive while Jeb was in jail?"

She shot a sharp look at Jennifer, then turned away. "I managed."

"Randy told me he'd attended school at one time. Did you live in a town?"

"Yes."

Jennifer felt uncomfortable, as Beth's answers were terse and short. She figured there would be no information given. "I hope you plan to enroll the boys in school next year. They could ride their bikes to our place, catch the school bus, then ride home when they were dropped off after classes."

"If we're still here, I'll for sure enroll Randy. Not sure if Earl will go."

Jennifer studied Beth for a moment. "What do you mean, 'If you're still here'?"

Beth shrugged. "One never knows."

"Regardless, try to talk Earl into finishing his education. It would help him in later life to at least have a high school diploma."

"I know and I'll definitely try, but it will be between him and his father."

Jennifer headed for the door. "I better get on my way. I'll bring the cereal in a couple of days."

"At the rate Randy is improving, I could send him down on his bike."

"If he's up to it, that will be fine. I'll talk to you soon," she said, stepping out the door.

Driving home, Jennifer had the distinct feeling Beth had given her the brushoff. She'd definitely not gotten any information, and the look she'd given her made her shrink inside. The woman knew when someone tried to probe where they didn't belong, and immediately put up her guard.

Beth seemed distant and very private, not like other women Jennifer knew, who were eager to share their private lives. Of course, the possibility existed she had something to hide. Jennifer felt like Beth would never take her into her confidence and she'd never find out the secrets the woman held within her heart, other than by sheer accident.

When Jennifer reached home, she didn't feel like going to town; it could wait until tomorrow. Instead, she went to her chair. Miss Marple hopped into her lap, then Jennifer swiveled around and stared out the window over the lake as she habitually ran her hand down her pet's back.

***

In his Medford office, Hawkman pushed back his chair, yawned and stretched his arms above his head. He'd rather be out in the field, than working over books, but he'd found out you do both when you become a private investigator. He had several cases pending, but didn't want to take on much more right now, not until he got a handle on the Hutchinson case. He glanced at the computer clock, and decided to wrap it up, then take a ride over to 'The Big Mug'. The outside appearance of the establishment made him very curious about the interior, so a beer might just be in order, or possibly, the house drink.

He tacked things up, grabbed his briefcase, shoved on his hat and left. While driving through town, he thought about

Jennifer and wondered if she'd had any luck with Beth. He'd tried to warn her not to expect much, but hoped he'd be surprised.

When he reached the tavern, cars were already parked in the lot. He took an empty space and ambled toward the fancy front entry. He pulled the heavy door open, and stepped into a dimly lit foyer. A large room at his left appeared to be a dining room: soft lighting, with large round tables covered with white tablecloths, each set with glassware, utensils and a small vase with a single rose gracing the center. The area to his right revealed the cocktail lounge. A long oak bar followed the wall down one side and across the end of the room. The closed curtain on a stage filled the other side of the chamber. Small square tables lined the small dance floor.

Hawkman strolled into the bar, and hoisted himself onto one of the tall stools next to another patron. The bartender arrived within seconds.

"What can I get you, sir?"

"How about the house liquor?"

"Coming right up."

Hawkman turned to the man next to him. "This is a fancy place. I've never been here."

"It's fairly new," the fellow said. "I bring my wife occasionally for dinner."

"Do they serve good food?"

"Excellent, but pricey."

"Who owns this establishment?"

"Moss Atkins." The man glanced around. "He was here just a few minutes ago. I imagine he'll be back shortly. He runs a tight ship."

"I've never heard the name. Has he lived in the area long?"

"About three years. He bought the property and built this place in less than ten months."

"Where does he hail from?"

"Oregon."

"I'd like to meet him." About that time, the barkeeper set Hawkman's drink before him, and he took a swig. "Whoa, that's good stuff." He knew exactly where it'd come from.

"Oh, there's Moss," said his drinking buddy. He gestured at Atkins.

"By the way, my name's Tom.

"I'm Cliff."

The two men shook hands before Moss Atkins had a chance to get to them, due to being stopped several times on the way. When he finally stood in front of them with his bald head glistening under the lights, and his short barrel shaped body, Hawkman knew immediately, this man had bought Jeb's hooch on Saturday night. The thing he hadn't been able to see that evening were pockmarks that riddled the man's face.

Cliff introduced Moss to Hawkman, and they shook hands.

"Great place you have here."

"Thank you. Glad to have you as a customer. Hope you come in often."

Hawkman raised the mug. "Man, this is good stuff you serve as the house brand. Where'd you get it?"

Atkins threw back his head. "Trade secret. Have another on the house."

Hawkman grinned. "I think I'll do that. Thank you."

The bartender brought over another round for Cliff and Hawkman.

Hawkman scooted the mug in front of Cliff. "I've got a drive ahead of me, so I better not

have any more. Pleasure meeting you.
Have a good night."

  After he left the place, it made him wonder
why an owner would take the chance to buy
moonshine with such an expensive looking
establishment. Maybe he was losing money
and hoped to get more customers with the
rotgut.

CHAPTER THIRTY-SIX

Driving home, Hawkman didn't even tune his radio to one of his favorite talk show hosts. Instead, his thoughts seemed focused on the Hutchinsons. If it weren't for Jennifer's attachment to the family, he wouldn't have delayed calling in the law officers. Moonshine, mostly brewed in the Appalachians, rarely emerged in this part of the country. He had a feeling Jeb's dad got him into bootlegging, since the still was ready and available when the Hutchinsons moved in.

Impatient to get home, he thought about pushing the accelerator a bit, but didn't want to take the chance of hitting a deer. Good thing his good sense won out, because when he made a sharp curve, a doe jumped out of the trees onto the pavement. She seemed hypnotized by his headlights and stood in the middle of the road, staring at the vehicle. Hawkman made a screeching stop, inches from the animal. She quickly took off and he exhaled a whistle in relief. He didn't need a dead deer on his hands, or a huge auto repair bill. Going slowly, and keeping a lookout for a fawn, he continued toward the lake.

He finally arrived home, and pulled into the garage. Walking into the kitchen, he noted Jennifer sat in her chair with Miss Marple on her lap, and the television going.

"Hey, why the sullen expression?"

"I'm not happy tonight."

"Oh, why not? Tell me about it," he said, placing his valise on the counter, and grabbing a beer from the refrigerator. He joined her in the living room.

She related her experience with Beth. "I think in so many words, she told me to get lost."

"I wouldn't go so far as to say she didn't want to see you anymore. It sounds more like her telling you not to tread into her private life."

"Maybe, but what are friends for if you can't confide in them?" she asked.

"Honey, I've tried and tried to tell you, Beth doesn't get close to anyone, not even her husband or kids. She's a very distant person, and will only let you in on what might help her in life."

"I'm beginning to see it now. Don't worry, I'll live through it. Enough about my day, how'd yours go?"

He told her about seeing one of the cars that picked up the liquor from last night unloading its stash behind The Hut. Then he continued about meeting Moss Atkins at his pub. "He's one ugly man, with a very pockmarked face. The tavern is really luxurious. I might even take you there for dinner one night."

She shook her head. "I don't think so. No way will I patronize a man who's contributing to the downfall of a family."

Hawkman raised a hand and slapped his thigh. "Nix that plan." Then he told her about the man he'd met in the bar. "Cliff told me Atkins came from Oregon. I thought it interesting, because so did Tami. There's the possibility she and Moss knew each other."

Jennifer eyed him questionably. "Isn't that sort of far-fetched; Oregon's a big state."

He shrugged. "Maybe, but I'll look into anything that might give me a clue."

"Why worry about Tami, she's just the in-between. She could deny knowing any of them and no one could prove any different."

"Except Beth."

"You might have something there. She hates the woman." Jennifer rose from her chair. "It's getting late. Have you eaten?"

"I had plenty of hors d'oeuvres at the tavern, so I'm not hungry."

"I'm hitting the sack."

"I'm right behind you."

***

Tuesday, Jennifer decided to go to town and do her weekly shopping. She'd get the rice cereal for Marcy, and if Randy didn't come to get it, she'd take it to Beth on Thursday. While driving into Yreka, thoughts of the Hutchinsons lay heavy on Jennifer's mind. She couldn't figure out why Beth had gotten so under her skin, like no other female acquaintance. Maybe because she tended to be so distant, or was it her American Indian heritage? Regardless, she didn't know how to cope with it; but deep in her heart, she knew the thought of an enduring friendship had ended.

Walking the aisles of the grocery store, Jennifer concentrated on her list and stood at one of the bins checking the bananas when her gaze drifted to the woman opposite her. She quickly closed her mouth before speaking. "Tami."

The woman looked up. "Pardon."

"Aren't you Tami?" Jennifer asked.

The woman dropped the apple in her hand. "No, my name's not Tami." She abruptly turned and walked away.

Staring at the woman's back, Jennifer watched her exit the sliding doors. Why would Tami deny her identity? Jennifer felt rattled after the encounter. Not dilly-dallying like she sometimes did, she hurried through her shopping, and left.

Reaching home, Jennifer put away the groceries, then paced the floor. She knew the woman at the grocery store was Tami Spencer. No one could duplicate her looks. Why did she repudiate it? Did she recognize me? Jennifer wondered. Did she feel threatened?

She sat down at her computer, and suddenly a thought hit her on why she'd received the 'butt out' signal from Beth, and Tami had avoided her. They'd found out about Hawkman being a private investigator. It still didn't fit all the puzzle pieces together, but a few. She could understand Tami's denial better than Beth's, because her line of business would prevent her from being too friendly. However, Randy surely told his mother about Hawkman before they went up to meet the family. Of course, with Jeb now selling the hooch, she might want to keep her distance, so he wouldn't be exposed. The explanation made some sense, but still didn't satisfy Jennifer completely.

When Hawkman arrived home, she ushered him to his chair in the living room, where a cool drink and treats awaited.

"Okay, what do you want?" he said.

"Nothing but your expert opinion." She sat on her seat, and swiveled to face him, then told about the encounter she'd had with Tami, along with her conclusion of why Beth had turned against their friendship.

Hawkman took a swig of his drink, placed it on the table and took her hands. "Honey, you don't have a criminal mind. There's no way you can tell what these people are thinking."

She frowned. "It doesn't make any sense to you?"

"On the contrary. Any normal, down to earth person would think along those lines, but these people don't. Upmost in their minds is how they'll make money. The more the better.
Also, they don't care who they hurt."

"So, you don't think it matters you're a private investigator?"

He shook his head. "None whatsoever. They'd just as soon shoot me as they would you, if you got in their way."

She fell back against her chair. "Darn, I thought I had it all solved." Then, she came forward again. "One more thing. Do you think Randy would have told his mom about seeing you on the property?"

"Have no idea, but it wouldn't matter. He's a kid, and it was late. His imagination could have been working overtime."

She sighed. "I think my best option is to stay away from the whole bunch."

"Excellent decision. I'd certainly feel better if you did."

"By the way," he said, pointing at the box on the counter. "Who's the baby cereal for? Has Miss Marple developed a stomach ache?"

"No, it's for Beth. She gave me a couple of dollars and asked me to pick it up when I went to the store. Marcy will start solid foods soon."

"Are you going to take it to her tomorrow?"

Jennifer shook her head. "She told me she'd send Randy to pick it up in a day or two."

CHAPTER THIRTY-SEVEN

Wednesday passed slowly for Jennifer. She kept checking out the kitchen window in hopes of seeing Randy come up the driveway on his bike, but it didn't happen. Already, she'd decided not to take the baby cereal to the cabin; instead she'd wait for the boy. Why expose herself to more rejection?

When Hawkman got home, Jennifer immediately started talking. "I'm so glad you're here and hope your day has been more exciting than mine."

"Actually, it's been boring."

"Mine too."

He eyed the box of cereal still on the cabinet. "No Randy?"

She shook her head. "Nope. It can sit right there until it gets weevils before I take it to Beth."

"So you're going to wait until it's bug infested?"

She laughed. "No, silly. That's just a saying."

He put his arm around her. "Giving you a hard time, my love." A car coming across the bridge caught his attention. "On second thought, I could hail Tami and let her deliver it for you."

Jennifer jerked her head around, then turned toward the kitchen window. "It's her all right. There's also a man in the passenger seat, but it's not Jeb."

Hawkman stared at the windshield until the car drove out of sight. "I'd swear that was Moss Atkins; bald head and big jowls."

"Doesn't he have a pub to run?"

"He might have run out of whiskey. I have news for him; Jeb won't have another batch ready until this weekend at the earliest. He sold the rest of that first run to 'The Hut'."

Jennifer leaned on the counter top with her elbows. "Jeb is going to find it hard to do business with no way to communicate with his prospective clients, other than going through Tami, or having them drive up themselves."

"On top of that, they have to rendezvous out in the boonies with Jeb, who meets them with a horse and wagon."

She grinned. "Nothing like going back to the good old days of a whiskey run."

"Yeah, but at least they had cars. Trying to outrun the authorities was much more exciting. Jeb will have a hard time getting away."

She shot him a look. "I'm worried about the family."

He patted her on the back and headed for the living room. "I think we better change the subject."

***

Thursday morning, Hawkman left for Medford, and Jennifer busied herself around the house. Shortly after lunch, the doorbell rang. When she answered the door, she looked into the face of a smiling Randy.

"Hello, good to see you. Looks like you've healed completely."

"Hi, Mrs. Casey. Yeah, I'm feeling great. I came to pick up the baby cereal for Marcy."

"Do you have time to come in for a minute?"

"Sure," he said, stepping into the house.

"How about a bowl of ice cream after such a long ride?"

His eyes lit up. "That would be great."

She pointed to the stool at the kitchen bar. "Hop up there while I dish it up."

After placing the icy dessert in front of him, she moved around the bar and sat on the opposite side. "How's everything going at home?"

Randy made a face. "Not real good. Mom and Dad fight a lot over Tami. I hate her. Like last night, she brought up some guy to see Dad. When the guy and Dad went for a walk, Mom went outside, climbed into Tami's car and gave her a talking to."

Jennifer looked at him wide eyed. "Did you hear her?"

"No, but I peeked out the door, and I could tell by Mom's expressions, she wasn't happy."

"Where'd your dad and this man go?"

"They were walking around in the field in front of the cabin."

"Do you know why Tami brought this man to your house?"

Randy shrugged. "Not really, but Mom said it had to do with Dad's business."

"What is his business?"

He frowned. "I don't know, but I think it has something to do with the two buildings beside the cabin. They're always locked, so I've never been able to see what's in them." He finished his treat, and just about jumped off the stool, when he spotted Miss Marple at the corner of the kitchen bar watching him. "Can I pet her?"

"Sure."

The cat welcomed the strokes to her back and purred, then wound around his legs.

"She likes you." Jennifer said, smiling. "Normally, she doesn't take to strangers."

"She's one of the prettiest cats I've ever seen." Then he glanced at Jennifer. "I better get home; don't want Mom to worry about me, since this is the longest ride I've taken since I got hurt."

Jennifer put the box of cereal, receipt and change into a plastic bag. "This sack has holes in the top on two sides; makes it easier to carry, or you can slip it over your handle bars."

"Mom said to thank you for picking this up, and I thank you for the ice cream. I really liked it."

She walked him to the door with Miss Marple trailing behind. "I think Miss Marple would like you to come see her again."

Randy laughed. "I will when I have time to play with her." He jumped on his bike and headed down the driveway, then turned west onto the road.

Jennifer watched his feet pedal as rapidly as a ten year old boy could go. She shook her head. "Boys feel they have to go fast, fast, fast," she murmured, closing the door. "Miss Marple, I hope the cereal gets there in one piece," she said, picking up her pet. She went to the glass sliding door overlooking the lake. Her thoughts went to Randy as she stared out over the calm water. Sam was this age when she and Hawkman adopted him. Maybe that's why she had such a tender place in her heart for this young Hutchinson boy. Sam had adjusted to a new home and parents, becoming their source of pride. If Beth's children were taken away, this could happen for Randy too. She prayed Beth wouldn't be involved, but she didn't see how it could be avoided with the still right there beside the cabin.

Wondering how long Hawkman would wait before talking with authorities, she put the cat on the floor. It made her smile as she watched Miss Marple stretch, then attack her stuffed bunny. It also made her happy that her pet liked Randy. It indicated he was a good boy. Animals seemed to know how to judge character, much better than people. She went to her computer. Maybe it would help to get this crap off her mind. If not, surely there was a story in all this.

Her mind finally focused in on her latest mystery novel, and the hours flew by. Before she knew it, Hawkman walked in the door. "Oh, my gosh, what time is it?"

He laughed. "Don't panic. I'm a little early and decided you didn't need to fix dinner tonight, so I went by and had Pedro make us a take home Mexican dinner for two. I'll tell you from the weight of this thing, there must be enough for six people." He carefully placed the large box on the counter.

"Oh, yummy. I love Mexican food." She immediately opened the box, closed her eyes and sniffed the aroma. "It smells delicious. Let's eat right now while it's still warm."

As they ate, Jennifer told him about the visit from Randy and the disturbing news about his folks arguing over Tami.

Hawkman put down his fork. "Speaking of her. I took the long way to work this morning and went to Yreka. Located her apartment on my GPS and drove by it. She lives in the crummiest part of town, in a rundown building."

"Are you sure you got the right address?" Jennifer asked.

"Yes, I spotted her car in front."

"She must not be making much money. I wonder if Jeb pays her for getting him customers."

"I imagine she gets a small percentage from both parties."

"Another good reason for Beth to be angry about her showing up at the cabin."

"If things get rolling and Jeb has to keep the still going twenty-four hours a day, Tami will demand more."

Jennifer put her hand in the air. "If he builds a good reputation, he might not need her services anymore. Then what happens?"

"He'll get rid of her."

CHAPTER THIRTY-EIGHT

Jennifer stopped eating and studied her husband. "What do you mean?"

"He'd fire her, but that won't be necessary as she won't be working for Jeb or any tavern owners before long. It'll all be shut down."

"Have you talked to the detective?"

"No, but I'm putting it on my schedule for the end of next week. I tasted Jeb's brew at The Big Mug, and it's good stuff. Once the word gets out, he'll have to keep the still fired up all the time."

Jennifer sighed. "Wonder how long it will take Randy to figure out what his dad's doing?"

"It wouldn't surprise me if Earl doesn't tell him soon. When the activity increases around the still, Jeb probably won't keep those sheds locked, as it's a pain to get into them. He may also have to teach Earl how to fix the mash. Once Earl is involved, he'll brag to Randy. He'll let him know how dad has put him in charge of a secret job, and he'll feel like a big shot."

She put her head into her hands. "Their household will erupt into complete chaos."

He reached over and took hold of her arm. "Honey, it already has."

She patted his hand. "I know. I've backed off now, and am ready for most anything. I even thought about how Sam adjusted to us after we adopted him. It worked out. The same can go for Randy, Marcy, and even Earl."

"Good point." He took a bite. "Let's not spoil this great dinner by talking about the Hutchinsons. We can get into them later."

"I agree."

They finished their meal and went into the living room.

"Now we can resume talking about the Hutchinsons. I've got a favor to ask of you." Hawkman said.

"Sure, as long as it doesn't mean going to the cabin."

"No, it doesn't. You can do it right here from the house. It might be boring, but I'll only ask you to do this for one day."

"Don't keep me guessing. What is it?" Jennifer asked, with a puzzled expression.

He leaned forward in his chair and rested his elbows on his thighs. "While I'm at work tomorrow, I'd like you to keep an eye out, not only for Tami driving by, but the bald headed guy that was with her the other night. I have this feeling, he's going to pick up his own moonshine."

"What'll he be driving?"

"Unfortunately, I'm not sure. It will be a strange vehicle to the area; just try to concentrate on the driver. Do you remember what he looks like?"

"Vaguely. Do you have a picture?"

"It's not clear, it's real fuzzy." He went to the kitchen counter and rummaged in his briefcase, then handed her the photo.

She frowned. "This definitely isn't a good shot, but I'm sure it's the man I saw with Tami."

"I could be all wet on this, but I have a feeling he'll want first dibs on this batch of hooch, and he'll come to get it to make sure."

"I'll do my best, but I can't guarantee I'll catch him going by."

"That's all I ask."

"Why are you interested in whether this man picks up his own moonshine or Jeb meets him in the boonies?"

"I need to be able to tell the detective how they're picking up the whisky so he can put a team of men on both sides. Otherwise, he could miss them all around."

***

Friday morning, Hawkman left for Medford, and Jennifer prepared for her surveillance duty. She opened the drapes, then moved her computer table around so she'd face the dining room window overlooking the bridge. Being able to spot an unfamiliar car or truck coming across the span would give her time to dash to the kitchen window, and check it more closely.

Miss Marple watched her mistress intently from a distance, then cautiously approached when she stopped shifting things back and forth. Timidly, she jumped upon the chair and then onto the table eyeing Jennifer with each movement.

"You're not sure about all this, are you? I get the feeling you don't like it much." She laughed, then gave her pet a loving stroke across her head. "Don't worry, it's only for today." Pulling up the extra chair to the side, she pointed. "There's yours."

The cat jumped down onto the seat and immediately curled up. Jennifer went to the kitchen and fixed a glass of cold water and brought it to the computer table. She booted up the machine, then made herself comfortable.

Hawkman didn't have any idea if this Moss Atkins would appear today, or at what time, but figured he'd make a run before the tavern opened at five. So Jennifer settled in for the long haul. She wrote on her latest book for a couple of hours and just as she hit the printer key to print out a chapter, she spotted a deep green colored pickup with a fitted cover over the bed, turn onto the bridge. She'd never seen the vehicle before. Most people on the lake had black Fords, but this looked like a Chevy. She hurried to the kitchen window with her binoculars, and focused on the man's face. Even though he wore a ball cap, she could tell it was Moss Atkins by Hawkman's description.

Writing down the time, she happened to glance outside again, just as Tami drove by. "Wow, I almost missed her," she said aloud.

She thought it odd Tami would be coming so close behind Atkins, almost as if she knew he'd be going to the Hutchinson place. Jennifer tapped her chin with the pen, and wondered why Tami would even be going there. Maybe she got paid for each sale, and wanted to make sure she didn't get screwed.

Jennifer made a call to Hawkman. "Moss Atkins just went by with Tami following close behind. Why would she be tailing him?"

She listened for a moment, then nodded. "I thought as much."

After hanging up, she went back to her computer and checked the time. Hawkman figured Atkins would be there about an hour if Jeb had the whiskey ready, otherwise, he'd be out sooner. Keeping her gaze on the bridge, in a little over an hour she spotted Atkin's pickup traveling back toward town.

Jennifer kept a close eye on the rode, thinking Tami would follow, but she never appeared. Doubting Beth had welcomed the woman with open arms, Jennifer wondered if by some chance, she'd gone out the back way.

Hawkman soon arrived, and Jennifer told him the time Atkins had come and gone, then told him about Tami never coming back.

"Do you think she went out the back way?" she asked.

"I doubt her car would make it over the rough trail from the cabin to the road. She'd hit bottom, or wreck the underside. You probably just missed her." Hawkman said.

"I'm sure I didn't, but I can't believe she'd still be up there."

"Maybe she collected her money, and left sooner than Moss."

"I did run to the bathroom right after she went by, but surely she didn't do a turn around that fast."

"Did you take a book with you?"

Jennifer laughed. "No."

"Maybe Beth invited her for dinner."

She rolled her eyes. "Not unless she had it in mind to poison her."

"Now that's a thought."

Wrinkling her forehead, she scowled. "You're not amusing."

"You started this dialog."

"I think we'll end the subject of Tami Spencer. She must have snuck by me."

Hawkman raised his hands. "Fair enough."

"Let's talk about Moss Atkins."

"Why him?"

"If the law catches these guys selling moonshine, will they shut them down?"

"I doubt it, if it's their first offense selling hooch. They'll probably give them a stiff fine and warning."

"So you're telling me the authorities will be tougher on Jeb than the taverns?"

"Yep, because he's making and selling it. The state gets no taxes from his business."

CHAPTER THIRTY-NINE

Saturday morning, Randy could hardly wait to get outside on his bike. He threw on his jeans, tee shirt and light jacket, then charged out the door. Earl and his dad had ridden the horses off on a hunting trip, so he knew he wouldn't be bothered. He jumped on the two-wheeler and rode in the area close to the cabin, but soon found it boring. The idea struck him to go see Mr. and Mrs. Casey.

He started down the path and almost gained the road when a flash of light to his left grabbed his attention. Skidding to a stop, he could see the sun rays striking something metal or glass, so he decided to explore. Riding toward the glare he soon saw a car parked in a grove of trees. As he approached, he recognized the vehicle as Tami's beige Toyota.

"What the heck?" he mumbled.

When he reached the car, he rode to the driver's side and hopped off his bicycle. He could see Tami's form through the window. Her eyes were open, so he knocked on the glass.

"Hey, Tami, are you okay?" he called.

When her fixed stare didn't change, nor her body move, he yanked at the door handle trying to force it open, but found it locked. Running around to all the doors, he discovered they were secure and the windows closed tight. He noticed she'd still not moved, nor had her fixed gaze changed. When he spotted the ribbon around her neck, which looked like one his mother used to tie back her hair, his stomach churned. He put his hand to his mouth, and backed away.

***

Hawkman went outside to turn the sprinklers on the front lawn when he spotted Randy coming down the street riding his bike much too fast. The boy skidded onto his driveway and almost slid sideways on the gravel.

"Hey, Randy, slow down. You're going to hurt yourself." When he got a good look at the boy's face he saw fear in his eyes. "What's the problem?"

Randy jumped off his bike and grabbed Hawkman's arm. "I'm sure she's dead. I'm really scared."

"Who?"

Jennifer had been standing at the kitchen sink, looking out the window when she saw Randy frantically hop off his bike and grab Hawkman. She sensed something wrong, and stepped out the front door.

Hawkman pointed toward the entry. "Why don't we go inside and you can tell us all about it,"

Randy nodded, while wringing his hands. "I don't know what to do."

"Maybe we can help."

Jennifer took a soda from the refrigerator, popped it open and placed it in front of Randy as he climbed upon the bar stool. His hands shaking, he took the can and swallowed a big gulp.

"Thanks."

"What's got you so frightened?" Jennifer asked, as she stood at his side.

Hawkman walked around the kitchen bar, sat down, and studied the boy.

"She's in her car and I couldn't get her to answer, but her eyes were open."

Jennifer put a hand on his shoulder. "Start at the beginning."

Randy looked up at her. "You mean from when I got up?"

"Yes."

"Okay. I had breakfast, then went outside and got on my bike. I rode around close to the cabin for a long time, then decided to head for the road. About halfway, I saw the rear end of a car off the path and thought someone must be having car trouble, so I pedaled over to it. That's when I recognized Tami's car."

"Then what happened?" Hawkman asked.

"I could see the outline of her head from the rear, so I went up to the driver's side and thought she was asleep, but when I knocked on the window, she didn't answer. That's when I saw her eyes were open and she was just staring into space. I tried to open the doors, but they were all locked."

Jennifer shot a look at Hawkman, then back to Randy. "Did you tell your mom?"

Randy shook his head, and tears welled in his eyes. "No, I was too scared, cause I could see a ribbon around Tami's neck that looked like the ones my Mom uses to tie her hair back. I figured she must have killed Tami. I didn't know what else to do, but come straight down here to you guys."

Hawkman stood. "Let's not jump to conclusions. I want you to show me where you found Tami's car. We'll go in my vehicle. You can leave your bike here."

Climbing off the stool, Randy, his head bowed, with shoulders drooping, went out the front door, followed by the Caseys. Hawkman moved Randy's bike to the garage, then they all climbed into the Cruiser. The boy remained quiet until they turned off the road onto the well-beaten path to the cabin.

"Her car is down there," he said, pointing to a cluster of trees.

Hawkman made a sharp right and as he approached the saplings, he could see the reflection off the rear of the Toyota Corolla. He pulled to a stop several yards from the car. "You two stay here. I'm going to have a look." He turned to Randy. "Tell me, when did you discover this?"

"Just before I came to your house."

Leaving Jennifer and Randy, he strolled toward the car. Not touching anything, he peered into the driver's window. The boy was right, Tami Spencer was definitely dead and a ribbon was wrapped around her neck. He hurried back to the vehicle. "I've got to call the police."

Randy began to sob. "They'll take my Mom away."

"We don't know that will happen, so try not to worry about it right now."

He drove quickly back home, and called Detective Bud Chandler in Yreka. After hanging up, he turned to Jennifer. "They're on their way. I told them to come to our house and I'd take them to the car. The coroner is also coming. You and Randy stay here. We'll take this one step at a time."

In less than an hour, two police cars pulled into the driveway. The coroner's wagon and tech van parked off the street in front. Hawkman walked out and met them.

When the officer stepped out of the first patrol vehicle, Hawkman knew he was not a person one would mess with. He estimated the man at six foot tall, two hundred pounds of brawn with no fat. A ruddy complexion with sandy colored hair made his blue eyes really stand out. He held out his hand. "I presume you're Tom Casey?"

"Yes."

"Detective Bud Chandler." The two men shook hands. "Detective Williams from Medford, Oregon, told me to expect a call from you. However, he said it would have something to do with bootlegging, not bodies."

"It still might connect to booze running. However, I didn't think it would go this far."

The detective gestured toward the patrol car. "Hop in and show us what you found. We can go over the other parts of the story later."

Hawkman climbed in, and directed them to Tami's car. They parked several yards back from the Toyota and on foot approached the vehicle from the front. Once the technicians examined the area around the car, took many photos and made impressions of the footprints they found on the ground, they dusted for fingerprints on the handles of the car.

"You'll probably find bike tire tracks, kids foot prints, along with mine, child's prints on all the doors, as a young lad found the car and tried to get inside to help the woman, but found all the doors locked," Hawkman said.

One of the technicians nodded and jotted down some notes on a clipboard. "How old is the boy and was she alive when he found her?"

"He's about ten years old. I don't think the woman was alive from his description. When I came to verify his story, she was definitely dead. The boy is at my house and I'm sure the detective will want to get his statement."

Soon the coroner examined the body in the car, then took many pictures, as the techs visually examined the inside, then told the detective, they'd need to take the vehicle in to the lab. He put a call in through his radio. Once the coroner finished his inspection, they put the body on a gurney and wheeled it into the wagon.

"From my surface appraisal, it appears the woman died due to strangulation, and she's been dead approximately twelve to twenty-four hours. I won't know for sure until I do an autopsy.'

Once they'd loaded the body, the coroner left. Soon the technicians approached

Chandler. "Have this area corralled off. I think we've covered everything, but we might need to come back and check it out again."

After the tow truck came and placed the car on the rack, the detective had his men yellow tape the area. He stood next to Hawkman as he watched the two officers fasten the ribbon around several trees. "Those technicians are so good, they usually don't miss a thing. However, if they want me to fence it off, we fence it off." He pointed behind them. "I noticed a car path going north. Where does it lead?"

"The Hutchinsons. They live on this property."

"Okay, we better pay them a visit."

CHAPTER FORTY

Hawkman directed the officer on how to get to the cabin. The other patrol car followed.

"What do you know about this family?" the detective asked Hawkman, as they drove over the rough terrain.

"More than I have time to report right now."

"Does that mean you'll be coming into town to give me a statement?"

"Yes, I'll be there tomorrow."

The detective smiled. "This should be interesting."

"Believe me, it will be."

When they got to the Hutchinsons, Chandler motioned for the officers in the other car to stay put. Hawkman followed him to the entry, while eyeing the building containing the still and noticed the padlock, although locked, dangled loosely from the handle. Beth opened the door and her eyes widened at the sight of Hawkman.

"Is Randy okay?"

"Yes, he's at my place with Jennifer. He'll be home later."

She frowned. "What's going on?"

The detective showed his badge. "Are you Mrs. Hutchinson?"

"Yes."

I'd like to ask you some questions. May we come in?"

She stepped aside and gestured for them to come inside.

Chandler took a notebook from his pocket. "Do you know Tami Spencer?"

"Yes."

"How long?"

"We've been friends for years."

"When was the last time you saw her?"

"A couple of nights ago. Why?"

"We found her dead body in a car on this property."

Beth put her hand to her mouth, stepped back, and clutched her waist. "Oh, my God!"

"Who else lives here?"

"My husband, baby and two sons," she said, her voice cracking.

"One of those sons is with Mrs. Casey. Where's the other boy, and how old is he?"

"He's sixteen and with his dad hunting."

"When do you expect them home?"

"Not until evening."

Chandler put his notebook back into his pocket. "Mrs. Hutchinson, I'll be back. Tell your husband and son not to leave. I want to talk to all of you at once."

She nodded.

Back in the car, Detective Chandler turned around and headed toward the main road. "You notice that ribbon she had around her hair?"

"Yeah," Hawkman said.

"Sure looks similar to the one around the victim's neck."

Hawkman suspected the detective noticed many things. He was the type.

When they reached the Casey's, Chandler stepped out of the car. "I want to speak to the boy. What's his name?"

"Randy."

"You said he told you about finding the car; am I right?"

"Yes."

The two men went inside. Randy quit playing with Miss Marple on the floor, and stood up. Jennifer arose from her chair and advanced toward the two men. She held out her hand. "I'm Mrs. Casey, and assume you're Detective Chandler."

"You're right," he said, smiling. "A pleasure to meet you."

She turned toward the boy. "This is Randy Hutchinson."

After the introductions were over, Hawkman said, "Randy, Detective Chandler would like to speak to you."

A wave of fear swept across the boy's face. "Okay."

"Let's have a seat on the couch, son," the detective said, giving the boy a pat on the back.

Randy slid to the far end of the sofa, not taking his eyes off the big man.

"I promise not to bite," Chandler said.

Randy threw him a nervous smile, but immediately turned somber.

Chandler reached into his chest pocket, pulled out a small recorder, and placed it on the coffee table. "I'm going to record what you tell me, because I won't be able to remember everything. I hope you don't mind. First, I want you to tell me your name."

After the initial recording, the detective started the interrogation in a soft voice.

"Tell me how you found the car this morning."

Randy started talking, but almost in a whisper.

"You're going to have to speak up. I can barely hear you."

He took a deep breath and started again. "I was riding my bike and decided to come see Mr. and Mrs. Casey, when I saw a reflection in the trees. I'd never noticed it before, so decided to go see what was causing it."

"When you found the car, did you look inside?"

Randy nodded.

"I need you to say yes or no."

"Yes."

"What did you see?"

"Tami, sitting under the steering wheel. I thought she was asleep and knocked on the window. When she didn't turn her head, I looked closer and her eyes looked glassy like marbles. I tried to get the doors open, but they were all locked. So I rode down here to tell Mr. and Mrs. Casey."

"How come you didn't tell your mother?"

Picking at a hole in his jeans, he shrugged. "I don't know, guess cause I was scared."

"Why?"

Never taking his eyes off the threads, he said, "Cause, she looked dead, and she was my Mom's friend. I didn't want to make her cry."

"What made you think Tami wasn't just asleep?"

"For one thing her eyes were open, and she never blinked or moved, even when I kept calling her name. She just stared straight ahead."

"Did you notice anything else that might make you question whether she was dead or not?"

Randy shot a look at Jennifer and Hawkman, his lip quivered, and his eyes filled with tears. "Yes," he said, his voice a little above a murmur.

"Could you tell me?"

The boy took a deep breath, then blurted, "There was a ribbon wrapped around her neck. Looked like she'd been choked."

"Are you sure it wasn't a piece of jewelry, like a necklace?"

Randy finally made eye contact with the detective. "I don't think so. There were two or three layers, and her neck was red."

"Have you ever seen a cord like that?"

"Not really. My Mom uses bands to hold her hair out of her face, but they're usually just torn from rags, nothing fancy."

"Did you like Tami?"

"No."

The detective shifted in his seat, and scratched his chin. "Want to tell me why?"

"She always caused trouble when she came to our house."

"What kind?"

"I don't know, but my Mom always acted angry after she left."

Detective Chandler reached over and turned off the recorder. "I think I've asked you enough questions. I'm going to go back up to your cabin and talk to your folks. When do your dad and brother usually get home from hunting?"

"Before dark."

The detective stood, then approached Hawkman and Jennifer. "I'm going back to Yreka and check with the coroner. The boy doesn't have to be there when I question his folks. It's up to him."

"Can I stay with you Mrs. Casey?" Randy asked, with pleading eyes.

"Of course, but the detective will have to let your folks know when he goes there tonight." Jennifer said.

"I'll tell them. Are you going to spend the night or be home later?"

"Just tell them, he'll spend the night with us. If he wants to go home later, I'll take him," Hawkman said.

CHAPTER FORTY-ONE

Beth fed Marcy, put her down for a nap, then paced the cabin, wringing her hands. She peeked out the small window numerous times or opened the door to see if she could hear Jeb and Earl riding in on the horses. When Mr. Casey told her Randy had stayed with Jennifer, she wondered what part he'd played in this Tami deal. She stopped in the middle of the floor and put her hands to her face. "Dear Lord," she said aloud. "He must have found her body and rode down to tell the Casey's. They had to be the ones who called the police."

Suddenly, she jerked her head around at the sound of hooves beating against the ground. She hurried and flung open the door, then ran into the yard.

Jeb yanked his horse to a short stop. "What's the matter? Looks like you've seen a ghost."

"Have Earl take care of the animals. I need to talk to you quickly, before the police get here."

Jeb frowned, as he dropped to the ground, removed his shotgun from the scabbard, then motioned for his son and handed him the reins. "Earl, take the mounts to the barn. Remove the saddles and brush both horses. While you're at it, put the game in the smoke house." He followed Beth into the cabin, and placed his rifle in the gun rack on the wall. "Now, what's this about the police?"

"They'll be here shortly. Tami's dead body was found inside her car on this property."

The color drained from Jeb's face. "Damn! Where?"

"I don't know, but I think Randy discovered it, then hightailed it to the Casey's. They must have called the authorities, as Mr. Casey came with the detective earlier. He told me Randy had stayed with Jennifer."

"What did you tell the police?"

"They only asked if I knew Tami, and of course, I told them I did. This was before I knew she was dead. He wants to talk to you, me and Earl together, so he said he'd be back tonight."

Jeb frowned. "Finding her on our property puts us in a real predicament."

Beth bit her lower lip, then looked into her husband's face. "Did Tami show up here last night?

He shook his head. "No, Atkins came by himself. He said he would have no use for her anymore, now that he knew where to come. He'd just pick up his own whiskey and not have to share the profit."

Beth sat down on the couch, shoved her hair out of her face, and tied it with the ribbon she had draped around her neck. Marcy had awakened, but lay cooing at the strand of colorful ornaments strung across top of the crib. Beth stared at the baby. "Jeb, I'm scared. What will we do if they think we had something to do with Tami's death? They'll take my babies away from me."

He sat down in the chair opposite her. "Before that happens, I'll get you out of here."

She threw up her hands in despair. "How? In the buckboard? How much of a chance do you think I'd have getting away?"

"That's the way we got here."

"Yes, but we weren't running from the law."

Earl came in the door and placed his rifle in the gun rack. "Got everything done." He studied his parents for a moment. "Is something wrong?"

Jeb turned toward his son. "While you were on watch last night, did you see Tami?"

"No, I only saw the guy in the truck drive up. You were out there, and said he was all right to let in."

"Where'd you head afterwards?"

"I walked the boundary behind the barn, then came in for supper. I didn't think I needed to go toward the road, as you and that man were out in front talking."

"The police found Tami, dead in her car on our land." Beth said. "We don't know where, but they'll be here shortly to talk to us."

Earl's mouth dropped open. "Did someone kill her?"

"We don't know how she died," Jeb said.

"Where's Randy?" Earl asked, glancing around the cabin. "I didn't see him outside."

"He's with Jennifer Casey," Beth said.

Earl grimaced. "What's he doing there?"

"I think he found Tami. He didn't know what to do, so he went to them."

"Why didn't he come to you, Mom?"

"I have no car, no way to make an emergency call, and you guys were gone."

The boy nodded. "Yeah, makes sense." He jerked his head toward the outside. "I just heard a car."

The sound of slamming car doors echoed through the room. Fear crossed Beth's face as she clasped her hands together, stepped back, and stared at the entry. A rap on the wood sent Jeb to the door. A man in a dark suit, with three uniformed police officers flanking him, met Jeb's gaze.

"Yes, what can I do for you?" Jeb asked, his attention drawn to the detective's shiny badge he held out for him to examine.

Chandler folded his wallet and pushed it into an inside pocket of his jacket. "Are you Mr. Hutchinson?"

"Yes."

"I'm Detective Chandler from the Yreka Police Department. May we come in? I'd like to talk to you about Tami Spencer."

Jeb moved aside and motioned for the men to enter.

The detective turned to the officers behind him, and pointed. "You two stay out here. Mike, you come with me."

Just as they stepped inside, Marcy let out a yowl. Beth picked her up and headed for the bedroom.

"Where are you going, Mrs. Hutchinson?" Chandler asked.

She stopped, and turned on her heel. "It's time to feed my baby and I don't care to do it in front of strangers."

He motioned toward the officer. "Mike, check the room for any guns. Mrs. Hutchinson, leave the door open, and come back in when you're through."

Mike returned in a matter of seconds. "Room clean."

Meanwhile, Earl had moved behind his dad, and eyed the officers.

"Is this strapping young man your other son?" The detective asked.

"Yes, this is Earl," Jeb said, then gestured toward the small sofa. "Have a seat."

"Before I forget, the Caseys said to tell you Randy will spend the night with them. I've already spoken to the boy about the Spencer woman."

"Did he find her?" Jeb asked.

"Yes, and he's a bit traumatized by the whole event."

Jeb ran a hand over his neck. "I can imagine. Where was she?"

"In her car, pushed into a covey of trees just before you get to the paved road. My team has already removed her body and the car. How well did you know her?"

"She's been a friend of my wife's for years, but they'd never been close enough to visit until Tami moved to Yreka some time ago."

"What did Ms. Spencer do for a living?"

Jeb shrugged. "I have no idea."

Beth wandered back into the room holding Marcy. She put the baby in the crib with some toys and faced the detective.

"Mrs. Hutchinson, do you know what Ms. Spencer did for a living?"

"She used to be a waitress in a small cafe, until it closed. I don't know what kind of job she had recently," Beth said.

"I thought you were good friends?"

Beth shrugged. "To a point, but you have to realize we live quite a ways from Yreka, and gas is very expensive. I have no way of getting into town, unless I use the buckboard or ride one of the horses, which is a bit hard with a nursing baby. So we really didn't see each other very often."

"When did you see her last?"

"It was two or three nights ago when she brought a man out to meet my husband. She said he might have a job for him."

Chandler turned toward Jeb. "What kind of work, Mr. Hutchinson?"

"Something to do at his bar, but being we have no vehicle, it didn't pan out."

"I see." The detective put his attention back on Beth. "How many ribbons do you have?"

Beth stared at him in shock. "Are you talking about my hair ribbons?"

"Yes."

"I have a drawer full, because I'm always losing them."

"May I see them?"

"I can't imagine what they have to do with Tami's death," she mumbled as she opened the chest and handed him a handful.

The detective sorted through them. "Looks like most of these are handmade."

"They are, I tear them off of rags."

He pulled a red satin one out of the pile and held it up. "This one looks store bought."

"Yes, I had a couple of those, a red and a blue. I lost the blue one somewhere; they're so slick they slide off real easily. It's probably out in the yard. They were on a gift I received when I moved here." She frowned. "Why are you interested in these?"

"Because Ms. Spencer was strangled with a blue ribbon."

CHAPTER FORTY-TWO

Beth narrowed her eyes as flashes of red anger exploded. Jeb and Earl both stepped back when she grabbed the hair ribbons from the detective's hands and tossed them on the chair. "How dare you come into my home and suggest one of us strangled Tami. You can buy these for a dime a dozen." She pointed to the door. "Get out! And don't return."

Taken aback by the sudden outburst from Beth, Detective Chandler stood, held up his hands, and retreated toward the entry. "Mrs. Hutchinson, I didn't mean to insinuate any such thing. I just wanted you to know how she died."

"That's a bunch of bull," she said, advancing toward them, then she reached for her husband's rifle on the gun rack.

"We're not murderers, but you may make me one if you don't get off our property."

Chandler shook his head when he saw his officer going for his gun. "We're going, Mrs. Hutchinson, we're going. Don't leave town. We'll want to talk to you again." When he stepped out the door, he motioned to the two officers guarding the front. "Okay, boys, let's get out of here,"

Beth stood in the doorway, the gun aimed at the detective. The officers all hurried to their cars, jumped in and took off without any argument.

Jeb stood behind Beth, and watched the cars disappear down the path. "After your tirade, they'll never leave us alone."

She shoved the gun into his hands, and stormed into the kitchen area. "I certainly didn't intend to stand there and listen to our family being accused of murder."

"Did you kill her, Beth?" Jeb asked.

She glared at him. "What if I did? I had every reason to strangle her. Are you going to turn me in?"

Earl stepped in front of his mother, his eyes wide with horror. "Mom, you didn't kill her, did you?"

"What if your dad did?"

His mouth dropped open, and he stared at his father. "Dad?"

"It sounds like one of your mother's hair ribbons was used. Maybe you stole it from her stash and killed her."

Earl stuck his thumb into his chest. "Me? Why would I want to get rid of Tami?"

"Did you like her?" Jeb asked.

"No, but not enough to murder her."

Beth stood listening to the two. "It appears any one of us could be a suspect. I think we ought to leave this place. We've had nothing but trouble ever since we moved here."

"Then we'd really look suspicious. They'd find us for sure, as we have no way to travel but in the buckboard," Jeb said, flopping down on the couch. "Besides, I don't want to go right now. I've finally found a way to make some money."

Beth had her fists clenched beside her body. "You'll get caught at it soon, too, and you'll be hauled off to jail."

"It beats a murder rap."

***

Hawkman stood staring out the sliding glass door overlooking the lake when he spotted the police cars moving across the bridge toward town. His gaze traveled to Randy sitting on the floor holding Miss Marple, his attention glued to the television set where Jennifer had tuned in cartoons. He glanced at his wife at the computer, and nodded his head toward the deck. She arose and followed him outside as he slid the door shut.

"Detective Chandler and his troops are headed into town. They've finished up with Beth and Jeb for the night," Hawkman said.

"Could you see if they had any one in the car beside the officers?"

"I couldn't tell, too dark to see inside the vehicle, but doubt they made an arrest. Not enough evidence except for the hair ribbon around Tami's neck, and that's not enough to put Beth behind bars."

"Wonder if Chandler has any inkling what's in those buildings?"

"He'll know by tomorrow night. I'm going to go in and give him the skinny on the Hutchinsons and their customers."

"Do you think we should take Randy home?"

"Not unless he wants to go."

Jennifer hugged herself. "I think he's scared."

"After seeing the dead body of a woman he knows and a cord around her neck he recognized as one of his mother's hair ribbons, I'd say I don't blame him."

"I can't believe Beth would kill her friend, even though she has a good reason to wring her neck. None of the family liked Tami, except maybe Jeb. Randy hated her, but he's out of the question. However, Earl's another story."

Hawkman rubbed the back of his neck. "Or someone doing business with her."

"Then how come 'her' body was found in 'her' car on the Hutchinsons' property?"

"That's a good question. Maybe I'll get some answers when I talk to the detective tomorrow."

A knock on the glass caused both of them to turn around. Randy stood at the door with Miss Marple in his arms. Jennifer slid it open.

"You tired of the cartoons?"

"No, but I'm lonesome for my Mom and Marcy."

"You're more than welcome to spend the night. We have an extra bedroom," Jennifer said.

"Thanks, but I think I want to go home."

"You can't ride your bike in the dark, so we'll put it in my vehicle and take you," Hawkman said.

Randy gave Miss Marple a big hug, then put her on the floor with her stuffed toy. "Now you be a good girl until I see you again." He looked up at Jennifer. "I really like Miss Marple."

"She really likes you too, and she's going to miss you. It's been a long time since she's gotten so much attention."

Randy smiled. "I'll come back soon."

They trooped out to the Cruiser and Hawkman lifted the bike into the back of the vehicle while everyone piled aboard. He wondered what sort of reception the boy would receive. Randy remained extremely quiet on the trip to the cabin. When they arrived, the faint glow of the lanterns could be seen through the windows. Randy and Jennifer climbed out and stood until Hawkman lifted out the bike.

"You don't have to stay," Randy said, parking the two-wheeler at the side of the dwelling.

"We want to see you inside," Jennifer said.

Randy shrugged and pushed open the door. The threesome met the surprised stares of Beth, Jeb and Earl, who stood planted with his rifle, aimed to fire.

"Hi, everyone. Put the gun down, Earl, it's just me." Randy said.

"The detective said you were spending the night with the Caseys," Beth said.

"I decided I wanted to come home."

"We told him he could, if he so desired," Jennifer said, in a stiff voice.

"Thank you, for bringing him."

Hawkman touched Jennifer's shoulder. "We better get on our way. It's late and these people probably want to get to bed."

They stepped outside, closing the door behind them, and climbed into the 4X4. On the way back to their place, Hawkman asked, "Could you read any of their faces?"

"No. I couldn't tell if they were happy to see Randy or angry with him. At least we know none of them were taken to the police station."

"It'll only be a matter of time before one of them is arrested for running moonshine or murder."

CHAPTER FORTY-THREE

Randy could feel the stares of his family as he slowly walked toward Marcy's crib.

"Don't bother her, she just went to sleep," Beth said, sternly.

"I wasn't going to wake her."

"I want you to tell us about this morning," Jeb said.

"Yeah, creep. The police have been here," Earl chimed in.

"Enough out of you," Beth said, pointing a finger at the oldest son.

Randy slumped down on the cot, and clasped his hands together. His gaze cast to the floor, he told his story. "I went riding on my bike this morning and got bored, so thought I'd go down and see Mr. and Mrs. Casey. Just before I reached the road, I saw a bright reflection coming from the trees, so thought I'd see what caused it.

When I got close, I recognized Tami's car and thought she'd fallen asleep inside. I yelled her name, and when she didn't move, I knocked on the window. Her eyes were open, but she never turned her head or anything. I tried to get in the doors, and they were all locked. I really got scared when I saw a ribbon that looked like one of Mom's hair bands wrapped around her neck. I didn't know what to do, so I went to the Caseys' and told them about it. We all piled into Mr. Casey's Cruiser and I showed him where I'd found the car. He got out and looked, then drove back to his house where he called the police. Later, one of the policeman asked me a bunch of questions." He glanced up and studied the faces of his family. "That's what happened."

Beth walked over and knelt in front of her son. "Why didn't you come and tell me?"

Tears welled in Randy's eyes. "Because she was your friend and when I saw the hair ribbon, I really got scared."

She took his hands. "Did you think I'd killed her?"

"I don't know what I thought," he sobbed.

She folded him into her arms. "You did the right thing. I couldn't have done anything, since I had no transportation. Your dad and Jeb weren't here, so I'd have probably sent you to the Caseys for help."

Randy wiped his cheeks with the back of his hand. "I'm happy you think I did right by going to them. I wasn't sure. That's why I didn't come home any sooner; I thought you might be mad at me."

Beth patted his back, then stood. "I can imagine seeing a dead body is horrifying. It would frighten me too."

Randy gazed up at his mother. "Did somebody kill her?"

"It appears so," Jeb intervened.

Randy peered up at his father, wide eyed. "Who would do that and leave her on our land? It makes it look like one of us did it."

Jeb nodded. "Yes, we could be in deep trouble."

***

Sunday morning, before making the trip into town, Hawkman called Detective Chandler to verify if he'd be in his office. He told him, unless an emergency occurred, he'd be there. Hawkman took off for Yreka. Not having been to the department since they'd moved into the old library building on Miner Street, he looked forward to seeing it.

When he pulled up to the station, he didn't dare park in the fifteen minute zone in front, as he knew he'd be there longer. He couldn't park across the street, because of the fire station. Taking a right, he circled the building where he found an empty slot on the right-hand side.

Strolling along the sidewalk to the steps leading to the door, he was impressed by the neat square building with an oval shaped entry. Maybe one day they'd see fit to remove the Library sign at the top.

As he stepped inside, the receptionist at the front desk quickly averted her eyes, then told him where he'd find Detective Chandler's office. Hawkman grinned, knowing the eye-patch always intimidated some women. He meandered down the short hall and knocked on the door with Chandler's name printed in copper letters.

"Come in," a loud voice called.

Opening the door, he had to smile, as Chandler's large desk stacked with papers reminded him of Detective Williams' desk in Medford.

"Glad to see you, Mr. Casey. I'm anxious to hear what you have to tell me."

"It seems you have gobs of paperwork here too. Every time I drop in on Detective Williams, his head is bowed over many reports awaiting his signature."

Chandler shook his head. "It never ends. Have a seat," he said, gesturing to a chair in front of the desk.

Hawkman sat as Chandler stretched, made a yawning sound, then wiped his hand across his chin. "The last two nights have been buggers. Not only did Mrs. Hutchinson kick us out of their place, but kids don't know how to have calm and quiet graduation parties, causing chaos with the neighbors who'd like to get some sleep."

Hawkman frowned. "Did you say you were kicked out of the Hutchinsons'?"

"The lady really got fired up when I asked to see her hair ribbons. She thought I was accusing her family of killing the Spencer woman, and ordered us out of the house. I'll have to get a warrant if I want to speak to them again. Which I might have to do. Obviously, you know these people better than me, so give me a little insight."

He told the detective about how they met Randy first, then went up to welcome the family and were met with gun totting Earl and Jeb. "The property belongs to Jeb's father, Jacob Hutchinson."

"Did you meet the father?" the detective asked

"Yes." He then related meeting Jacob at his stinky home and learned Jacob's invalid father lived with him.

"When did Jeb and his family move into the cabin?"

"Can't give you an exact date, but figure six months to a year ago. Jeb had been incarcerated for five years, for vehicular manslaughter, but let out in three for good behavior. From what I can gather, he's been out of prison for close to three years, couldn't get a job, so his dad let him move to the cabin. I'm not sure what the deal is, but there's a huge still on the property, and Jeb has been making moonshine. Whether this is a deal between his dad and him, I don't know, but the still cost a bundle and I'm sure it's been on the place for a while, definitely before the Hutchinsons settled in."

"Do you think he's selling the whiskey?"

Hawkman nodded. "I've witnessed it twice. This was where the Spencer woman came into the picture."

"How?"

"The go between. She sets up the buyer, then arranges for Jeb to take his buckboard and meet them on a back road."

Chandler scratched his chin. "Interesting. Wonder why she didn't pick up the order."

"Probably scared of getting caught."

"How did you see this happen?"

"I'd rather not say, but I can tell you I saw the exchange of cash for the product."

"Trade secret?"

Hawkman chuckled. "You might say so."

"Why would someone murder the go between? Doesn't make much sense."

"This is hearsay, but Jeb Hutchinson and Tami Spencer had an affair some years ago. When Beth Hutchinson found out, she almost left him. Needless to say, she wasn't happy to have Tami show up on the scene."

Chandler scowled. "Odd, I understood they were good friends. This information gives me a new look on things."

"She probably wanted to save face in front of the children, since the woman did come to their cabin a couple of times that I know about. However, I don't think she convinced Randy. The boy really disliked Tami."

"Tell me about these two boys. Are they going to school?"

"No. My wife, Jennifer, talked to Beth about getting them enrolled. She told her next year she'd see to it." Hawkman shrugged. "Whether she will or not is up to Jeb. Earl is Jeb's sidekick."

The detective leaned forward. "If one of those people killed Tami Spencer, those children might end up in foster homes and there won't be a decision whether they go to school or not. They'll be enrolled."

"Have you heard from the coroner yet?

"Yes, we've gotten a few reports back, still waiting for the bulk. We do know Ms Spencer was killed by both ligature and manual strangulation. It appeared the ribbon didn't do the job, so the hands and fingers were used to squash the larynx. There were bruises on her neck and signs of a struggle. Also human flesh was found under her fingernails. Appears she scratched this person mighty good before she died. The residue has been sent off to see if we can get a DNA reading. Whoever killed her used gloves as we didn't find a fingerprint. However, we did find footprints on the back seat floorboard. Looked like they were made with boots."

"Did the Hutchinsons say when they'd last seen Tami?"

"That's what threw me. They said they hadn't seen her for a couple of days. If they're telling the truth, it's hard to believe she'd be found on their property."

Hawkman furrowed his brow. "That's puzzling, as my wife and I saw her drive by as if she were headed for the their place the night before Randy found her. We spotted her shortly after seeing Moss Atkins go by. We never did see her return."

"Who's Moss Atkins?" Chandler asked.

"The owner of The Big Mug restaurant and tavern."

"Is he one of the moonshine customers?"

"Yep."

"Know anyone else buying the stuff?"

"Claude and Luke, owners of The Hut."

CHAPTER FORTY-FOUR

Detective Chandler wrote down the names of the tavern owners, then glanced up at Hawkman.

"Want to work with me on this case? Can't pay you, but would sure like your viewpoint."

Hawkman laughed. "Sounds like you've been talking to Detective Williams."

Chandler put his hand in front of him and wiggled it. "Yeah, we talked a little about you."

"Sure," Hawkman said, "I'll work with you, since I've got a bit of a head start."

Chandler put his forefinger in the air. "Before I forget. We did a search on trying to find the next of kin of Tamara (Tami) Spencer. Came up with nothing. Do you think you could find out from Mrs.

Hutchinson? Apparently, she's known the woman for several years."

"My wife has become friends with Beth. I'll put her on it."

"Great, get back to me when she finds out anything." The detective glanced down at his notes. "This Moss Atkins looks like not only a suspect in buying illegal booze, but also murder."

Hawkman nodded. "Definitely."

"The problem is I have nothing on the man to bring him in for questioning at this time. Just because he drove by your house, doesn't mean he went to the Hutchinsons. I don't want to get
ahead of myself, so I think my first plan is to question Jeb Hutchinson."

Hawkman rose. "About as good a start as any. I think I've covered everything about the family. If you think of any questions I didn't answer, give me a ring." He handed Chandler one of his business cards. "Keep me informed and I'll do the same for you. If I spot a whiskey run is in the making, we can probably catch them red-handed."

"Sounds good. Thanks for your help."

Hawkman left the station and headed for Copco Lake. When he reached home, he didn't pull into the garage. He hopped out and went inside. Jennifer sat at the computer and raised her head when he entered. "How'd it go? Sure didn't take you long."

"Real well. I think we're going to get along fine." He put his briefcase on the counter. "Are you busy right now?"

"No."

"Let's go to the Hutchinsons."

She frowned. "Why?"

"The detective would like us to find out if Beth knows where he could find any of Tami's kinfolk. I told him I'd put you right on it. Since you've experienced some tension with Beth, thought we'd go together."

"I like the idea too. Give me a second."

She left the computer, and ran back to the bedroom, soon to return with hair combed, and fresh lipstick. They jumped into Hawkman's SUV and headed up the hill. Within thirty minutes they pulled up in front of the cabin.

Jennifer shot a look at Hawkman. "There's something wrong."

"Yeah, it's mighty quiet."

Hawkman looked toward the corral. "I don't see any of the horses."

They hopped out and went to the door. When Jennifer knocked, the portal opened a crack on its own accord.

"Beth," she called, then poked her head inside. "Oh my."

He reached over her shoulder, pushed it wide open, and they stepped inside.

Jennifer's gaze searched the room. "They're gone," she said. "She pointed toward the cabinets, where all the doors stood ajar. "All the essentials for cooking and what little foodstuffs Beth had are missing. It appears they took Marcy's crib and the cot." She hurried to the master bedroom, Hawkman at her heels. A bare mattress sat on the frame and the open closet had been stripped of clothes. Some items were strewn across the floor. "Looks like they left in a hurry."

They checked Earl's room and found it empty, except for the bed. Hawkman went outside, where he checked the still and fermenting room. He found them both padlocked. Putting his ear to the wall, he could hear the bubbling of fermentation.

Jennifer stepped up beside him. "What are you doing?"

"Put your ear to the wall."

She grimaced. "Sounds like something bubbling."

"Fermentation. They haven't gone far. Jeb is making moonshine and has to get down here to tend to it. Both of these buildings are locked up."

"Is there another cabin on the property? Even a shack would give them some protection from the elements."

Hawkman stood with his thumbs hooked in his jeans back pockets and stared out over the forest covered land. "I don't think so, but I can't be sure. They aren't afraid of the weather, and with summer coming on, I suspect they'd pitch some sort of lean-to or tent, and it would suffice for several months."

Jennifer gazed at the ground as she made circles in the dirt with the toe of her tennis shoe. "It makes me sick at my stomach to think one of them is guilty of killing Tami."

"Even though picking up and running looks bad, we don't know who murdered the woman. The Hutchinsons are scared, because they know everything points to them. Especially, with Jeb being an ex-con; and the ribbon around Tami's neck appears mighty suspicious."

"Do you think we'll ever see them again?"

"Hard to say. Depends on how well they're hidden, and how bad the police will want to find them. This is rough country and would take many hours of personnel to search these hills."

"What about spotting smoke from a cooking fire?" Jennifer asked.

"I'd imagine they'd wait until nightfall before lighting one, as you wouldn't be able to see the plume." He took Jennifer by the arm. "Let's go home. I need to call Detective Chandler and tell him not to bother about an interview with the family. He may still want to come out and look the place over."

"Does he know about the still?"

"Yes."

"Will they destroy it?"

"Not unless they have proof that it's being used for illegal purposes."

Jennifer remained silent as she stared out the passenger side window on the way home. Hawkman immediately went to the phone and dialed Detective Chandler. When he received no answer, he left a message for the detective to call as soon as possible.

Within the hour, the phone rang,
Hawkman picked it up and punched on the
speaker phone. "Tom Casey, here."

"Casey, Detective Chandler, returning your
call."

"Thought I'd let you know. My wife and I
went up to the Hutchinsons this afternoon
to see if we could find out about Spencer's
next of kin. We were surprised to find the
place deserted. The entire family has left
with their belongings."

"That's interesting. You have any idea
where they've gone?"

"More than likely into the hills, as the only
transportation they have is the buckboard.
However, I don't think Jeb is giving up on
his moonshine business, because I could
hear the bubbling of fermentation going on
in one of the locked buildings. Which sort of
indicates they probably aren't camping too
far away."

"You think he's going to keep the same
customers?"

"Don't know. I'll just have to keep an eye
on the place and get back to you."

"I had a chat with Moss Atkins and he
admits nothing. Says he doesn't know a

Jeb Hutchinson or Tami Spencer. However,
I think he's lying through his teeth."

"What makes you think he's not telling the
truth?"

"His hands were scratched up and he had
a big red abrasion across his cheek. I
asked him where he got the wounds. He
told me he'd had a rowdy customer he had
to throw out and the guy didn't want to go. I
asked him if he knew the man's name. He
said he'd never seen him before. All very
convenient answers."

"Unfortunately, you can't prove him wrong,
as his employees will stand behind him."

Chandler harrumphed. "You got that right;
I already questioned them, and each one
verified his story."

"Right now, things are at a standstill, but
I'll get back to you if anything develops. If I
see Atkins pass my house, you'll have to
hightail it up here, because it might be your
only chance to catch them red-handed."

"We can do that."

CHAPTER FORTY-FIVE

Earlier the same day, Jeb walked into the cabin with sagging shoulders. "Beth, how fast can you clear this place out?

She glanced at him in shock as she fed Marcy. "What's happened?"

"Nothing, yet. I just figure we better go. One of us could be blamed for Tami's death."

Beth removed the baby from her breast. "With everyone's help, we could load everything into the buckboard in less than two hours. Where are we heading?"

"There's a place in the hills we can get to in the wagon, and it's well hidden. I think we'd be safe there for a long time."

Beth put Marcy into the crib. "Get the buckboard rigged to the horses and bring it up to the cabin. We can start loading immediately."

She turned to Randy, who'd been listening with his mouth open. "Take the case off your pillow and load it with your books and clothes. Then place it on the middle of the cot. I'll make satchels out of the sheet and covers to pack other things."

They all got into high gear as Jeb left for the barn. Beth tossed cooking items out of the cabinets onto Randy's bed, along with her hair ribbons. Then she nestled the iron skillets into the big iron pot, along with other utensils she'd need on a campfire, and placed them near the front door. Once she cleaned out her small kitchen, she headed for the bedrooms. Grabbing her's and Jeb's small amount of clothes from the closet and small boxes on the floor, she piled them in the middle of their bed, pulled the corners of the sheet together and tied them so they could be easily carried. Going into Earl's room, she did the same. Then she set the lanterns together on the small table in the front room.

Jeb soon entered with Earl, and they began to carry out the guns, along with other items and loaded them into the buckboard. Beth lifted Marcy out of her crib.

"Earl, I'll need her bed, break it down so it won't take up too much room. Randy, when your dad takes the stuff off the cot, fold it up. I'm sure we can squeeze it into a corner."

Jeb took an empty box out to the smokehouse and loaded it with foodstuffs, placed a clean rag over the contents, and put it into the wagon. "I'm leaving one of the lanterns here, because I'll need it when I check the cabin. Don't want any wild animals making it their home."

Soon, they were packed. Jeb closed the door, then climbed onto the seat of the buckboard. Earl mounted one of the horses; two were pulling the wagon, Jeb's steed was saddled and tied to the back. Beth had Randy hold Marcy while she climbed onto the seat next to Jeb. Once situated, she took the baby, then grabbed Randy's hand and pulled him up, where he got a foot hold and could climb into the corner of the wagon left for him.

Jeb picked up the reins, "Hee Yah," he called, as he slapped the back of the steeds with the straps. The horses neighed and strained against the weight of the load.

Once started, the family settled in for the bumpy ride to their temporary home.

"I do hope you know where we're going, and we don't fall off in a canyon somewhere," Beth said.

"Don't worry, I made sure we could get the wagon through."

The cart of people and belongings silently traveled seemingly uphill for hours as night fell. Beth finally broke the stillness.

"How much farther?"

"We're almost there," Jeb said.

Her sight had grown accustomed to the darkness and she could make out a clearing up ahead, surrounded by a grove of trees. Jeb headed the horses right to the area and soon came to a halt.

"We'll bed down in the wagon for now and tomorrow we can make the area more livable."

"Beth handed Marcy to Randy as she rummaged through the items in the wagon, dropping some over the side to make room for her brood. She soon came up with blankets for each of the family. Earl had removed the horses from the front of the wagon and tied the reins to a large oak. He tethered his and Jeb's mounts to another tree, then made himself a sleeping area on the soft grass. Randy rolled his cover around him and used the buckboard seat as his bed. Beth, Jeb and Marcy lay on the floor of the buckboard. Soon, they were all crooned to sleep by the sounds of birds, crickets and the distant hoot of an owl, along with an occasional howl of a coyote.

The sun rose early, shining its beams on the sleeping family, disturbing their peaceful sleep. Beth's eyes flickered open, and for a moment, she glanced around with a questionable expression. Then she remembered. A smile settled on her lips as she surveyed the area. It brought back memories of her childhood living in the Indian village. Many times she'd gone into the forest with her father as they hunted game and collected wild berries. They'd spent nights in the forest foraging for food. She took a deep breath, loving the smell of fresh air, mixed with the aroma of pine. After feeding Marcy, she climbed from the wagon, and made plans to build the fire pit in the safest spot so as not to start a forest fire. After a careful surveillance of the area, she decided the best place to set up the tent for sleeping, so that smoke wouldn't permeate the inside. Since the nights were pleasant, the boys could sleep in the buckboard, as the crib would take up quite a bit of space in the tent.

Her plans forming, she set up Marcy's bed, so she could watch all the activity, then sent the boys to find large rocks as she dug out the fire pit with the small pick they'd brought from the cabin. Jeb took care of the horses; then he, Earl and Randy unloaded the wagon, stacking the items in a pile, then manually pulled the wagon to a location where Beth directed.

Jeb, carrying a bucket, called to Beth. "Come with me." He took her for a walk and pointed out a small stream not far from their camping site. "This is clean fresh water coming from an underground source higher up." He knelt down and filled the container.

"You've thought of everything. Now, all we can do is pray we don't get caught."

They headed back toward their campsite. Jeb placed the bucket near the cooking utensils and covered it with a clean rag he found in one of the pots. "I'll have to go down to the cabin several times a week," He said. "I'll check your garden and bring home any ripe vegetables. I brought what little smoked meat we had, and hung it in a tree quite a ways from the camp. Earl can get what you need. Hopefully, no animals will feed off it, before we can eat it."

Beth nodded. "I'll fix it soon. I'll have the fire pit done by supper time, so a hunk of it could be used tonight. Everyone will enjoy a hearty meal after working all day. There won't be anything ready in the garden, it's too early, but you might throw some water on it."

"I'll do that. Just remember not to start the fire before dark. Smoke would give away our hiding place."

"Yes, I know."

When they reached the site, Randy had sat down on a log in front of Marcy's crib and had her giggling. Earl had collapsed on the opposite of the clearing. "Did we get enough rocks?" he asked.

Beth glanced down at the pit which the boys had encircled with large round stones. "Perfect," she said. "Rest awhile, then you'll need to gather some kindling and small logs before night falls."

Jeb went to the buckboard, loaded one of the rifles and brought it to Beth. "Here's a loaded gun, in case you need it against a bear or varmint." He handed her some extra bullets. "I'm saddling the horse and going down to the cabin. It will take me several hours to and from, so don't expect me back until after dark."

She took the gun and found a safe place to set it against the crook in a tree trunk, not far from her reach, and dropped the bullets into the pocket of her jacket. Knowing why Jeb was going back to the cabin gave her an uneasy feeling. What if he got arrested and didn't return. She knew he'd never disclose their hideout, but what would she do? Shaking the thought from her head, she watched him walk toward the tethered horses.

Once he'd galloped out of sight, Beth turned her attention to the children. "I'm sure you're hungry. I can't fix anything hot until after dark, but I think I've got some cold biscuits." She rummaged through the things she'd brought from the cabin. "Yes, here they are, along with some wild berries."

Both boys hungrily stuffed the biscuits into their mouths, washed them down with a cup of water, and then ate the berries.

As they ate, Beth studied Earl. She reached over and touched his neck, then ran her fingers down some wounds on his arms. "Where did you get these scratches?"

His face turned red. "Uh, I was picking blackberries a couple of days ago, slipped on some squashed ones I'd dropped, and fell head first into the briars."

Beth frowned. "A couple look infected. I better put a salve on them."

CHAPTER FORTY-SIX

Monday morning, Hawkman decided to stop by the Yreka Police Department on his way to work. He'd have to take the long way to Medford, but he had nothing pressing on his calendar. When he reached the station, he went directly to Chandler's office. The door stood open so he poked his head inside and found the detective at his desk, concentrating on signing papers. Hawkman gently knocked on the siding.

Chandler glanced up and smiled. "Come in. I need a break."

Hawkman slid a chair up to the desk. "I just wanted to ask a couple of questions about Tami Spencer."

"Shoot."

"When you went through her things, looking for relatives, did you by any chance find an appointment book?"

The detective shook his head. "The closest thing we came to that was an address book and after checking the few phone numbers listed, we discovered none were relatives." He stood and pulled open a file drawer where he removed a medium size box. "It appeared she was very poor; all the personal belongings we found from the car and in her apartment fit in this. She didn't even have a bank account. We found a couple of hundred dollar bills taped to the underneath side of a dresser drawer. Probably to pay rent."

"That bad?"

Chandler nodded. "Here's the book."

Hawkman thumbed through it and found an entry he studied for a moment. "This is interesting."

The detective raised his brows. "What?"

"Looks like an appointment. "JH and MA four p.m., It could be Jeb Hutchinson and Moss Atkins. However, there's no date or reference it happened."

"Yeah, I spotted it, but like you, couldn't figure out who, when, or where."

He checked through the rest of the pages. "Nothing of interest here but a grocery list.

Doesn't look like she wrote down anything to indicate her setting up moonshine runs."

"No, unfortunately, it's a shame there's no connection. I talked with the owners of The Hut, Claude and Luke Graham."

"I didn't realize they were kin," Hawkman said.

"Brothers."

"They swore they'd never heard of Tami Spencer or Jeb Hutchinson. So at this moment, I have no suspects in her murder, except the Hutchinsons. My suspicions have really heightened since you told me they'd up and disappeared. Any signs of them?"

"No. I think I'll go by and talk to Jeb's father, Jacob Hutchinson, and see if there's another cabin on that property."

"Get back to me if you find out anything."

"Will do," Hawkman said, standing.

He left the station, and drove over to the old man's house. Maybe he could somehow persuade Jacob to step into the yard so he wouldn't have to go inside the stinking house. He knocked on the door, and heard the dog bark, then Jacob tell him to shut-up. When he opened the door, he squinted, "Mr. Casey, is that you."

"Yes, I'd like to talk to you a few minutes. Would you like to step out here so we don't disturb your father."

"He can't hear a damn thing. Nothing disturbs him. Come on in."

Hawkman took a deep breath and entered the room. Surprisingly, the stench wasn't nearly as bad as the first time he'd visited. Someone had cleaned up a little. Even the dog looked like he'd been bathed. Relieved, Hawkman took the chair Jacob offered.

The old man flopped down on the couch, and placed his cane across his thighs. "What can I do for you?"

"I'm wondering if there's another house on your property, besides the cabin Jeb and Beth live in?"

Jacob slowly shook his head. "Nope, why do you ask?"

"It appears Jeb and his family have moved out."

Jacob scowled and slapped the couch arm. "Really. Now why in the hell would they go and do such a thing?"

"Not sure unless they had something to do with the murder of Tami Spencer. Her body and car were found on the premises."

The old man's mouth flew open. "Shit, who would have murdered Tami?"

"So you knew her?"

"Sure, I met her when she and Beth were close friends. But Tami got sweet on Jeb, and Beth didn't like it one bit. So it ended their friendship. Then Tami appeared here in Yreka a few years back and asked me about work. I hired her for a little while, to take care of Dad, but she didn't like the job and she needed more money, so she quit." Jacob scooted toward the edge of the cushion. His eyes sparkled. "You think Beth might have killed her?"

"I have no idea. I'd just like to find where they've gone, so I could question them. I figure they've just gone up into the hills, as their only transportation is the buckboard."

The old man raised a finger in the air. "There are many places one could camp in that forest and stay hidden for a long time. Beth could survive anywhere, being an American Indian."

"Tell me about the still. Did you put it there?"

Jacob narrowed his eyes and glared at Hawkman. "Ain't none of your business."

"If Jeb is running moonshine, it will be the police's business."

"I think I'm through talking to you. You can leave my house now." He raised his cane.

Hawkman rose and hurried out the door before the old man could whack him or sic the dog on his butt. He'd definitely hit a sore spot with Jacob.

Driving down the block, Hawkman turned the corner, made a U-turn and parked on the opposite side so he could see Jacob's place. Just as he thought, the old fellow opened the garage from inside and backed out his pickup. He then jumped out and closed the big door. Following from a distance, Hawkman knew from the route Jacob had taken, he was headed for Copco Lake. He'd have to keep a good space between them, as the road had little traffic and Jacob might spot him.

When they reached Copco Lake, Hawkman let Jacob get across the bridge before he crossed. Then he quickly drove into his own driveway and jumped on the four-wheeler.

Jennifer stepped out the front door. "What's going on?"

"Don't have time to explain right now, I'll tell you later." He gunned the machine and took off toward the back road he'd used before to spy on the Hutchinsons.

He parked a bit closer to the cabin area, since he knew the family had moved out, then hiked up to the corral area. Skirting the outside, he ducked behind some bushes when he heard the old pickup coming toward the cabin. Also about the same time, he heard a horse neigh, and a rider drew up at the front.

Hawkman recognized Jeb as he dismounted and waited for his father to alight from the truck.

"What the hell's going on?" Jacob yelled, shaking the cane at his son, as he hobbled toward him.

"How do you know any thing's going on?" Jeb asked, holding the reins of the horse, to keep it from shying away from the old man and his stick.

Hawkman didn't have to adjust his hiding spot, as he could clearly hear the men conversing.

"The private eye fellow came to see me this morning, I forget his name."

"Casey?"

Jacob nodded. "Yeah, yeah, that's his name. He asked a bunch of questions."

"Like what?" Jeb asked.

"Wanted to know if there was another house on the property, and he told me you, Beth and the kids had moved out."

"Did he tell you why?"

"Yeah, said Tami Spencer had been murdered and they found the body on the property. I figured Beth must have killed her since you guys have gone into hiding."

"Don't believe everything you hear. It all points to us, but neither Beth nor I had anything to do with it; but with my record, we're suspects and didn't want to be hounded."

"He also asked if I'd put in the still."

Jeb jerked up his head. "How'd he know about the still?"

Jacob shrugged. "He didn't say."

"Guess I better stay low for a while. Sure don't want to get caught selling moonshine, on top of being suspected of murder."

"With Tami gone, you might have trouble finding contacts," Jacob said.

"I have a few customers. One is coming in tonight to buy a load. I came down to bottle it up."

"So where are you holed up?"

"Camping up in the hills."

"When can I get my percentage? I'm running short of funds for grandpa's medicine."

"I'll put it in the smokehouse under a rock. You can pick it up tomorrow."

Jacob leaned on his cane. "Keep on selling; you'll only get a slap on the wrist if you're caught."

CHAPTER FORTY-SEVEN

Hawkman watched Jacob limp back to his worn out pickup and leave. Jeb tethered his horse in the shade of an oak tree, then strolled to the fermentation building. After unlocking it and going inside, he remained there for several minutes before reappearing, carrying a barrel. He then unlocked the other shack and disappeared within. Hawkman couldn't see the interior from his hiding place, but could smell the fire being started under the still.

Sensing Jeb would be here for several hours, Hawkman crept away and hurried to where he'd parked the four-wheeler. Since it was still early afternoon, he didn't worry about Jeb hearing the machine, as many people rode them in the area. He gunned it up, and took off for home. No way could Hawkman follow Jeb back to his campsite on the noisy Polaris; he'd need a horse, and even that would be risky.

He turned at the driveway, then into the shade of the lean-to, hopped off, and ambled into the kitchen. Jennifer quickly rose from the computer.

"Something distract you from work today?"

"Sure did. Before I talk to you, I've got to call Detective Chandler."

"Can I listen?"

"Sure, it will save me from having to tell my tale again."

He sat down at the kitchen counter, picked up the receiver, punched it on speaker phone, then breathed relief when Chandler picked up.

"Tom Casey here."

"Any news?"

"Yeah, a tidbit of information." He told him about the encounter he had with Jacob, how he'd followed him out to Copco Lake, then rode his Polaris out to the Hutchinsons. "Jeb rode up on horseback and I think he was surprised to see his father. I hid close by so I could hear the two men talking."

"Does it appear a rendezvous will take place tonight?"

"Yes, but here's the dilemma. If you come out and arrest these two guys, we'll never find the rest of Jeb's family. He'll never tell where they are, even if you torture him."

"I see what you're saying. Have you got a better plan?"

"Let me run this by you, and see what you think."

"Okay, shoot."

"If I can follow Jeb tonight back to his campsite, we'll know where the family is."

"How will you do this?"

"Can't use my Polaris, too noisy, so I'll borrow a horse from my neighbor, and just hope I can keep the animal in line so he doesn't give me away. I'll follow Jeb, and find out where they're camping out."

"That's damn risky. You could get shot."

"It's hard to shoot a moving target in the dark."

"Are you that good with directions in the middle of the night? You could guide the police to them?"

"Yes, I've had training in that field. I might be a bit rusty, but feel it will all come back when I get into the situation."

"I'm going to trust you. Detective Williams said you were good. I'm going to believe him."

"Thanks. If I can do this without Jeb getting suspicious, he'll continue his moonshining business and we can catch him later. Right now we need to find where they're hiding, in case one of them murdered the Spencer woman."

"I'm hoping to get some reports back next week. I'd sure like to match the DNA."

"I'll give you a call first thing in the morning and let you know how it went."

"Good luck."

"Thanks."

When Hawkman hung up, Jennifer stood on the opposite side of the kitchen bar, staring at her husband.

"Where are you going to get a horse? Not only that, you haven't ridden in years."

"The Martins. They have a couple of mounts, and ride them often. No doubt, I'll be sore tomorrow, but riding a horse is like pedaling a bicycle; you never forget how."

"Well, you better get over there, and make sure they're home."

"Yeah, you're right. If they're not, I could have a big problem on my hands."

Hawkman hoofed it over to his neighbor's house and knocked on the door. He exhaled in relief when Carla answered.

"Hi, Hawkman, come on in."

Wayne walked in from the back of the house. He held out his hand. "Howdy neighbor, long time no see."

After greeting him, Hawkman scratched his chin. "Got a favor to ask."

"Sure, what can we do for you."

"I need to borrow one of your horses for the night."

They glanced at one another, then at Hawkman. "Why for the night?" Wayne asked.

"I'm working on a case." He gave them a short version of his plan. "I can't use the Polaris, it would give me away."

"I can see the predicament," Carla said.

"How long has it been since you've been on a horse?" Wayne asked.

Hawkman hung his head. "Years."

Wayne laughed. "You do know how to ride though, right?"

"Yes," Hawkman said grinning.

"I think it best you take Jasper; he's my horse and used to the weight of a man. Let's go get him saddled up and you can ride him a bit before you take on this adventure."

"Does he spook easily?" Hawkman asked.

They both shook their heads. "No, neither Nellie nor Jasper do; they're both very calm. About the only thing that might make them nervous is a mountain lion, but we haven't heard of any sightings of the big cats lately." Wayne said.

The two men left through the front door. Wayne hopped onto his four-wheeler. "Get on the back and we'll go to the barn."

The Martins boarded their horses on a small plot of land they owned at the end of the road. When they approached, the horses came right to Wayne, who gave them each a carrot he had in his pocket. Hawkman then followed him inside the barn where he unlocked a small room which held an array of tack for the animals. Handing Hawkman the blanket and bridle, he carried out the saddle.

Wayne saddled Jasper, a beautiful deep brown colored quarter horse, then he turned to Hawkman. "Mount him, and I'll adjust the stirrups. Your legs are much longer than mine."

Hawkman did as he said, and Jasper didn't move.

"Looks like he's comfortable with you," Wayne said, as he moved the foot rings down to Hawkman's ankle bone. "How does that feel?"

"Great," he said, placing his cowboy boots into the stirrups.

"Ride him around a bit until you get used to each other, then have him go through his gaits. He's a good horse, and minds well. The best of luck to you tonight on your adventure."

"Thanks, Wayne. I appreciate you letting me borrow your steed. I'll bring him back good as new."

Wayne opened the gate for the rider and horse to get through, then closed it. He gave a wave, hopped on his four-wheeler and drove down the road. Jasper gave a whinny, then obeyed Hawkman as he reined him around. He rode for almost an hour out in the field around the enclosure, letting the mount get his feel and taking him through the different gaits. Nellie trotted back and forth at the fence line and called to her friend. Soon Hawkman reined Jasper's head away from the corral and guided him toward his house. When they came up the driveway, Jennifer came out the door grinning.

"You look like a regular cowboy."

Hawkman touched the brim of his hat. "Thank you, ma'am. All I need is a pair of chaps."

"Do you plan to take up cattle driving?"

He swung his leg across the saddle and dismounted. "No, I think one long night on his back is going to be all I need."

"Where are you going to put him until you're ready to go?"

He handed the reins to her. "Hold him here for a minute; I'm going to get a rope out of the garage. I'll put him in the back since the grass needs mowing. It'll give him something to nibble, and he can drink from the lake."

Jennifer talked to the horse and rubbed his forehead while Hawkman rummaged in the garage until he found a cord that would do the trick. He then led the horse around to the back, tied the end of the reins together and placed them over the horn on the saddle. Loosely securing the rope around the horse's neck, he tied the long end to a tree trunk, which would keep

Jasper in the shade but insure he had
plenty of room to maneuver without getting
tangled in the cord. He'd keep an eye on
the steed until the time came to leave for
the cabin.

CHAPTER FORTY-EIGHT

After dinner, Hawkman kept an eye on the bridge. He didn't figure Moss Atkins, the bar owner, would come to pick up his batch of booze until late, but just in case, he didn't want to miss him.

"Hon, do you have some carrots?"

"Yes, why?"

"Wayne gave the horses some when he went to the corral. Thought I'd carry two or three to let Jasper know I appreciate him."

"Not a bad idea," she said, opening the refrigerator and pulling out three long roots. "These are long, but you can just break them in half. The horse won't know the difference."

"Great," he said, snapping each one in two, then stuffing them into his jacket's zippered pocket.

She pointed toward the bridge. "Here comes a pickup."

Hawkman hurried to the kitchen window, and recognized the truck. "That's him. Wish me luck."

She reached up and gave him a kiss on the cheek. "Be careful."

"I will."

He went out the back sliding glass door, and approached the horse. Jasper didn't shy away when Hawkman removed the reins off the horn, and untied him from the tree. Wayne had put a small saddle pack behind the cantle, which held a water bottle, flashlight, his night binoculars, the carrots and his GPS which he'd loaded with a map of the area. He put his boot in the stirrup, threw his leg over the saddle, and could already feel the stiffness of this new adventure setting in.

He rode around the house, down the driveway and onto the road. Hawkman decided to go the front way to the cabin since there was enough distance between the road and the buildings which ensured he wouldn't be seen, especially, on this pitch black night with the moon hiding behind a layer of clouds. Since Earl wouldn't be there, he could stay hidden in the trees until Atkins left, then follow Jeb when he took off for the campsite. He sure hoped his calculations on the timeline were right.

Hawkman came to the turnoff and guided the horse up the small knoll, then took a sharp right and stayed along the tree line as he advanced closer. Soon he could see a faint light up ahead, and cut into the darkness of the forest. He dismounted and led Jasper as he neared the cabin. The glow of a lantern on the stoop outlined Jeb's horse tied at an oak tree nearby. Hawkman prayed the two animals didn't decide to converse. He took a part of a carrot he had in his jacket and fed it to Jasper, hoping the steed would get the message.

Atkins had backed up to the still which suited Hawkman, so that when he left, his headlight beams wouldn't bank off the trees where he and Jasper were hidden. Hawkman couldn't hear what the men were saying, but he watched their movements as they packed the bottles of hooch into the bed of the pickup. When they finally finished, he saw Atkins hand Jeb a roll of bills; then they both tied a large tarp over the goods. The two men shook hands, then Moss got into his pickup and left. Jeb took the money out of his pocket and peeled off several bills and went to the smoke house. Hawkman knew this was the percentage he owed his dad. Jeb strolled to the barn and brought back a muck bucket which he placed in front of the horse. Soon he returned to the still where he removed the barrel, and placed it in the other building.

Jeb took the lantern inside the cabin and before long Hawkman could smell the wood burning stove. He figured Jeb was preparing the next batch of mash. Settling on a stump, Hawkman assumed this procedure might take awhile. In less than an hour, Jeb came out carrying a large heavy pot, went to the fermentation shack and disappeared inside. He came out a few minutes later with an empty pan, and locked up the building. Double checking the lock on the still, he went back inside the house. He returned with a bucket, which Hawkman assumed was full of water, as he headed for the horse and set it down in front of him. After the horse drank, he picked up both containers and walked back to the cabin, where he placed them outside the door. Jeb went inside the house, and the glow from the windows faded. He closed the door and headed for his horse.

Hawkman removed the night binoculars from the pack, put the strap around his neck, took out the GPS, turned it on and slid it into a deep pocket in his jacket. He readied himself for a long ride as he watched Jeb mount, remove his rifle from the scabbard, place it across the seat between his body and the pommel; he then reined the horse due north.

Hawkman waited until they disappeared, then brought Jasper out of the shadows and climbed onto his back. He flipped up his eye-patch since he didn't need it for protection during nighttime. As they walked past the front of the cabin, Hawkman could see Jeb's silhouette moving through the tall grass.

When they forded the small stream that flowed nearby, Hawkman let Jasper drink for a few seconds, then gave him a gentle kick in the flank to move ahead. He figured Jeb could travel about fifty yards in front and he'd still be able to locate him with the night binoculars.

Not wanting to be surprised by some big cat or bear, he unsnapped his jacket and flipped up the flap on his shoulder holster, so his gun would be handy. He figured Jeb knew the territory better than he did. Seeing him with his rifle ready made Hawkman aware of all sorts of noises. Also, he'd pay attention to Jasper, especially his ears, as animals tend to sense danger immediately.

They moved along at a steady pace with no incidents for a half hour. The hooves of the walking horses were silent as the ground cover was heavy along the route they traveled. The only sound was the brushing against the bushes as they passed. Hawkman pulled on the reins and stopped Jasper for a few seconds to see if he could hear Jeb. If he couldn't hear anything downwind, then he knew Jeb couldn't hear him.

Suddenly, a loud whinny and the deafening blast of a gun echoed through the still night. Jasper let out a big neigh and reared up a bit. It took Hawkman a minute to settle the horse, then he quickly put the night binoculars to his eyes. He spotted Jeb, holding his rifle high, as he and his mount thrashed up the mountainside at a hard gallop. He doubted Jeb would have heard Jasper as he thundered through the brush.

Not wanting Jasper to get any more skittish, which he might if they came across a dead mountain lion or bear, he decided to skirt the scene. Keeping Jeb in his sight, he moved in a semicircle, then gave Jasper a slight kick in the flanks. The horse took off in a gallop and soon Hawkman had Jeb back to the fifty yards distance and slowed Jasper down to a steady walk.

They'd been on the trail for well over an hour. Hawkman scanned the mountainside with the binoculars as he rode. Unexpectedly, a movement caught his attention among the trees. He backtracked and discovered what appeared to be a horse tethered, but he couldn't see much else due to foliage, and distance.

Hawkman kept a close eye on Jeb, as he didn't want him to circle back and catch him on his tail. When they got closer to the area where he'd seen the horse, he could make out a tent and the glow of a smoldering fire pit. The buckboard came into view on the outer edge of the camp, everything sheltered by a large covey of trees. He turned Jasper under a large oak and reined him to a halt.

He watched Jeb ride into the camp, unsaddle his horse, give him a quick brush, and tie him next to the other mounts. Carrying his rifle, he entered the tent. Hawkman knew he'd have no trouble finding the campsite again on horseback; in a vehicle it might be questionable.

He urged Jasper out from the trees and they started the long trek down the mountain. Things looked transformed, coming from a different angle, and he wasn't sure exactly where Jeb had met with the beast. Before he knew it, they rode right into the area. Jasper shied away and made low growling noises deep in his throat as he sidestepped around the carcass of a huge mountain lion.

"Wow," he muttered. "That's one big cat. Let's hope there's no more around." Hawkman rode Jasper to the corral, unsaddled the horse, brushed him down, and turned him loose to be with Nellie.

***

The man stomped along the floor of the small living room, wringing his hands and kicking at the wastebasket as he passed. "The bitch," he mumbled, "even though I hired her, I knew I wouldn't need her long. She surely knew that, so why did she come and threaten me to pay her more than I owed or she'd tell my clients how I'd cheated them. If she thought blackmail would save her butt, she had another thing coming."

Nervously, he glanced out the window at every passing car. Then he continued talking to the dog who lay on the floor watching him with soulful brown eyes. "They'll never connect me with the murder. No one had any idea I'd hired the woman or would be there waiting for her. I didn't leave any fingerprints, and I've thrown my boots away. Damn she was hard to strangle. For a little woman, she put up quite a fight, and those damn long fingernails of her's kept clawing at me. I just had to use brute force and crush her windpipe."

He finally flopped down on the soiled couch, and closed his eyes. "Gotta get some rest."

CHAPTER FORTY-NINE

Tuesday morning, Hawkman groaned as he rolled out of bed. The results of not riding a horse for years had taken it's toll on his body. Jennifer grinned as she watched him limp to the bathroom.

"Little sore this morning?" she asked.

"My butt hurts like hell. I can hardly walk."

"Did you find Beth and the kids?"

"Yes, a hundred miles from here." He waved a hand. "Well, probably not that far, but my bones feel like it."

She climbed out of bed, smiling. "I'll get the coffee started. Then you can hobble in and tell me all about it."

"You're enjoying my pain, aren't you?"

She gave him a quick kiss on the cheek. "Of course not. I'm just happy you're home safe."

Later, over a cup of coffee at the kitchen bar, he told her about finding the campsite and how Jeb had shot the mountain lion.

"Sounds like it turned into a very hazardous ride. Sure glad you didn't come face to face with one of those critters. If Jasper had bucked you off, I'd probably never find you deep in the woods."

"Believe me, it ran through my mind." He reached for the phone. "I've got to call Detective Chandler and give him my account of the hunt."

Jennifer made breakfast, while Hawkman spoke with the detective. When he hung up, she studied his face. "Looks like you just received some bad news."

"I'm not sure. Chandler said they received the DNA results from under Tami's fingernails, but so far no matches. They've contacted the prison Jeb spent time in, but haven't received a response. They're going to see if Atkins will volunteer a sample; otherwise, they'll have to get one or arrest him."

"On what grounds?" Jennifer asked.

"Suspicion of murder."

"This is becoming one complicated mess," Jennifer said, throwing up her hands. "Do you think he killed Tami?"

Hawkman let out an audible sigh. "I wish I could answer, but I have no idea. It has to be connected somehow to the Hutchinsons, or a customer Tami dealt with to buy the hooch."

"Who hired Tami to do this job?" Jennifer asked.

He looked puzzled. "That's an excellent question. I have no idea."

"I doubt Jeb hired her; he has no money. I wouldn't think the bars would, as they probably hadn't even thought of moonshine until she brought it up. So someone had to mention it to her and know Jeb was making it."

He jumped off the bar stool and moaned. "I forgot I'd been on a horse for ten hours."

"Where are you going in such a hurry?"

"Into Yreka, and talk to Detective Chandler. I want to look through Tami's personal stuff again. She had a small address book with only initials written inside. I want to check those again. It may hold a clue of who killed her."

"Are you going into work today?"

"I have nothing pressing right now, so I can miss a day or two." He grabbed a Stetson off the Hawkman coat rack, and his cell phone off the counter.

Jennifer shook her head as she watched him hobble out the front door.

Once Hawkman got a short distance from Copco Lake, his cell phone could find a signal and he called the detective.

"Hi, Detective Chandler, Tom Casey here. You going to be in your office for a while? I need to look at Tami Spencer's address book again."

He listened for a moment. "Great, see ya in a few."

Soon, Hawkman pulled into the police station and parked. When he went inside, he found the detective hovering over a stack of papers. "All you detectives seem to have come from the same mold. Always signing papers."

Chandler raised his eyes and grinned. "Yeah, but they didn't tell us about this in the academy." He motioned at the chair in front of his desk. "Have a seat."

Hawkman carefully lowered himself and the detective grinned.

"You act like you've been in the saddle for a while. Guess you've got a sore ass."

"Yep, you've got that right. My body will never be the same."

Chandler rose and went to the filing cabinet. "So what made you want to see Spencer's address book again?"

"My wife asked me a question this morning that sent my brain into overdrive."

"Oh, yeah. What about?"

"She asked who hired Tami Spencer to be the in-between person. I figured it had to be someone who knew Jeb had a still."

"How many do you think knew?"

"Very few, and she may have demanded more money as she began to bring customers in, especially after seeing them come to Jeb's place after the initial meeting, and collecting the hooch themselves. This could have gotten her killed."

Chandler handed Hawkman the small book. "Do you think you saw something in there that would give us a clue?"

"I'm not sure. I wanted to check the grocery list I spotted the first time. It could be a code indicating meetings, and who she reported to."

Hawkman flipped it open and went through it page by page. He stopped at the grocery list he'd seen before. Shaking his head, he began examining the book. It appeared the plastic cover could be separated from the rest, so he carefully fiddled with it and eventually pulled the pad out of the binding. A folded piece of paper fell to the floor. Picking it up, he smoothed the sheet out on the desk. After scanning it, he glanced up at Detective Chandler. "This might be the motive for murder!"

Chandler's eyes opened wide. "What?"

He turned the paper around so the detective could read the writing. Chandler's eyes then narrowed as he absorbed the information. He ran his finger across a line. "If this is her handwriting, which I'd assume it is, she has it dated when Jacob hired her and he obviously owed her a large sum of cash. Everything from gas bills to hush money, which he obviously never intended to pay." He pointed to a note scrawled at the bottom of the sheet. 'Tell Moss Atkins how he's cheated them'. "It appears she might have threatened Jacob that she'd tell his clients they were being ripped off if he didn't pay up, so he shut her up for good."

"It certainly looks that way," Hawkman said.

"The thing that bothers me is why did he kill her on the Hutchinson's property?"

"To make it look like Beth had done it. He doesn't like her, and he knew the story about Tami having an affair with Jeb. He probably found the ribbon out in the yard when he went up there earlier."

"Okay, that fits. But how did he know Tami would be there?"

"It's possible he told her Jeb would be getting paid by Atkins that night, and he'd meet her at the cabin after he got his percentage; then they could settle their debt. He might have even told her to park where we found the car and body."

Detective Chandler rose from his seat and attached his gun belt around his waist. "I think it's time to have a talk with Jacob Hutchinson." On the way out, he motioned to a couple of his officers. "Need a back up."

Hawkman directed him to Jacob's place, and before they got out of the car, he warned the detective of the pungent smell in the house. "Also, he told me he takes care of his father, who is bedridden.

Probably, much of the odor comes from such a situation."

The detective nodded as they walked up to the entry. Flanked by two officers, Chandler stepped upon the stoop and knocked firmly. Hawkman could hear the growling of the dog, then a male voice shouting for him to shut up.

When Jacob opened the door and saw the police officer along with Hawkman, he frowned. "What's up?" he asked.

Chandler displayed his badge. "We'd like to come in and talk to you about Tami Spencer."

When they stepped into the room, the odor hit the men like a slap in the face. Nonchalantly, they covered their noses with their hands.

"Sorry about the stench," Jacob said. "My Dad wets and shits on his bed faster than I can clean him up."

"I'd like to talk to your father," Chandler said.

Jacob furrowed his brow. "Why, he's not even coherent. He couldn't tell you a thing."

"Just the same, I want to see him."

Shrugging his shoulders, he led the detective to a bedroom off the main part of the house. Chandler walked over to the still form, and yanked back the filthy covers. "Dear God," he murmured. He stormed back into the living room, and spoke to one of the officers. "Go out to the car and call an ambulance. That man needs to be in a hospital. He's skin and bone, with sores all over his body." He swirled around and pointed a finger at Jacob. "How could you neglect your own father to this point?"

"He's never seemed to be in any pain," Jacob said.

Chandler scowled. "You stupid man. He's got bed sores all over his body. Do you ever feed him?"

"Yeah, but he won't eat much."

"He's sick," Chandler yelled. "He needs medical attention."

The officer came back from outside. "Ambulance on the way."

"Good, you two go outside and wait for it," he instructed the two officers. "When it arrives lead them to the poor man." Turning back to Jacob Hutchinson, he glowered. "Sit down. I've got some questions for you, and by God you better answer truthfully."

CHAPTER FIFTY

The ambulance arrived and the paramedics rolled the elderly man out on a gurney. A clipboard in hand, the driver approached the detective.

"What's his name?"

Chandler pointed at Jacob. "Ask him."

"Jacob Ross Hutchinson, Sr. I can't afford no long hospital stay for him."

Chandler glared at Jacob. "So you're a Jr.? Your father will stay there as long as needed. That poor old fellow has been neglected long enough. You'll find the money."

Hawkman stepped back and leaned against the wall with his arms crossed as he watched Detective Chandler in action. He also noticed scratches on Jacob's neck and on his right arm where he had his shirt sleeve rolled up.

After reading Jacob, Jr. his Miranda rights, Chandler began his questioning. "How well did you know Tami Spencer?"

"She was Beth's friend. I only saw her a few times."

"I told you I want the truth, Mr. Hutchinson. I have some indication that you owed Tami Spencer quite a sum of money."

Jacob shook his head. "I still don't know what the hell you're talking about."

"When did you install the still on the property near Copco Lake?"

"I ain't put in no still anywhere."

"Mr. Hutchinson, I can find that out through the company when you ordered it. So I'd advise you to tell me."

Jacob slammed the end of his cane on the floor. The dog jumped and so did Hawkman. "Five or six years ago. Don't remember the exact month."

"Did you plan to make moonshine and sell it?"

He stared at Chandler. "Never had the opportunity."

"I see. So when your son got out of prison and couldn't find a job, you figured this was the time to put the still to work?"

"Beth didn't want him to do it. She didn't like the idea of him going back to jail."

"You bribed him with a free place to live with his family, didn't you? Along with a little money each month to keep them in staples and ammunition for hunting?"

"I don't have that kind of money."

"You've got enough to hire someone to be an in-between for moonshine running, even though you didn't pay her."

Jacob jerked up his head. "What are you talking about?"

"Mr. Hutchinson, I did a search on your son, Jeb, when I found out we had an ex-con in the area, and guess what else I found? A whole lot about the Hutchinson clan. Your dad made a fortune, but it's still in his name. You've been skimming off the top, just enough to not draw attention to yourself. When the old man dies, you'll inherit the whole shebang, but you know it has to be a normal death or your son, next in line for the inheritance will get all his money."

Hawkman listened intently to Detective Chandler, and liked the way this man worked. He'd definitely done his homework.

Jacob fidgeted with his cane, never making eye contact with the detective. "What are you trying to say?"

"When Tami Spencer approached you about the money you owed her for finding customers to buy the moonshine, you told her to meet you at Jeb's place, where you'd be getting cash. You instructed her not come to the cabin, but park in a cluster of trees. That's where you killed her, making it look like Beth had done the deed."

Jerking up his head, Jacob narrowed his eyes. "You're crazy. There's no proof I did anything to Tami. I hardly knew her. I ain't answering no more of your questions."

"It's up to you Mr. Hutchinson, but I'm putting you under arrest for the abuse of an elderly person. Please stand up so my officer can put on the cuffs."

"I treated my Dad good. He's still alive."

Chandler scowled. "Barely."

"I can't walk without my cane."

"My officers will assist you to the car."

"What about my dog?"

"Has he got a name?"

"I call him Mutt."

The detective eyed the thin, dirty dog on the floor beside the couch. "I'll get the

SPCA out here to take him in. He definitely needs help too. Doesn't look like you take good care of living things that supposedly mean something to you."

"How much will it cost me to get him out?"

Chandler shot a look at him. "Get him out of my sight before I pull my gun. Take him in and book him for elderly abuse for now."

The two officers got on each side of Jacob and practically carried him outside. The dog watched with soulful eyes, but didn't move to object to his owner being carted out. The detective closed his notebook, then turned to Hawkman. "Let's get out of this hell hole. Would you mind going with me to check the hospital to make sure the poor old man is being looked after?"

"Sure," Hawkman said, as he stepped outside and gulped in the fresh air.

On the way over, Chandler called the SPCA and told them to pick up the dog. The door was unlocked. He gave a little history of the animal's malnutrition, its name, and told them the owner was being incarcerated for a while.

After hanging up, he shook his head. "Boy, this guy is one loser. The DNA should prove he's the murderer."

"Did you notice the scratches on his neck and right arm?" Hawkman asked.

"Vaguely. He made me so mad, I couldn't see anything but red. Glad you spotted them; We'll take pictures at the jail."

They arrived at the hospital and went straight to the emergency room where Detective Chandler did all the talking. One of the nurses led them into one of the rooms where Jacob Hutchinson, Sr. lay on a bed with an intravenous tube in his arm. His eyes were closed and Hawkman noticed Chandler's lip quivered as he stared at him. He quickly regained his composure and said, "How could anyone starve his own father."

Before Hawkman could respond, the doctor strolled into the room. "Hello, Detective Chandler. You sent us a good one this time. I think we can save him, even though he's in bad shape. He told us to get him well; he had a score to settle. The old fellow's got spunk"

"Really. Good for him," Chandler said, with a grin. "I knew I liked this old codger. You tell him I'll be back to see him in a couple of days. We need to talk."

The detective and Hawkman walked back
to the car. On the way to the station,
Chandler shot a look at Hawkman. "What
did you think about everything that went
down today?"

"I thought you did a great job. The one
thing that baffles me is I didn't know the old
fellow's name, so just assumed the Jacob,
Jr., the land where Jeb and family had set
up housekeeping. Now, I'm doubting it. I'm
going to go back to the courthouse and
recheck the title."

"You think Jacob, Sr., is really the owner?"

"I have my suspicions."

"Let me know if you get verification. I'd like
to add another abuse charge against
Jacob, Jr."

They reached the station lot where
Hawkman hopped out of the police car and
went to his own vehicle. He waved at
Detective Chandler as he drove out of the
lot and headed for the courthouse.

When he entered the section of properties,
he saw the young woman who'd helped him
before and walked straight to her desk.

"Hi, Mr. Casey. What can I do for you
today?"

He explained what he needed and her fingers flew over the keyboard of her computer. Within in a matter of seconds, she had the title in front of her and turned the monitor so Hawkman could see it. She pointed out the owner of the property.

"It's owned by Jacob Ross Hutchinson." She paused. "Wait a minute. On the second line is 'Sr.'. Looks like there wasn't enough room to put that on the first line."

"All I needed to know. Could you make a copy of the deed?

"Sure. Give me a few minutes," she said, leaving her desk. She soon returned and handed him the papers.

"Thank you." He got up and left the room.

CHAPTER FIFTY-ONE

Hawkman drove back to the police station and went inside. The receptionist told him to wait in Detective Chandler's office as he'd be there shortly. Within a few minutes, the detective came in and sat down at his desk. "Sorry for making you wait. Been at the holding cell where we have Hutchinson. We took pictures of those scratches. She clawed him bad; doc said a couple of them were infected. Then I had to give the doctor instructions about getting a vial of blood for me to send out for the DNA test, so had to sign some papers. Got a message from the SPCA; they've picked up Mutt and taken him straight to the veterinarian. They said the poor animal was in bad shape. What news did you find?"

Hawkman leaned forward. "The property is owned by Jacob Hutchinson, Sr." He handed the copy of the deed to the detective.

After he studied the document, he glanced at Hawkman. "Wonder if Jeb knows?"

"I doubt he'd even question the consent to his living there, even if he knew his dad didn't own it. He probably figured his grandfather had said it was fine." Hawkman shrugged. " Who knows, maybe he did. Sometimes it pays to have people on your property, rather than have it available to vandals."

Chandler brushed back the sandy colored hair that had fallen across his forehead. "This has been quite a day."

Hawkman rose from the chair. "It's moved along at a rapid rate. Let me know about the DNA."

"I'm putting a rush on it. I can keep him behind bars for a while with the abuse charges, hopefully until I receive the report."

"Has Jacob hired a lawyer?"

"Not yet. I don't think he realizes he's in a pot of boiling water."

"Keep me informed."

"Will do."

Hawkman left the station and drove home. He and Jennifer talked for hours over what had happened and the repercussions it could have on Jeb and Beth.

"How will they know what's occurred?" Jennifer asked.

"We'll take it a step at a time. It'll work itself out, and we'll know what to do to help."

***

Several days passed. Hawkman kept his regular routine of going to the office in Medford, trying not to think about the Hutchinsons, but working on cases he'd taken on in the past two weeks. The phone rang just as he sat down at the desk with a cup of coffee. He punched on the speaker.

"Tom Casey, Private Investigator."

"Tom, this is Detective Chandler. Where are you right now?"

"Medford, at my office."

"How soon could you get to Yreka?"

"In forty-five minutes to an hour."

"Would it be too much to ask you to come to the station right away?"

"Not at all. I can leave now."

"Great, I'll explain everything when you get here."

Hawkman closed down shop and headed for Yreka on Interstate 5. Since there was little traffic, he made the trip in record time, and walked into the police station in about forty minutes.

Chandler looked surprised. "My word, man, did you fly?"

"Want to thank you for clearing the freeway. Had it all to myself," Hawkman said, grinning.

The detective chuckled. "I'm sure you're wondering why I wanted you here. Two things. The first is the DNA report came back a perfect match. So we have our murderer behind bars. The second thing is, I received a phone call from Jacob, Sr.'s lawyer. He wants you and me to meet him at the hospital."

"Why me?" Hawkman asked.

"The old man requested it. Says he knows you've been involved with his family. Now, don't ask me if that's good or bad; we'll soon find out." Chandler stood. "You ready?"

"Why not."

They climbed into the police car and drove to the hospital. On the way over, Hawkman asked about how the older Hutchinson was doing.

"I've made a few calls, checking his progress, but haven't seen him. The doctor told me, he's been amazed at Jacob's recovery. He said, he definitely has a will to live."

They reached the hospital and found out the room number, and were soon sitting around the bed of the senior Jacob Hutchinson. Hawkman couldn't keep from staring at the old fellow. He could hardly believe he was the same man he'd seen taken out on a gurney from that filthy house. He'd been cleaned up, his blue eyes sparkled, his face had some color and he smiled at Hawkman.

"You didn't think this old man would make it, did you?"

"Sir, to be honest, no. I'm looking at a miracle."

He introduced Hawkman and Detective Chandler to his attorney. "This man has been my lawyer for many years. Jacob never let him come and see me after he put me in that rat infested room. Always made up some excuse, especially when I got so weak I couldn't do anything about it. Then you two men entered my life. I want to thank you from the bottom of my heart. You came just in time; otherwise, I would have died for sure."

Detective Chandler reached over and took the man's hand. "When I saw you, I wasn't leaving until I could get you to the hospital."

Jacob patted his arm. "I've got a few things to do in this world before I leave it, and one thing is, to make life easier for Jeb and Beth. My son was greedy and mean. From what I understand, he'll be spending the rest of his life in jail. Good riddance as far as I'm concerned. He won't be around to tempt Jeb into doing wrong things. Jeb's a good man; he didn't intend to kill anyone. His wife is wonderful. I've always loved Beth." He pointed a not so feeble finger at Hawkman. "You know where they disappeared to, don't you?"

"Yes," Hawkman said.

"Good. I've got a job for you, Hawkman, and I'll pay you nicely. I want you to tell them I said to get back to the cabin. Let them know about Jacob, Jr. and tell them Great Grandpa will come and see them soon. Tell Jeb to destroy the still and get it out of there. We're going to raise cattle, not moonshine."

Hawkman smiled. "I'll do that, but I won't take a dime for it. It will give me much pleasure to follow your orders. Tell me, how did you know to call me Hawkman?"

Jacob chuckled. "You'll never get rich that way. To answer your question. I've lived in this area a long time, and when I saw you at Jacob's house, sporting the eye-patch, I knew exactly who you were. You'd worked for the Agency, then married that petite little widow, Jennifer, that lived at Copco Lake. I know lots more about you, but now is not the time to go into it." Then he turned to the detective. "I want you to tell my son, he's no longer in my will. I've had my lawyer write up a new one. That'll take the starch out of him real fast."

"I'll do it," Chandler said, nodding.

"Okay, gentlemen, that's all I have to say right now. I need my rest, so I'm in good shape to go to the cabin to see my grandson and his sweet wife. I want them to look upon me as strong and able. Hawkman, you let me know when they're back."

"I'll certainly do that." Hawkman said, shaking his hand.

The two men left the hospital, and on the way back to the police station, Hawkman noticed Chandler's stern expression. "You okay?" he asked.

The detective slapped his hand against the steering wheel. "Just makes me so mad to think his son let him get in such bad shape. I'm sure he's not much over eighty years old, but when I saw him in that bed, I'd have sworn he was a hundred. Thank God, we found him in time."

"True," Hawkman said. "After a few months of good nourishment, and some physical therapy, I'd say he'll be like a new man."

"I lost my Dad when I was ten years old, and I've missed him all my life. Just so hard for me to see anyone treat their Dad so badly. When I'd give my eye teeth to have mine back."

Hawkman now knew why Chandler got so angry when he saw Jacob in the filthy bed with sores all over him. "I have a feeling it's going to give you a great deal of pleasure to tell Jacob, Jr. he's no longer in his dad's will."

Chandler smirked. "Oh, you bet." Then he glanced at Hawkman. "By the way, Jacob, Sr. sure knew a lot about you. So your nickname is Hawkman. How'd you come by that handle?"

"Yeah, when we have more time, remind me to tell you."

CHAPTER FIFTY-TWO

Hawkman realized time had slipped by and today, being Friday, it was possible Jeb would be at the cabin finishing up a batch of moonshine. When he arrived home, he told Jennifer about the events of the day, and informed her he was going to the cabin.

"I'll go in the front way, so maybe I'll catch him off guard, and he won't shoot me.

She put a hand on her hip, and looked him in the face. "I'm going with you."

He frowned. "Honey, it could be dangerous, and he might not even be there."

Ignoring his comment, she continued, "If he's not there, we'll borrow the Martins' horses and ride up to their campsite in the morning. Let's go on the four-wheeler tonight. If Jeb's there, seeing me at your back might prevent him from shooting."

Loudly exhaling, he glared at her. "Guess there's no way of talking you out of your crazy idea."

She threw back her head in a haughty manner. "Nope. When do you want to leave?"

"Now. Let's get this over with."

Jennifer strapped on the fanny pack holding her gun, then they went outside and climbed onto the Polaris. When they approached the cabin, Hawkman noted Jeb's horse wasn't there. The two buckets were still by the cabin front door. He jumped off the machine, went to the locked fermenting building and pressed his ear against the wood. The bubbling sounded faint, but he could still hear it. He turned to Jennifer, who'd checked the cabin.

"Anything different?" he asked.

She shook her head. "Nothing in the house."

"Come here, and tell me what you hear."

She stepped closer and listened. "It's still fermenting, but it doesn't seem real strong."

Hawkman hooked his thumbs in the back pockets of his jeans, and looked out over the countryside. "I'm thinking, he'll come tomorrow."

They walked back to the four-wheeler. "How long does it take to reach the campsite on horseback?" Jennifer asked.

"Hour and a half to two hours. It's a rough ride, mostly uphill."

"We better get back home so we have time to talk to Carla and Wayne before dark. We'll need a very early start in the morning to catch Jeb before he leaves."

They left the cabin site, and stopped at the Martins' house. When they told them of the plan, they both agreed to lend Jasper and Nellie. Wayne took them to the corral, saddled the horses and gave Jennifer a couple of small buckets of grain. He then wished his two friends luck, and went back home.

Jennifer looped the buckets over the handle bars and drove the four-wheeler back to their house. Hawkman rode Jasper and led Nellie by the reins. They tied the horses in the back, as Hawkman had done before, and Jennifer fed them a couple of carrots. He snapped off the small pack under the cantle and brought it inside the house. Doubting he could make contact up in the hills with his cell phone, he still charged it and decided to take it in case of an emergency. He cleaned his gun and shoved extra ammunition into the pack. He prayed they wouldn't come face to face with a cougar or bear. It might take more than a few shots to knock a big animal down. Jennifer also added extras to her fanny pack. They had a light dinner, then went to bed.

Saturday morning, the couple arose before the sun. Hawkman went out and fed the horses the grain Wayne had given them while Jennifer dressed in jeans, boots, sweatshirt and a cowboy hat. After eating breakfast, she made sure they each had a tall bottle of water, and extra carrots to carry for the horses. They were soon ready, went outside, and mounted their steeds. Jennifer stayed abreast of Hawkman until they got into the hills, where she dropped behind him since he knew the way. After an hour in the saddle of hard riding, Jennifer knew she'd be one sore female tomorrow. It had been a long time since she'd been in the saddle too. Fortunately, Nellie was an easy riding horse.

Hawkman turned in his saddle. "Be on the lookout for mountain lions or any other varmints; this is near the area where Jeb killed the one I told you about." He pointed to the ground ahead of him. "In fact, there's the remains."

They steered around what the scavengers had left and continued their journey. Suddenly, Hawkman pulled on the reins and stopped Jasper. Jennifer rode up alongside him.

"What's the matter?" she asked.

"Jeb is coming."

She shaded her eyes with her hand. "Where?"

"He's just disappeared into a gully. You'll see him in a moment."

"What are we going to do?"

"Confront him."

"You think he spotted us?"

"Probably. We'll stay put for a few minutes." Hawkman surveyed the area around him, but saw no signs of Hutchinson. However, he figured the man had good tracking skills and could come upon them swiftly.

Sure enough, out of nowhere, a voice demanded. "Put your hands up and dismount."

"Do as he says," Hawkman told Jennifer.

Climbing off their horses, but holding onto the reins, they both hopped to the ground with their hands high in the air.

Jeb stepped out from behind a tree with his shotgun pointed at them. "What the hell are you two doing up in these hills?"

"Looking for you," Hawkman said. "We've come to give you some news."

"What kind, good or bad?"

"A little of both."

"Let's hear it."

"We'd like to tell Beth, too," Jennifer said.

"You tell me first, and I'll decide whether she needs to know."

"Can we lower our arms?" Hawkman asked.

"Yeah, as long as you keep your hands in view."

Hawkman began telling Jeb that the murderer of Tami Spencer had been arrested. "The man's DNA matched what they found under Tami's fingernails. He's behind bars, so no longer are you and Beth suspected."

"Who is he; do I know him?"

"This is very hard to tell you. Your father killed Ms. Spencer."

Jeb stared at Hawkman. "You're telling me the truth aren't you?"

"Yes, your grandfather was admitted to the hospital in bad condition, but he's much better. He asked me to tell you and Beth, to come down out of the hills and move back into the cabin. He will come and see you when he's strong enough."

Jeb lowered the rifle, and rested the butt on the ground, then rubbed the back of his neck with his free hand. "You two mount up. Beth needs to hear this from you; she'll never believe me."

"There are other things we haven't told you yet," Hawkman said.

"You can tell us at the campsite. No need for you to have to repeat it."

Jeb gave a whistle and his horse came from behind a cluster of trees to his master. Slipping his rifle into the gun scabbard hanging from the saddle, Jeb got astride his horse, and signaled with a wave of his hand for them to follow.

They climbed the hillside for close to an hour before they came to a clearing where Jennifer spotted Beth and Randy sitting on a blanket in the shade, playing with Marcy. Earl stood against a tree with his gun at his side. He jerked up and grabbed his rifle when Jeb trotted into the campsite with two companions.

"Jeb raised a hand as he dismounted, "It's okay Earl, they're bearers of good news."

Hawkman and Jennifer climbed off their horses and stood with the reins in their hands. Beth rose and walked slowly toward them.

"How did they find us?"

"I don't think it matters now." Jeb said. "Hear what they have to say."

"Tie up your horses, and come into our humble home," she said, pointing to a huge log. "I don't have any refreshments to offer, other than water."

"We don't need anything; we have our own water, so save yours. Thank you, anyway," Jennifer said, as she looped Nellie's reins over a low branch and tied them. She fished out a water bottle from the small pack, and strolled to the log where she sat down. Hawkman did the same.

Once everyone had huddled around them, Hawkman told the family what had happened. When he told of the DNA matching Jeb's father, Beth covered her face with her hands. Then when he told about the old man, her face broke into a big grin.

"He's okay?" she asked. "I loved him, but Jacob wouldn't let us see him, once he took him into his home."

"Obviously, he loves you too, he can hardly wait to visit with your family."

Hawkman pointed at Jeb. "The message for you from your grandpa is to tear out the still, get rid of it. You're going to be a rancher and raise cattle. He's going to make an honest man out of you."

A rare smile crept across Jeb's lips. "He actually said that?"

"Yes, and I have no doubt that's what he plans on doing."

After Hawkman finished with all he had to tell, Beth jumped up and said, "Let's get packed up and go home. The first thing I'm going to do is fix a place for great grandpa to come and live with us when he gets out of the hospital."

"He'll love that, Beth," Jennifer said. "Can I help you do something?"

CHAPTER FIFTY-THREE

Hawkman and Jennifer helped the Hutchinsons pack the buckboard. Once they had things all tucked in securely, Jeb hopped up on the driver's seat and took the reins. Earl rode on a horse with his dad's mount in stride; Hawkman and Jennifer brought up the rear. The family started the long journey down the mountain.

The pace proved to be slow and tedious. Several times Jennifer shifted in her saddle, as her legs were aching, along with her butt. Once the idea ran through her mind to get off and walk, but she didn't want to look like a sissy in front of Randy.

They had plenty of daylight ahead, so if all went well, they'd make it to the cabin before dark. Hawkman studied the wagon and it appeared very durable. Jeb handled it with care and avoided going over rocks as he kept a strong rein on the horses so they wouldn't go too fast.

Hawkman had to hand it to the man; keeping the cart under control, took much patience and concentration.

Suddenly, Randy started clapping. "We're almost home, I can see the road."

When the path leveled, Jeb let the horses have a little of their head, and they notched up their gait as if they knew rest was not far off. They came in on the northwest corner, forded the small stream and soon rolled up to the front of the cabin.

Beth handed Marcy to Randy, then hopped down from the buckboard. She hurried into the cabin and whirled in a circle. "It's so wonderful to be here," she sang in a loud voice. Then she dashed back outside. "We've got to get unpacked before dark."

When Hawkman and Jennifer started to dismount, Beth ran to their sides. "No, no. You've done enough. We can do this without help. It won't be hard as we know where everything goes."

Jeb stepped up behind her. "Tonight is my last night to sell the rotgut. You can tell my grandpa, the still will be gone when he comes to see us."

Hawkman leaned down and shook Jeb's hand. "I'll tell him."

They waved goodbye, and took off for home. When they got to the road, Hawkman turned in his saddle toward Jennifer. "Wanna race?"

She looked at him with disgust. "Have you lost your mind. I probably won't be able to walk now. All I'd need is more bouncing on this horse before I'd be crippled for life."

He threw back his head and laughed.

They took the horses to the Martins' corral, and brushed them down. Hawkman started looking for the grain when he heard Wayne drive up on his four-wheeler.

"Saw you two go by. Figured you could use some help. How'd it go?" he asked in a good-natured voice.

"I can hardly walk," Jennifer said. "Other than that, things went great."

Wayne chuckled and pulled out the grain sack.

"Oh, shoot, we left the buckets at our house. "Hawkman said.

"No problem, got plenty."

They finished tending to the horses and closed the big gate.

"How about coming down to the house for a drink?" Wayne asked.

"Can we take a raincheck on that?" Jennifer said. "I'm beat."

"Sure. Why don't you jump on the back of my machine and I'll take you to your front door."

"I wouldn't think of turning you down," Jennifer said, laughing, as she climbed on behind him."

"We'll let the big guy walk," Wayne said.

"He's had an extra day of practice riding a horse. He can't be as sore as me," Jennifer said, waving at Hawkman as they drove onto the road.

***

Sunday morning, Jeb arose early and ventured outside. He opened the door to the still and began working on the dismantling. Beth came out, leaving the children inside.

"So how are you going to get rid of this thing?"

"I've already sold it to Moss Atkins, the tavern owner who bought the last of the moonshine. He's offered me enough money to buy a vehicle."

"When is he picking it up, and what's he going to do with it?" Beth asked.

"He's coming today with a couple of men and a big covered truck to carry it back to town. I didn't ask him what he's going to do with it, and really don't care, as long as it's out of here."

She walked back toward the cabin, whispering a prayer. "Thank you, grandpa."

"Send Earl out, I'll need him to help me," Jeb called, before she got to the door.

Soon, a big truck rolled onto the property, and hauled the copper still away. The whole family stood watching until the large vehicle disappeared.

"Good riddance," Beth said.

Jeb turned and handed her a roll of money. "Put this in a safe place until I have time to look for a good pickup. Our next project is fixing a place for grandpa."

They strolled back into the cabin. "We might hold off for a while, until we know if he's capable of taking care of himself," Beth said. "I thought about putting him in the boys' room at first. That way he's close to the kitchen where I work most of the time, and I can easily take care of his needs."

"Where will the boys sleep?" Jeb asked.

"Randy can sleep on the cot where he's slept most of the time while recovering from his wounds. Earl can sleep on the couch until we decide what to do."

Jeb walked over to the small back door and opened it. He could see Beth's garden and the edge of the stream. He then meandered outside and studied the side wall. "I could build a small covered porch out here, big enough to hold a couple of beds. It wouldn't be fancy, but it'd do the job. I think I'd have enough good lumber from the still buildings."

"That's a good idea," Beth said.

While they were outside discussing the room, Randy ran in the house calling for them. Beth poked her head in the door. "What is it, Randy?"

"The Caseys are here."

Hawkman and Jennifer came in, carrying baked ham, and beans. "Didn't figure you had much in the pantry for dinner tonight," Jennifer said.

"Oh, thank you," Beth said, taking the dishes and putting them on the counter. "How are you feeling today? You didn't look too comfortable on that horse yesterday."

Jennifer laughed. "Very sore."

Beth pointed out toward the back. "Jeb and I are trying to figure out where to build an extra room for the boys, as I want to give Grandpa their room when he comes."

Hawkman went out the door and started chatting with Jeb about the structure. The two men soon came back inside. "I've got some lumber and nails at the house you can use. I'd like to help you build this project."

"I'd appreciate the help," Jeb said.

On the way back to their house, Jennifer turned toward Hawkman. "I wonder where the still went?"

Hawkman shrugged. "Who cares; it's gone and Jeb's looking forward to his grandfather coming once he's stronger."

Jennifer bit her lip and glanced at her husband. "Are you going to pursue the moonshining case against Jeb?"

He raised his brows. "What moonshining? There's no proof of any such thing." He turned and smiled. "I think their lives might be ready for a big turn around, and I see no reason to interfere with it."

Jennifer reached over and kissed him on the cheek. "I sure hope so. Do you think the old fellow will have that much influence over Jeb?"

"Yes, I have the impression he has quite a bit of respect for his granddad."

Hawkman went to the Hutchinsons after work for the following several weeks. He even took Jeb into town and helped him pick out a used truck by a reputable dealer, and got the price down so there was enough money left over to keep Jeb in gas for a few weeks.

Once the new room was completed, the men spent another week making built-in beds for the boys, while Beth hand-sewed small mattresses filled with goose down for each. The impatient boys finally moved in, and loved their new quarters.

Detective Chandler drove out to the Hutchinsons and informed them the hospital had transferred grandpa to a rehabilitation facility for a month of therapy. Jeb and Beth immediately made plans to go visit him the next day in their new pickup.

They stopped by the Casey's that evening and reported they were very pleased with the service where grandpa would be staying for a while. They'd also picked up Mutt from the SPCA.

They had him tied in the bed of the pickup so he wouldn't be thrown out on their way home.

Hawkman reached over and patted the animal. "I had no idea the dog belonged to your grandpa. He looks great; his eyes are bright, shiny coat and I believe he's gained a little weight."

Jeb nodded and smiled. "They took good care of him. Grandpa had talked to them over the phone. They updated his shots, dewormed him and said he's in good health now. He's a great animal. Grandpa's eager to see him again. He calls himself and his dog, 'the survivors'."

"Have the kids ever met Mutt?" Hawkman asked.

"They saw him once, about three years ago. Grandpa had just gotten him, and he was only a pup."

Mutt let out a happy bark, and both men laughed.

Soon the time arrived when grandpa could come home. The Hutchinsons prepared to pick him up in their new pickup, but Hawkman talked them into letting him take them into town in a more comfortable vehicle.

As he prepared to go pick them up, Jennifer said. "You go ahead without me, so there'll be plenty of room in case the whole family wants to go. I can meet grandpa later."

When Hawkman arrived at the cabin, Beth and Jeb climbed into the Cruiser. "The boys are going to take care of Marcy and will greet their great grandpa when we return," Beth said.

They arrived at the nursing home and the nurse brought Jacob, Sr., to the vehicle in a wheelchair. He climbed into the SUV with assistance, as Jeb and Beth stood on each side of the still frail body.

A big grin formed on his lips and his blue eyes sparkled as he put his hand out. "Hawkman, good to see you again."

Taking the old man's hand, he was surprised at the strength of his grip. "You're looking good," Hawkman said, as Beth climbed into the passenger seat. After hoisting the wheelchair and a walker into the back of the Cruiser, Jeb scooted in beside his grandpa

"How's Mutt doing?" Jacob asked.

"Great," Jeb said." The kids have spoiled him rotten, but he's partial to Randy. Goes with him everywhere."

They soon arrived at the cabin and the kids were waiting outside. Randy held Marcy in his arms. Earl stood beside him, grinning from ear to ear. Jacob was lifted out of the van and placed in the waiting wheelchair. Tears trickled down his cheeks, and he grinned at his family. Mutt jumped around them, barking happily.

Hawkman decided to get out of there and let the family have their reunion in private.

Several days later, Randy pedaled his bike furiously down to the Casey's house; Mutt ran behind him.

When Jennifer answered the door, he spewed out in an excited voice, "Mrs. Casey, guess what Great Grandpa's going to do?"

Jennifer laughed. "Slow down, I can hardly understand you."

"He's going to put in a road going to our house, have electricity wired in so we can

have electric lights, maybe even a
television and install running water so we
can have bathrooms.

Then he said, if all went well, he just 'might'
build us a new house and save the cabin
for people he'd hire to help take care of our
cattle ranch. We're going to have real live
cows in our field."

Jennifer gave him a big hug. "Randy, that's
absolutely wonderful. I hope you boys are
going to get enrolled into school now."

Randy nodded. "Oh, yeah, Grandpa said
Earl and I both have to go to school and
graduate, or he wouldn't hire us as ranch
hands."

She smiled. "Your Great Grandpa sounds
like a good man."

Randy hopped back on his bike. "He's the
best. Gotta go, Grandpa might need me.
Come on, Mutt, let's go home."

Jennifer watched him ride like the wind up
the road; one happy young boy. She was so
thankful, Jacob, Jr. was in prison for a long
time and would never bother this
Hutchinson family again.

THE END

ABOUT THE AUTHOR

Born and raised in Oklahoma, Betty Sullivan La Pierre attended the Oklahoma College for Women and the University of Oklahoma, graduating with her BS degree in Speech Therapy with a Specialty in the Deaf.

Once married, she moved to California with her husband. When her husband was killed in an automobile accident, she was left with two young boys to raise. She is now remarried and has had another son through that marriage.

Ms. La Pierre has lived in the Silicon Valley (California) for many years. At one time, she owned a Mail Order Used Book business dealing mainly in signed and rare books, but phased it out because it took up too much of her writing time. She's an avid reader, belongs to the Wednesday Writers' Society, and periodically attends functions of other writing organizations.

She writes Mystery/Suspense/Thriller novels, which are published in digital format and print. Her Hawkman Mystery Series is developing quite a fan base. She's also written two stand-alone mystery/thrillers and plans to continue writing.
'BLACKOUT,' Betty's story about a bingo hall (of the Hawkman Series), ranked in the top ten of the P&E Reader's Poll, and won the 2003 BLOODY DAGGER AWARD for best Mystery/Suspense. EuroReviews recently picked 'THE DEADLY THORN' (One of Betty's stand alone thrillers) for their 2005 May Book of the Month.

Betty Sullivan La Pierre's work is a testament to how much she enjoys the challenge of plotting an exciting story.
Visit her personal site at:
http://bettysullivanlapierre.com

Proof

Made in the USA
Charleston, SC
06 December 2011